CANDLELIGHT
Ecstasy Supreme

**"DID YOU FORGET SOMETHING?" DAVID
DEMANDED.**

"Forget something?" she echoed. "What do you
mean?"

David walked slowly around the desk. "Oh, just idle
curiosity. You are Susan Anderson?"

"Yes," she answered, no longer apologetic. "As you're
well aware. We've met before."

"Sorry, I'd forgotten." He forced a pleasant smile. "I
assume you forgot something. I thought you would have
taken everything you wanted by now. But then, vultures
do come back to the scene of the kill until the bones are
picked clean, don't they?"

"What?" she demanded, her temper soaring.

"Didn't you get enough out of my father when he was
living? Well, don't worry, I'm sure he remembered you in
his will. I'm not quite sure what your talents were with a
man his age. But they must have been very good. You
were certainly well paid."

CANDLELIGHT ECSTASY SUPREMES®

QUANTITY SALES

Most Dell Books are available at special quantity discounts when purchased in bulk by corporations, organizations, and special-interest groups. Custom imprinting or excerpting can also be done to fit special needs. For details write: Dell Publishing Co., Inc., 1 Dag Hammarskjold Plaza, New York, NY 10017, Attn.: Special Sales Dept., or phone: (212) 605-3319.

INDIVIDUAL SALES

Are there any Dell Books you want but cannot find in your local stores? If so, you can order them directly from us. You can get any Dell book in print. Simply include the book's title, author, and ISBN number, if you have it, along with a check or money order (no cash can be accepted) for the full retail price plus 75¢ per copy to cover shipping and handling. Mail to: Dell Readers Service, Dept. FM, P.O. Box 1000, Pine Brook, NJ 07058.

HANDFUL OF DREAMS

Heather Graham

A CANDLELIGHT ECSTASY SUPREME®

Published by
Dell Publishing Co., Inc.
1 Dag Hammarskjold Plaza
New York, New York 10017

Dell ® TM 681510, Dell Publishing Co., Inc.

Candlelight Ecstasy Supreme is a trademark
of Dell Publishing Co., Inc.

Candlelight Ecstasy Romance®, 1,203,540, is a registered
trademark of Dell Publishing Co., Inc.

ISBN: 0-440-13420-X

Printed in the United States of America

June 1986

10 9 8 7 6 5 4 3 2 1

WFH

For my cousin, Gene Fowler, and my aunt,
Christine Ventresca, with lots of love

To Our Readers:

We are pleased and excited by your overwhelmingly positive response to our Candlelight Ecstasy Supremes. Unlike all the other series, the Supremes are filled with more passion, adventure, and intrigue, and are obviously the stories you like best.

In months to come we will continue to publish books by many of your favorite authors as well as the very finest work from new authors of romantic fiction. As always, we are striving to present unique, absorbing love stories —the very best love has to offer.

Breathtaking and unforgettable, Ecstasy Supremes follow in the great romantic tradition you've come to expect *only* from Candlelight Ecstasy.

Your suggestions and comments are always welcome. Please let us hear from you.

Sincerely,

The Editors
Candlelight Romances
1 Dag Hammarskjold Plaza
New York, New York 10017

PROLOGUE

She should have been forewarned by the receptionist's nervous attitude; Susan wasn't. She had agonized long and hard about coming here, and even so, she still wasn't sure she had made the right decision. Peter's mind was set: He loved his son, and he didn't want David to know the truth.

So why was she here? She who believed so deeply in other people's rights to choices and privacy?

She stared out the window of the penthouse office to the street far below. Snowflakes were falling in a gentle flurry, soft and gentle and mystical. They misted before her like a tender veil, such a contrast, she noted absently, to the deep red polish on her nails.

How long was David Lane going to keep her waiting? Each moment made it harder. She had practiced so many openings for the words she intended to say. Still, none of them sounded right; none of them could ease the reality that Peter Lane was dying.

But David was a mature man, grown and responsible. He

would accept the truth, be able to understand. He had sense and strength of character, as Peter so often told her.

"I almost lost the whole thing once," Peter had told her when they had first met. "Right after Mary died I fell to pieces, I did. David pulled it all back into shape—paid off the debts, found new backing, worked around the clock. And then he was ready to hand the reins back to me. I wouldn't take them. Didn't mind arguing with him now and then, but it was his turn at bat. He'd kept the game going; he'd earned it. And me . . . well, I was ready for some peace and quiet. The beach house full-time, and my own crotchety company most of the time."

Thinking about Peter, Susan smiled a little sadly. Her smile faded, and she lifted her arm to glance at the face of her watch. She'd be late meeting Peter if his elusive son didn't hurry along.

She felt that the receptionist was watching her and lightly pulled at the brim of her hat, bringing it farther over her eyes. Her ear bobs tinkled lightly. David Lane's slender secretary looked up with a nervous smile that was still genuine. Susan smiled back, a little perplexed by the woman's discomfort.

What was she going to say? *I understand that your business pressures have been very heavy lately, Mr. Lane, but I'm afraid it's more imperative that you come to the beach house now and then. You see, your father—*

A buzzer interrupted her thoughts.

"Yes, Mr. Lane?" the slim secretary asked.

Susan didn't hear the answer. The secretary rose quickly, smiled nervously again, and indicated the double wooden doors with the attractive brass handles. "You can go right in, Miss Anderson."

"Thank you," Susan said softly.

She pushed open the doors, quickly taking in the room. All the glass windows here looked out on the river. It was a beautiful view, with the ships below, the ever gentle snow-

10

flakes. The carpet was a deep, deep maroon, and the shelves were lined with books, appropriate for a publishing mogul. A very large desk stood in the center of the room in front of those shelves, but not even the size of the polished Georgian desk could diminish the stature of the man who sat behind it. His hair was very dark, sleek and shining; his shoulders were broad; his jacket impeccable.

That was all Susan could really see, because he did not bother to look up from what he was writing. She hesitated, annoyed by such pointed rudeness. He knew she was standing there; he had certainly heard the door open and close. After he had kept her waiting all that time, he couldn't bother to look up and put his pen down?

She clenched her teeth together, trying to control her temper. After all, he couldn't begin to understand the meaning of her visit. But he should have been interested. He should have wanted to meet her. Surely he had heard her name. . . .

She cleared her throat softly. He still stared down at his papers, writing quickly with a monogrammed pen.

The hell with delicacy, Susan thought angrily.

She strode across the room, stopping directly in front of the desk and abstractedly studying the things there: a polished pipe rack; a few books; piles of manila envelopes; an icy glass of water sitting on a coaster just beyond the blotter.

"David Lane?" she inquired crisply.

He still didn't look up. His voice was a cool drawl made more mocking by its natural husky tenor.

"Yes. What do you want? If it's more money you're after, talk to my father. You're his mistress—not mine."

Money? Mistress?

She tried to open her mouth to speak, but she was so furious that her vocal cords wouldn't work. Never in her life had she been so angry that she shook with it, burned and saw nothing but white light. The thoughts were all there—

11

the things she wanted to call him, to tell him—but still she couldn't speak.

Susan reached calmly for the glass of water on his desk and tossed it into his face.

Then she turned around and walked regally out of David Lane's office, closing the double doors on the thunderous oath that followed her.

The tears didn't burn behind Susan's eyes until she had left the Lane Building behind. It wasn't business that kept Peter's son away, it was her!

She tried at lunch to convince Peter that she should move out of the beach house, but he grabbed her arm in protest. She stared down at his hands, once large and powerful, now long and slender, from age and illness. She felt the trembling in them.

"Please, Susan. I need you." His voice trembled too. He who was always so realistic, so strong, so serene. "I need you."

"What if it's me that's keeping your son away?" she asked softly.

"David?" He seemed quite surprised. "David's just glued to New York, and I can see him here anytime I want. When he gets time, he'll come around. Ah, Susan! This project is so important to me. It can't be completed without you. . . ."

She knew she wouldn't leave him, not when that catch touched his voice—a voice usually so strong and courageous. Susan realized that she was indeed making it all easier for him. She couldn't leave. He had given her strength when she had needed it, and this was her chance to repay him.

"It was just an idea," she said pleasantly, taking a bite of her lobster salad.

"I wish you wouldn't insist on seeing that friend of yours tonight," Peter said wistfully. "You could come to dinner with David and me. I'm so anxious for you to meet him." There was a fraction of a pause. "And for him to know you."

12

"Yes, well, I'm sorry, Peter. This is my only chance to see Clarisse." Thank God she'd already made plans for the evening, she thought.

"Ah, well, he'll come sooner or later. It's a pity we have to go back tomorrow. But the work is important now, lass. You understand."

"Yes," she said very softly. "I understand."

CHAPTER ONE

Standing on the rough wood porch of the beach house, David paused. He could hear the wind whispering around him, rising to moan and howl as if it, too, mourned.

David clutched the raw wood railing and stared out at the water, a blue so deep that it almost appeared black today, roiling against the rocks and sand, whitecapped and thunderously brooding. The day was overcast, a storm threatening.

And that, too, seemed right. Peter Lane had loved storms. He'd loved the wind; he'd loved the sea and the tempest of the waves.

Standing there, David closed his eyes. His knuckles went white where they gripped the rail. Pain lashed through him like the onslaught of the waves, and he clenched his teeth together to keep from crying aloud with anguish. Peter had been old; this was not a tragedy, just the natural way of life.

At length David's grip on the rail relaxed. He smiled a little bitterly. It was just the beach house. It brought so

14

much back. Days when he had been a kid; when his father had taught him to fish and to swim, to endure the cold water, to love the wind.

They had quarreled here too. Ferociously. In the library, in the kitchen, in the bedroom—they'd quarreled throughout the house. Both stubborn, determined, and willful men.

David turned to stare at the house. Leaning against the rail and staring into the parlor through the windows, a wistful curve touched his lips as he saw his father's rocker. He could almost imagine it moving.

"Hey, Dad," he whispered softly, "I was only being your son. You taught me to follow my mind. To stand up for my . . ." His words faded as he groaned deeply and pressed his temples between his palms. "Oh, God, Dad! I miss you so much! Why . . . ?"

The anguish of the question hung on the wind for a moment, then seemed to be swept away by it. David squared his shoulders, stiffened, then relaxed. He smiled again and ran his hand over the railing. This place *was* Peter Lane. All the good, all the memories.

He reached into the pocket of his jeans and pulled out the little ring of keys to the place. He opened the screen door, then the wooden one, and stepped into the foyer. Instinctively he turned left to the library. His father's desk sat there, massive cherry wood, the swivel chair behind it slightly out, as if the desk awaited its owner.

David walked around and sat at the desk. He folded his hands prayer-fashion and touched his forefingers to his lips, surveying the floor-to-ceiling bookshelves that covered two walls. Everything imaginable was held in those shelves, from Sophocles to Chaucer, Steinbeck to Poe.

Peter Lane had loved the written word. Books had been his life.

David's eyes roamed as he turned the swivel chair. Directly behind him was a dog-eared copy of *The Adventures of Huckleberry Finn*. Smiling with affection and sadness, he plucked the book from the wall; large, strong hands roamed over the engraved cover, and the man remembered how the boy had loved it, how he had sat on his father's lap and listened, entranced, to the story.

David replaced the book. His eyes were watering when they fell, unseeing, to the top of the desk.

He stood restlessly and idly paced around the desk to perch on its corner as he picked up his father's old corncob pipe, the stem well chewed. Peter had owned a vast range of pipes, exquisite and exotic and beautiful pipes. Anyone who had known him and wanted to give him a gift had given him a pipe.

But the old corncobs were the ones he had loved most.

David glanced up, fingering the pipe. On the one wall not covered by windows or bookshelves was a large portrait. His father, his mother, and himself. An eager-looking ten-year-old. Peter had already been thoroughly gray; he'd been fifty at the time.

"Gray, but damned good-looking," David said aloud to the portrait. "You were one distinguished man, all right!"

And he had been. Lines had wizened his face; his nose had been something of a beak, but fierce arctic-blue eyes had ruled his face, and the simple character of his features had made him striking. Tall, lean, and proud. And why not? He'd fought his way from a penniless Irish immigrant to the owner of a book publishing house, and he'd done it all honestly, never once losing sight of his principles or beliefs.

Once again David stood restlessly and walked around to sit in the swivel chair. There was brandy in the bottom left-hand drawer. David leaned down and pulled it out, ignoring the crystal glasses beside it. He stretched his legs out over the desk, leaned back in the chair, and took a long swig.

They'd always quarreled. As a kid, David had fought for independence. Having had his own wild fling in his teens, Peter had been determined to curb his son. Then it had been the war. David's friends all had been heading for Canada. Peter had insisted that David enlist.

"I don't believe in it, Dad, and damn it, you told me not to do what I didn't think was right!"

"Not to the exception of the law!" Peter had thundered back. "This country has been good to us; it's given freedom, succored and sustained us . . ."

And besides that, there had been some trouble in David's last year of high school: growing pains, peer pressure. Everyone had been experimenting with sex, drugs, wild driving, irresponsible drinking.

"The service is just what you need," Peter had determined, despite all of David's mother's tears. "You either sink or swim, son, and right now you're going to do one or the other!"

In a fury, David had run out and enlisted in the Air Force. Peter had been right—it was sink or swim, and so he learned the hard way how to swim. He also knew that his father had been right: if he'd stayed with a certain crowd, he'd have likely wound up in a prison cell, addicted, or dead on a highway. And so he'd served his time, learned even more about life on a certain leave, and then come home changed and matured—and more like his father than ever.

He'd wanted to get into the business then. There had been another argument, this one about the benefits of education. And so, in another huff of fury, he'd returned to school, managing to finish six years of education in three. All to get a start in the company at the lowest pay scale, in the most menial clerical capacity.

"If you don't learn to work the hard way, David, you're in a bind when hard times come along!" Peter had warned him.

He hadn't minded working "the hard way." He had done so with a dogged determination to best everything—all on his own. Every year of his life more of the resentment faded and was replaced by respect. They still argued over almost everything, but they became debates with intelligent reason-

17

ing on both sides. It was often difficult to be the son of a living legend; all a man could do was become a legend in his own right.

And then had come the time when they'd finally come close again, really close. The year his mother had died. She'd always been the quiet one, soft and gentle, Peter's shadow.

Or so it had seemed. Because with her gone, Peter had become the shadow. He had turned the reins of the company over to David completely and closed himself away from life in the beach house with all that he had left to love in life—his books.

And in the decade that followed, he had roused himself to a few lively debates with David, but in the end he had always waved a hand, saying, "Ach! Make your own mistakes in life. Pay for them and learn!" And then he would berate David again for not producing a few grandchildren, nice respectful bairns he could dangle on his knee and entrance with a rendition of *Tom Sawyer*.

"Dad, I'd do anything in the world for you," David would swear, "except get married when it wasn't . . . right. And you wouldn't want me to do that, now would you?"

"What have you got against marriage?" Peter would demand. And David would scowl and tell Peter to get off his back, determined that his father would never know about one of the mistakes he had made in life, the mistake that had taught him so much about women.

They were great people. To talk to, have fun with, enjoy. But not to trust and not to love.

He'd learned that lesson well—Peter apparently hadn't.

With that thought David scowled, his dark brows meeting over the straight line of his nose with the intensity of his sudden fury.

The last argument they'd had had been over a woman! And not one of his choosing, one of Peter's.

It had come up over lunch in the city. Peter had flown into New York for a week. He'd come into the office, taken an interest in everything, gone to a few shows, and had dinner every night with his son. On Friday afternoon they'd sat together over Nedick's hot dogs—Peter had loved them all his life—and Peter had told David all about Susan.

David had been stunned at first. There had been a time when he had tried to introduce his father to women, someone to ease the loss of his mother, someone with whom Peter could share the silver years.

But no one had ever appealed to him. "I was a one-woman man, David. Your mother, God rest her soul, was the only one for me, and God willing, we'll meet again in another world."

Then suddenly, out of the clear blue, Peter was talking about Susan. And during the conversation it became clear that Susan was not a gentle widow but a young woman. Peter talked of her glowingly. "You should taste a cup of tea that Susan has made!"

"Oh, Dad!" David had said with a groan.

"What?" was Peter's belligerent reply.

David had hesitated, rubbing a thumb over his can of soda. He didn't want to hurt his father, but it made him furious to think that some young . . . parasite . . . was using a man as renowned as his father. A man once strong who was now old and lonely.

"Dad . . ." He sighed deeply. "If this girl's so young and perfect and beautiful—"

"What's she doing with me. Is that what you're trying to say?"

"Dad—"

"That's it, isn't it?"

"Damn it—"

"Don't swear at me, lad!"

And ice-blue eyes had flashed at ice-blue eyes across the table.

"All right!" David had snapped angrily. "There's no fool

like an old fool! Can't you see, Dad? She's using you! You're old, lonely, and rich! She's after something."

"You're a damned cynic!"

"Don't swear at me, Dad!"

Peter's jaw set into its stubborn angle, and he stared heatedly at his son. "You went off to war and came back hard, lad. Then you took over the company and came out harder still. You're smart as a whip, sharp as a tack—and I think you'd dare the devil himself. I've been proud of you many a time, David. Real proud. Even when we were at odds. Hell, I wanted to give you the world. I wanted to give you everything that I never had. And somehow I managed to keep you from the most important things: trust and love."

"Ah, Dad! Come on. She loves you?"

"Love comes in many ways, David. And in her way, yes, she loves me." He'd leaned across the table eagerly. "Come up to the beach house, David. Meet Susan. You'll understand."

"No, Dad. I can't tell you what to do, but I can't come up and meet this . . . girl and be polite."

"David, she makes me happy."

"Then I'm glad."

Peter had left New York. His calls and his letters had been full of Susan. "Bought Susan a pair of emerald earrings the other day—they match her eyes. Hope I can get her to keep them," or, "Susan and I flew over to Paris on the spur of the moment—just for dinner!"

The next thing David knew, Susan had gone on the payroll as a personal companion. David had signed her checks out of the separate corporate account twice a month, and every time his fingers moved the pen across the paper, he'd been furious and ill and—a feeling totally alien to him— helpless.

But somehow David had swallowed it all. And finally he had met her—or almost met her. He learned to just keep quiet when his father talked about her; he told Peter that the

20

business kept him in the city—that, sure, he'd meet her sometime. Peter seemed happy with that.

She had come into the city with his father, determined to see David alone, to bleed them further, it seemed. What else would she be doing in his office?

He hadn't wanted to look at her. When his secretary had led her in, he'd kept his eyes on the contracts on his desk.

"David Lane?"

"Yes. What do you want? If it's more money you're after, talk to my father. You're his mistress—not mine."

He'd had a glass of water sitting there. The next thing he knew, it was splashing down his face. He'd started up with an astonished oath to see her sable-coated back disappearing through the door.

He'd almost run after her, but then remembered that his father was growing older and that Peter loved her—though the love she returned was bartered and bought. Clenching his teeth, he sank back into his chair and mopped the water from his hair and face.

Swallow it, swallow it all, he had cautioned himself painfully. And he had—until Peter had come to New York the next time. "Come on, David. Susan would love to meet you."

Susan has *met me,* David had thought. Apparently she'd had the good sense not to mention the meeting.

Then he had exploded. "Don't you understand, Dad? I love you! I just can't watch it! It hurts to see you make a fool of yourself over some little bitch!" Immediately he'd been sorry. Not over his opinion; only because he really wouldn't hurt his father in any way. "Oh, Dad, I didn't mean . . ."

Peter had been calm and dignified. "She isn't a little bitch, David, and I'd appreciate your not saying so again."

"If she makes you happy, then fine. I just don't want to meet her, okay?"

"It's not fine." Peter had sighed. "I wanted so badly for

21

you two to get to know each other. You'd be friends. She knows books, David. She writes. She's good."

"Dad, please!" David had winced. Oh, Lord! The woman wasn't just a parasitical whore, she wanted Peter to use his influence for her!

"David—"

"Okay, Dad. Sometime I'll come up, okay?"

And so the rift had been patched. And in the end David had promised to come to Maine for the Labor Day weekend.

Except that his father hadn't lived that long. A heart attack had claimed him—when he was with Susan.

Susan, perfect Susan. She had telegrammed immediately following his father's death to ask what funeral arrangements he wanted. He'd telegrammed back telling her to ship the body and then get the hell out.

He had to tolerate her when his father was alive. But his father was gone now, and he didn't ever want to see Susan.

David took another long swig of the brandy, closed his eyes, and rubbed his forehead. Regrets . . . were they always part of grief? All Peter had wanted was a grandchild. Someone to toss on his knee. David had denied him that simple pleasure.

"Not on purpose," he whispered aloud. "Ah, Dad, I loved you! I would have been with you—"

He started suddenly. He had been so engrossed in his thoughts that he hadn't heard the doors, but now he did hear the click of heels on the polished wooden floor of the foyer.

And then he was staring at a woman in the library doorway.

She was as startled as he at the confrontation, but she was quicker to recover.

He stared quite bluntly, his eyes narrowing speculatively. With contempt and dismay he realized that Susan Anderson was even younger than he had expected, not more than twenty-five. She was tall and slim, the height of fashion in a

22

sleekly cut red suit, cream blouse, matching red felt-brim hat and heels. Her nails were as long as talons, blood-red to match the suit. Her hair was russet, which should have made the outfit awful, but it didn't. It was swept cleanly from her features in some sort of a knot beneath her hat. Her eyes were green—the emerald his father had mentioned, David decided acidly—and her features were flawless: stubborn chin, wide, generous mouth; small nose.

She was beautiful. The perfect sophisticated woman. She could sashay into any city office with that little nose in the air and attract the eyes of any man.

But no, she had lit on his father like a smooth vulture. Her clothing should have been in the height of fashion—Peter Lane could afford the best.

"I'm sorry," she said quickly. Even her voice was perfect. Melodious. How long had she practiced to get just that tone? "I had no idea that you were coming here. I wouldn't have interrupted you."

"Interrupted?" he heard himself ask coolly.

She flushed slightly. "I heard you . . . talking."

Everything in him seemed to explode. She'd been listening to him, heard him, in a private moment of grief. A moment that was his by right while she . . .

And he was sitting here, tears still misting his eyes, a brandy bottle in his hand, his legs sprawled on the desk.

He set the bottle on the desk carefully and deliberately, then swung his feet to the ground with the same painstaking care and stood, crossing his arms over his chest to keep his fingers from closing around her and shaking her. He made no pretense of disguising his scorn and distaste as his eyes perused her in a pointed study.

"Did you forget something?" he demanded with quiet authority.

"Forget something?" she echoed, a frown knitting her delicate, cleanly arched brows. She took a step into the room. "What do you mean?"

David walked slowly around the desk, idly stroking his chin as he continued to survey her like meat at a market. "Oh, just idle curiosity," he said. "You are Susan Anderson?"

"Yes," she snapped, no longer apologetic. "As you're well aware. We've met before."

"Sorry, I'd forgotten."

He lifted his hands, forcing a pleasant smile. "I assume you forgot something. I thought you would have taken everything you wanted by now. But then, vultures do come back to the scene of the kill until the bones are picked clean, don't they?"

Susan couldn't help but gasp at the razorlike edge of his attack. She hadn't expected him to be pleasant, but neither had she expected such a vicious assault.

But why not? she wondered bitterly. It was all she had gotten from him that time she had tried to . . .

"What?" she demanded, her fingers clenching into fists at her sides as her temper soared.

"Didn't you get enough out of my father when he was living? Well, don't worry about it. I'm sure he remembered you in his will. I'm not quite sure what your talents were with a man his age, but they must have been damned good. You were certainly one well-paid whore."

If David had known her, he might have been forewarned. Her eyes became a sizzling shade of lime when her temper—usually serene—snapped. But he didn't know her. And so he was taken completely by surprise when she struck him.

It wasn't a ladylike slap. It was a full strike across his cheek that sent him reeling back a step in amazement.

He took that step back to her, ignoring the ache in his jaw to bite his fingers into her shoulders. She made one attempt to wrench from his hold, found it impossible, and tossed her head back, meeting his gaze with one of crystal fury and contempt. Her cool glare angered him further; she'd used his

24

father, carelessly half killed him with her penchant for expensive excitement.

And she had the gall to defy him now!

He gave her a little shake, clenching his teeth against the gamut of emotions that threatened his sense of control. The shake dislodged her perfect little hat; a stream of fiery rich hair, waving with the russet hue of a sunset, fell over her shoulders and down her back. That hair, tangling over his fingers, carried a subtle and haunting scent of perfume, like a drug that played upon the senses and made a man take pause, assessing her again, noting the elegant beauty of her features.

He offered her a grim smile as her eyes widened with the slightest touch of alarm.

"Miss Anderson, my father is dead now. I remember you attacking my manners once before. Well, sister, my manners are fine. I treat a lady like a lady. But you're not a lady, Miss Anderson, not in my book. I call a young woman who attaches herself to a man for his money a whore. I—"

The alarm was out of her eyes. They seemed almost yellow now with pure rage, and his sentence was interrupted by his own startled groan as she kicked him in the shin.

David's lips compressed ruthlessly. She wanted an all-out cat-fight, and she was going to get one. "Get your hands off of me, you arrogant bastard," she cried.

But she was interrupted this time by his movement. His ankle quickly shifted behind her own to lift her foot from the floor and send her flying down to it—with him quickly beside her, hands pressed to her arms with relentless force as he bent over her.

"Miss Anderson, you are a regular little tigress, a huntress with all the wiles of the jungle. But I've had all I'm going to take from you. You attacked me once and walked away from it with your nose in the air. Not again—lady." He sneered. "You see, my father is gone now. He's not around to protect

25

you anymore. So if you go at it with me, you're going to get it right back."

She barely blinked; she just stared at him with hate in her eyes, her breasts rising and falling, her delicate jaw set with anger.

"There's not an ounce of your father in you," she said at last, and the lilt in her voice made it the gravest insult he'd ever received.

"No?" David inquired politely. "I really don't think you were around long enough to tell. You knew and used a broken old man, Miss Anderson. You preyed upon him when he was weak and lonely and vulnerable. You should have known him in his prime, but then, you wouldn't have, would you? Because he would have known you for what you are if he had met you in his younger days!"

She returned his glare, undaunted by his words, and he had to admit that she had courage. She had to be aware that he knew she had brought on the heart attack that had killed his father, knew that he considered her little more than a cold-blooded murderess and deserved any violence the pain and tempest in him could deliver.

But she still defied him, loathed him. Offered him no remorse, only her sizzling stare of smoldering scorn . . .

Sizzling. Hot. Her whole body was warm, vibrant, and alive. And touching her, leaning over her . . . seeing her, he knew something of it. She was both slim and shapely. Narrow-waisted, full in the breasts, long and elegantly limbed. Kinetic with passion and anger, trembling, all her heat and fury shooting from the emerald sparks of her eyes . . .

To David's horror he found himself shuddering. The fire in her eyes raked his body. Incredulously he wanted her in a primal way that knew no logic or thought. His body grew tense and hot, then a pulsing sensation stirred in his groin.

So this was it, he thought. This was the web that ensnared. This promise of sensuality, of a pleasure that was unique and heightened above any other, of a passion that was as wild as a tempest . . .

He closed his eyes quickly, amazed that a man of his age and experience could be so touched by such a practiced huntress. He shook slightly again, disgusted with himself. His father's mistress! And he was actually here with her, pinning her to the floor in fury, only to discover that he envied his father because he had known what it was to touch her, to fill his hands with the weight of her breasts, taste her lips, know the searing fulfillment of that promised fire. . . .

He released her suddenly, as if she had burned him. She barely seemed to notice but quickly folded her legs beneath her to sit, facing him like a spitting, wary cat.

"I think I knew him far better than you did," she said coolly. "I never considered him a fool, and I never thought of him as senile, which quite apparently, Mr. Lane, you did. And, for the record, I never 'attacked' you. I made an attempt once to discuss a matter of importance. *You* attacked —with verbal blades, intending to draw blood."

David sat back, idly lacing his fingers around his knees. "You don't believe in calling a spade a spade, I take it?" he inquired.

"Your arrogance and insolence are both incredible," she returned after a moment's disgusted surveillance of him. With natural grace she rose, then stared down at him. "It's truly amazing that Peter could have created such a son."

She spun around. David was on his feet quickly, halting her with a sharp command as she reached the doorway. "Whatever it was you left behind, Miss Anderson, get it and get out."

She turned, smiling with a true glint of triumph and amusement. "Mr. Lane, I'm afraid that you're the one who is going to have to get out."

"What's your game now, Miss Anderson?"

No woman could have appeared more innocent, more

guilelessly enchanting as she stared back at him with that sweet smile still curving her lips.

"The beach house is half mine, Mr. Lane. Check with your lawyers—your father left it to us."

No physical blow could have stunned him or hurt him with such thorough precision. He wasn't aware that he moved; he didn't even know that he had walked to her, gripped her elbow, and locked his fingers around it like steel shackles.

"What?"

His face had gone starkly pale; apparently she realized his menace at last when he was unaware of it himself, for a pallor touched her cheeks, making her eyes seem enormous, her lashes appear like a forest of fire and pitch around them.

"My father left you an interest in this house?" he thundered.

She tugged at her elbow. "Yes! Now get your hands off me. And if you touch me again, so help me, Mr. Lane, I'll have a warrant sworn out against you!"

He released her not because of the threat, but because he was too stunned to do otherwise. He wandered, dazed, back to the desk where he sat in the chair and picked up the brandy bottle. Heedless of her perusal, he drank deeply, then drank some more.

And then he began to laugh, eyeing her afresh.

"I have to hand it to you, Miss Anderson. I considered you a nuisance, a bloodsucking parasite, and a few other things. But I really underestimated you! You must be very good at what you do!"

She kept smiling, the glitter of loathing touching the intriguing depths of her eyes once again, heightened by the array of dark and blazing hair that still fell, unheeded, in disarray around her.

"I am very good," she said blandly.

"I still don't believe it."

"Call your lawyers."

28

"I will."

Keeping his eyes locked with hers, David reached across the desk for the phone. In seconds he had tapped out his attorney's number; in another few seconds he was talking to Barney Smith. Barney spent several long moments eulogizing Peter; David was grateful, but he cut Barney off a little quickly.

"Barney, what's the status with the beach house?"

He knew she had been telling the truth when Barney cleared his throat uneasily.

"Uh . . . joint ownership, David. It's been left to you and Miss Anderson." Barney cleared his throat again. "I tried to talk your father out of such a provision, David, but he insisted that it was her home and your birthright."

Barney was saying more. David didn't hear him.

"Thanks, Barney," he murmured distractedly, and replaced the receiver.

"I'll be damned," David whispered, rising and smiling crookedly at her without taking his eyes off her as he started toward her. It was as if something sacred had been touched. It had been his mother's home; the family home. It was probably the only possession that had ever mattered to David. It was his childhood; his parents laughing; it was Huck Finn and Tom Sawyer and Euripides and all the things that had been his parents. It was growing up; it was a reminder of youth, of the happiness and pain that comprised personal lives. . . .

He stopped right in front of her.

"You conniving little whore!" he exclaimed softly.

She stiffened. The smile slipped from her features to display saddened and weary features that, despite all his scorn and fury and pain, somehow touched him again. She was unique. So enchanting that even while a man despised her, he wanted to reach out and crush her against him and taste the sweet hint of passion that curved her lip. . . .

She backed away from him. He smiled.

29

"You are an insufferable bastard," she retorted with a touch of uneasiness. "But you think what you like—I really don't give a damn. You're even welcome to say what you like. But touch me again and I'll have the police on the phone."

He laughed bitterly. "If I were to touch you again, Miss Anderson, you wouldn't be able to get the police on the phone."

He turned away from her, startled and dismayed by both the violence and tempest of his thoughts.

"What are you doing now?" she demanded, and he was glad that she sounded nervous—very nervous.

"I am going to get drunk, Miss Anderson. As drunk as I possibly can!" He smiled, sat on the edge of the desk, and picked up the brandy bottle, swigging deeply to prove his intent. He lifted the bottle to her and gave her a frigid, mocking smile.

"How rude of me! Won't you join me, Miss Anderson? A toast—to your absolute and amazing victory?"

She ignored him with distaste.

"How long are you staying here? Don't you have to go back to New York?"

"Maybe," David replied. Then he shrugged. "I don't know. All I know is that for the moment I'm going to finish off my dad's brandy. Unless this bottle, too, is yours?"

Susan turned around and started walking to the door.

"Where are you going, Miss Anderson? Surely you didn't sell yourself for a spit of property just to desert it?"

"I'm going out!" she called back without turning. If he hadn't seen her, hadn't come to know her fervor and outrage, he might have suspected a sob in her voice.

But he had seen her. And he'd been signing checks to her for the last year.

He was drinking brandy again as the wooden door slammed, then the screen door.

Brandy . . . Guzzled like this, it burned the throat and

created an inferno in the chest. It made him feel afire. He prayed that it would dull his senses. All the pain, all the grief.

All the anger.

And the worst of it, all the incomprehensible desire. A fever not of the heart or the mind, but somehow of the soul.

A door slammed again. He looked up. Had she come back already? No, he realized dimly, it was the wind. A storm was brewing. He had known it when he came. A northeasterly from the force and sound of it. Even now he could hear the waves pounding on the sand and rocks with a fury to match his own. Soon the rain would come down as if the heavens had opened.

He knew the weather here. He had loved it as a child; loved it still as a man. Fierce gales; roiling, gray skies of clouds that billowed and rumbled.

About to take another long sip of the brandy, David hesitated.

She was out there.

He shrugged. She'd been living here awhile. She should have learned the weather. And if the wind should take her, the devil would be welcome to her too.

He didn't drink the brandy. He set the bottle down, trembling with a sudden vision of that blazing mahogany hair spread against the whiteness of the sand, her features as ashen as the bleached driftwood along the beach. Long limbs, tangled and lifeless . . .

"Damn it all!" he swore violently.

Then he strode across the room, through the foyer, and out the doors, allowing them to slam behind him.

The sky had become patterned in surly gray and black. Trees were bending, sand was flying, and the waves were rising high, like white kites against the vicious swirl of the heavens.

David's long gait carried him quickly along the walk to

31

the sand, and there he hesitated, raising a hand against the wind.

He should just let her go . . . because the strangest feeling rippled through him. It was as if he had come face-to-face with a crossroad and she beckoned him with a force he couldn't deny. She had some kind of power, like a Circe whispering a sweet melody that cut through wind and water and tempest. . . .

Should he go after her now, he knew he would be inextricably involved. One more step and he would never be able to turn back.

Ridiculous, he thought, scolding himself. All he wanted to do was make sure that the fool woman didn't drown. Even if she did kill his father.

At least Dad had gone out smiling, he reminded himself bitterly.

Smiling . . . He wanted to see her smiling. Laughing, filling the air with the melodious sound of joy.

He gave himself a shake. For God's sake! The woman had been his father's mistress!

The rain started just as he headed onto the beach.

CHAPTER TWO

Susan was choking back tears as she stumbled out of the beach house; tears she had sworn she would never shed. After all, she had met Peter Lane because he knew he was dying, and she had known exactly what to expect from the son. . . .

Those logical, determined thoughts helped her a bit, but she couldn't, for the life of her, understand why. She didn't care what people thought; she never had. So why, she wondered, was she so disturbed now? Especially since she had known for months now exactly what David Lane's opinion had been.

Her shoe caught in the sand, twisting her ankle. She swore softly, then allowed her tears to join with mist that surrounded her to dampen her cheeks. She realized that she had come right up on the beach, where the water was spewing over boulders and sand—and her shoes.

They were ruined, of course. Leaning against one of the

gray rocks that rose over her head, she pulled them from her feet and slammed them viciously against the rock.

What was it about David Lane that infuriated her to such a degree? The cold contempt and disregard she had first encountered when she had attempted to see him and tell him the truth about his father? She should have stayed that day. But she who had learned such serenity from life had tossed water in his face, stunned by his blunt, unexpected accusation. She shouldn't have done it. She should have been as cold and contemptuous as he'd been and informed him scornfully that he was an insolent bastard, but for Peter's sake she would tolerate his rude and unjust behavior.

Oh, no! She was right to have thrown the water in his face. She should have just stayed afterward and straightened things out then.

Except that his mind had been so set, he surely wouldn't have believed a thing she had to say. Except, maybe, about his father.

She shouldn't have been there to begin with, believing as she did in the rights of the aged and the dying. Peter might have been old and ill, but his mind had been as sharp as a whip. Sharper. Until the very end. And he hadn't wanted his son to know.

"Took me thirty-six years to get the relationship right with David," Peter told her once, "and for whatever time I have left, I want it to be what it is now. We're friends. He calls me, he sees me, he cares for my every concern. He leads his own life, but he's careful never to forget me. You can't always say that for young people today, you know," he had said proudly. Then he sighed. "Don't you see, Susan? We've finally got it just right. He's there, but he still respects my opinions, my individuality, and my privacy. If he knew, it would all change. He'd want me to come to New York. He'd start doting on me, and then I'd grow very old and decrepit, become a liability. No. I've got it all just right now. And that's what I want it to be like—down to the end. There's nothing I haven't had, Susan. Nothing. It's all precious to me. It's been a hell of a life. I've enjoyed it, and I'll continue to do so until the end!"

It had been Peter's right . . .

"Oh, I think that's why I hate you so much, David Lane!" she whispered to the rising wind. "He loved you; he was so proud of you. He was an incredibly great man—and you didn't think enough of him to believe that someone could care about him and not his money!"

She lowered her head dejectedly just as the rain started. She barely noticed it in her bitterness. What was the matter with their world that no one could accept a young woman and an old man being friends? Peter had been there for her when she had been alone and stumbling and groping. And she had been there for him. Not as a lover but as a friend. Someone who really cared for him and loved to hear him talk about his past, about his days as an immigrant, about the wife he had loved so dearly that he had defied his own people to marry her and flee to a new world . . .

"Oh, you son of a bitch!" she cried, with no one to hear her but the whipping wind and the rain. Ruefully she realized that she was dripping wet, that not only her shoes, but also her entire outfit was probably ruined. And that she— like an idiot!—was standing in the water while lightning coursed the sky.

But still she stood there, such a sizzle of pain and anger and outrage that her mind seemed too overcrowded to function correctly. She couldn't shake the image of the man—not the father but the son. She had lied; he was a great deal like his father. His eyes were so much the same, such a sharp, keen blue, seeming to assess so much more than what was seen by the naked eye.

"The man is blind!" she said raggedly.

She closed her eyes against the rain, hating him savagely, remembering the way he had spoken to her, the way he had touched her. How dare he judge what he knew nothing

35

about? And, once, she had been so eager to meet him. Peter had always talked about his son and shown her pictures. David at sixteen, soot-smeared face, helmet in his hand, grinning away on the high school football field. David in his Air Force uniform, clean-cropped, solemn, and beautiful as only a handsome young man could be. David a few years later, in what Peter jokingly called his Bohemian years, a man with overly long dark hair, his arm around a beautiful blond, scowling at the photographer.

David as a chubby, angelic baby, naked on a bearskin rug, his dark hair a riot of curls, his toothless smile a mile wide.

"Bearskin rugs were 'in' in those days!" Peter had told her ruefully, his eyes sparkling. "David hates this picture. He always warns me that he'll box my ears if I show it to anyone!"

And then there was the portrait of David on the sailboat, standing tall as he held the rigging, his broad shoulders covered in a red turtleneck, muscled thighs arresting in jeans. He was looking out to sea in that picture, framed by the sail and the sky and the water beyond, and something about the photo denoted a man of pride, of vital interest in the world around him. All of the fine breeding of his father's features were in his own high cheekbones, square and level jaw, long straight nose, dark jutting brows, and eyes as deep and as endless as the sea. There was a slight smile on his lips; it gave him the look of an adventurer of old. It spoke of humor and sensuality and even tenderness, and it had made Susan long to meet such a man. He would be Peter's son, as fascinating as the father. . . .

Or so she had envisioned—until she had been shown into his elegant office and informed that she should go to Peter for money since she was his father's mistress—not his!

"I tried!" Susan muttered. "You despicable bastard! You can take your beach house and—"

She broke off as a wave rose like a blanket of gray darkness, smacking her in the face and filling her mouth and

36

throat with seawater. Her hand slipped from the rock with the force of the water, and as the wave receded, the sand was washed out from beneath her feet. She fell, flailing, but in no panic. She knew this shore. The wave would rush out and she would find her footing again. She berated herself for not paying attention to the storm, to the force of the wind and rain that had cascaded against her. It was that horrible David Lane! She'd never known such absolute fury in her life, and it had completely stripped her of wit and good sense.

Susan staggered to her knees, teeth chattering suddenly, as if her body had just realized how cold the sea and rain and wind were. She planted a foot in the sand but it slipped, and she was thrown into the next wave that ravaged the shore. This time the water filled not only her nose and mouth but also her lungs, and as the wave receded, it carried her body with it. She was picked up as easily as a feather, buffeted, dragged, and buffeted again. The water had closed around her like an icy shroud.

Then she did panic. She could swim; she knew the treacherous currents of the shoals. But she was pitched far beneath the surface, fighting nature's power, her lungs on fire. Think! she warned herself desperately, aware that her life hung in the balance. Calm, rational thought. Don't flail, don't fight, go with the current, get to the top.

The urge to open her mouth and gasp for breath was unbearable. Even knowing that all she could gasp in would be seawater, she didn't think she could battle the urge much longer. Splotches of black seemed to be exploding inside her skull. She was blinded and freezing, almost too numb to make an attempt to live.

And she began to wonder a little hysterically if this was it. She who had learned to ease others from life was about to leave it herself. No waiting period, no adjustment, no time for regrets or restitutions. It would come on her suddenly, coldness and blackness embracing her. . . .

Still, she didn't flail. Nor did her life flash through her mind as she had always heard. Her foot touched the bottom, scraped against one of the rocks. She felt the motion but not the pain. She kicked against the rock, and then the surface broke above her.

The rain was coming in such torrents that it was difficult to tell the difference between sea and air, but she managed to gasp and fill her lungs with more oxygen than water. Treading water with care, she blinked furiously, seeking out the shore. It was incredibly far away, and yet she had been standing there moments ago.

But the sea was strong. Anyone who knew it well knew that. To survive she was going to have to stay calm, to waste no motion, to save her strength.

Another wave crashed over her even as she cautioned herself. It swept her under, tossing her toward the shore, then pulling her back out. She let it. She touched bottom again, sprang against it, and surfaced, gasping for a deep, deep breath. Then she plunged below the surface and began to swim.

She could stand again but she didn't. She stayed low where she could balance herself against the rush of water. Her heart began to soar with hope. She was almost back to the shore. Blinking the stinging salt from her eyes, she could see the giant gray boulders rising out of the sand.

Susan found her footing. The muscles in her legs were burning, as if a thousand bees had stung her, she realized. But it didn't matter. It didn't matter at all. The sand—gray and barely discernible against the gusting rain—was before her. She pushed back a sodden lock of hair that clung over her forehead and took another step.

A wave was coming; she ducked to brace against it. But it was more powerful than any of the others that had come before it. Go with it, go with it, she warned herself desperately. Don't panic, don't panic. . . .

She went with it—and gasped out an involuntary scream

of pain as the wave hurtled her like a twig against solid stone. Pain exploded in her temple. She was dimly aware that she had been tossed against one of the low-lying boulders and realized that water had poured into her open mouth, that it was filling her lungs, that she was choking . . . drowning.

And still nothing passed before her. None of her life. All she saw was a wall of blackness engulfing her. She couldn't fight anymore. She couldn't even lift a hand against the power that pulled and dragged her . . . a power like arms, strong arms, lifting her, carrying her, holding her. Bringing her to the sand. Giving her warmth against the terrible cold.

The rain continued to beat down. Oddly she could feel it slamming against her. She wasn't dead yet, but she was still being poked and prodded. Her stomach was being kneaded, and she was suddenly gasping again, spouting water and choking. And then she knew that she was really and truly alive because she was certain that one had to be living to feel so horrible and wretchedly sick!

Hands were on her, twisting her. She retched out all the seawater she had swallowed, vaguely realizing that it was taken back by the rain. Sand filled her mouth. Blackness alternated with bouts of dizzying misery. Someone was touching her, issuing commands that she could barely hear. Fingers tore into her hair. The rain washed around her face like a bucket of cold water, taking with it the salt and sand. Then it was suddenly gone, and something was above her face, shielding her from the onslaught. Her throat was forced back. She opened her eyes, and for a moment she thought that either she had died or the rain had ceased, for all she saw was a glittering crystal blue.

Then there was warmth and force against her mouth. Air shot into her lungs, and she was fighting the thing above her because she was going to choke again with the goodness of it. She was breathing again *and she hadn't been!*

Her eyes opened, and a semblance of reason returned to

her. Through the pelting rain she saw a face. A handsome face, dripping with rain, dominated by shocking blue eyes. David Lane. The man who had sent her to the shore; whose image had made her so bleak that she had noted neither the encroaching sea nor the storm. She was crushed against his chest, and he was hunched low around her to fight the wind. She couldn't move; not against the strength of his arms and not against the chattering numbness that enveloped her.

But she did see something in his face. Irritation, anger. That ever-present scorn. He was annoyed that he'd felt obliged to save her! she thought with amazement.

She would have never needed saving if it hadn't been for him, she thought in a moment of near hysteria.

His eyes fell on her open ones as the rain stopped beating against them when they reached the porch to the beach house.

"I hate you!" she whispered.

She saw his face tighten furiously, and that was all. A lid seemed to close over her with the slamming of the door. She pitched into a dreamless void where pain and cold were gone, as was all else.

David frowned, worried. He'd taken lifesaving along with sailing classes, and he knew CPR. Things had gone pretty smoothly. He'd managed to get the water out of her and air back into her.

But what the hell did he do now? She had opened her eyes, she was breathing, and her pulse was steady. But her body felt as cold as ice.

He muttered a soft oath and carried her with him into his father's study, certain that the best thing to do would be to get some professional help on the phone. Cradling her against him, he dialed the emergency number and was glad to get Jerry Tyler, an old friend from way back, on the phone. Even as Jerry efficiently asked for a description of the situation, David marveled that the village was so small that everyone in the whole town really did know one another.

"Jerry, this is David Lane. I'm at the beach house. I just dragged Susan Anderson out of the water—"

"Is she alive?" Jerry asked anxiously, then remembered that he was supposed to be the calm expert. "Is she breathing on her own—?"

"She's breathing fine and her pulse is steady, but she's passed out on me and she's as cold as ice. Shouldn't I get her to a hospital or something?"

"You can't get her to a hospital; Bay Road washed out about fifteen minutes ago. Thank God she's breathing! I couldn't even get a helicopter to you right now—the wind is too fierce."

"Well, what the hell do I do?"

"Get her warm. Keep her from going into shock. Try to get some brandy into her. What was she doing out in this weather, anyway?"

"I don't know—"

"She swims like a fish," Jerry muttered. "And she's no fool about the water."

"I imagine that her mind was occupied and the storm took her by surprise," David said ruefully. "Oh, hell! Are you sure that road's out?"

"Positive. Get her warmed up, then call me back."

David carefully extracted the receiver from the crook between his shoulder and ear and hung it up. Get her warm, Jerry had said. That made sense; her lips were turning blue.

He carried her back into the foyer and up the steps, hesitating a second, then walking ahead to his room. He laid her on the brown comforter and then wrapped it around her.

He realized then that he was touching her as he might a cobra, and that was ridiculous. Whatever she was, whatever he thought of her, she was in bad shape at the moment, and he couldn't go tiptoeing around with concern for her feelings or his own.

41

He left her and hurried into the bathroom, quickly drawing water that was steaming hot but touchable. He left the tub to fill and hurried back to the bedroom. He hesitated only once, staring down at her ashen features. She looked like a porcelain doll; her features were so pure, her skin so smooth. Her dark lashes swept her cheeks like velvet spikes, black against the pallor of her skin. Her hair, even sodden and tangled about her, glittered with red highlights, and he shook his head a little, objectively admitting that she was a uniquely stunning woman.

He stiffened, determined to keep that objectivity and not to harm her by acting like a fool.

He knelt down beside her, swept away the blanket, and started stripping away her drenched clothing. He didn't watch his hands—they were almost as cold from his own soaking as her flesh—but watched her face as he found the zipper to her skirt, loosened it, and pulled away skirt, slip, and panty hose all in one, casting them to the floor. He rested her face against his chest to struggle with the red jacket and her blouse.

She moaned slightly as he at last did away with her bra, and he paused with her weight against him, thinking that it would be a hell of a thing if she regained consciousness then —hating him the way she had so assuredly informed him that she did. She would be certain that he was attempting to rape her.

He made a sound close to a growl as he lifted her again, hurried back to the bathroom, balanced her weight, and turned off the water. Thank God she was light! She stood about five-five, he thought, but she didn't weigh more than a hundred or a hundred and five. If she'd been much larger, he thought with a quirk of humor, he'd probably have dropped her by now.

The quick spurt of amusement left him as he carefully placed her in the tub, and still she showed no sign of life. Maybe he should have tried the brandy first.

He shook his head in self-disgust, wishing the damned road hadn't washed out. It wasn't doing much for his tangled soul to realize that he wasn't any bargain in an emergency. He winced. Somehow he'd always been all right before. In the service he had made do with whatever was around in far worse circumstances. Now a slip of a woman he had every reason to detest had passed out on him, and he was starting to get really frightened that he was doing it all wrong.

David managed to set her head on the rim of the tub, and he checked her pulse against her throat. It was still strong and sturdy; her breathing was even and natural. And the water was surely warming her. Maybe he should get the brandy now. . . . He hunched back on his heels, worrying that if he left her, she might slip into the tub.

And then he discovered that he was staring at her, that he really couldn't help himself. Her body was as perfect as her face. Her flesh was unmarred in any way, a lovely creamy tan color without a scar or scratch. David knew there were those people who were unique, so lovely that no one could deny their particular beauty. She was one of them.

Even in this deadened repose her length seemed to be all grace. Her legs were long, lightly muscled. They rose to an enchanting curve at her hip, and her waist was narrow—even her damned belly button was perfectly set in her taut stomach.

He felt uncomfortably like a voyeur but still couldn't help assessing her. Objectively, of course, he tried to tell himself. But the sensation he had felt when they had so crudely tussled in the library was with him again. Desire was something that a man controlled, not a thing to control him. And yet he couldn't help being seized by that same fire. The ache to touch her was painful; the fascination to hold her, to challenge all the soul and passion she seemed to promise streaked through him like molten steel. Everything about her was elusive and intriguing: the dark and haunting curls

43

that formed a tempting web between her thighs; the rise of her breasts, rounded and firm and rose-tipped; the nipples, still hard and taut from the cold. Just a glance could have beckoned him to her; she was the type of Circe who could lure a man to anything. . . .

He closed his eyes, swallowing painfully, allowing a jolt of self-fury to grip him. Yes, yes, she could lure anyone. *Had* lured anyone! She had taken his father's last days and made a mockery of them, made a fool of him, and she had been rewarded well. No one had ever claimed that beauty could not be mercenary.

He reminded himself sharply that he had brought her here because he was growing more and more desperate about her state of well-being. He couldn't get the brandy; he'd left it downstairs like an ass. If there were smelling salts in the place, he sure as hell didn't know where. He couldn't dump cold water on her because he was trying to warm her up!

"How the hell can I be so incompetent?" he asked aloud, aggravated. He spun on his toes to the cabinet beneath the sink and dug out a white washcloth, dipped it into the water, and held it against her neck. He moved it over the other side, then gently over her cheeks. Her lips, he noted gratefully, were no longer blue.

And then, to his vast relief, her eyes opened. They were dazed and disoriented at first—then very wide with shock and alarm at the sight of him. Color flooded back to her cheeks, bright red color to highlight each, and she scrambled to lock her arms around her knees, wincing as she did so. David was certain that she was going to start screaming accusations.

He pressed the washcloth firmly over her lower face and spoke irritably as he rose. "Don't you dare say anything! They can't get any emergency vehicles through, and I was told to warm you up before you went into shock."

She didn't say anything; she just shook her head, causing

the washcloth to drop. Her eyes remained on him, and suddenly he discovered that he was giving her an ironic smile.

"I promise—I wasn't trying to drown you. You were doing that all by yourself." He shifted on his sodden shoes impatiently. "Look, are you with me? Do you feel like you're going to pass out again? I'll run quickly for the brandy."

"I'm—I'm not going to slip," she said weakly.

David nodded, but he still wasn't certain. He raced down the stairs to the library, then raced back up, arriving just in time to see her grope for a towel, about to leave the tub. She saw him, paled again, turned red again, sat quickly back within the tub, and hugged her knees. For some reason he couldn't begin to understand, he felt a softening toward her. He spoke less harshly.

"I'm not trying to embarrass you. I can't leave you in there alone." He handed her the brandy, and then he couldn't quite contain a slightly wicked smile because she was studiously trying to figure out a way to take the bottle without exposing herself.

David slipped a hand about her nape and placed the bottle to her lips. He could see the suspicion in her eyes—sea eyes now, green and blue and luminous—and his grin deepened. "Take a sip carefully," he warned her.

She did, then wheezed and coughed, anyway. He went to pat her on her back; she raised a hand to stop him, then groaned miserably and hugged it back around herself as she realized that she had defeated the whole purpose of his assistance.

David laughed.

"Miss Anderson, the modesty is a little false, isn't it? I mean, we both know how you got into that tub."

"Oh, will you get out of here?"

"What gratitude!" he said, dryly mocking. "Not, 'Gee, thank you, I wasn't planning on drowning today.' How the hell did you get into that situation to begin with?"

45

Her eyes flashed to his with such fury that he was certain she was going to be all right.

"I was sorely aggravated!"

"Ah, the trials of youth, Miss Anderson! Give yourself a few more years—life is full of aggravation. You can't go throwing yourself in the water every time it comes your way."

"I did not throw myself in the water!" she snapped. "I did not plan on drowning today. Nor did I expect to come home and find you! Nor can I understand—knowing your very frank and abusive opinion of me—why the hell you bothered to drag me out. Now, will you please get out of here?"

There was no expression on his face. When he chose, his emotions could be totally shadowed and secret. "I've no wish for your physical injury, Miss Anderson," he said flatly. "I'll get out as soon as you get out, because I sure as hell don't want you to lose consciousness again and drown in a bathtub after I went through all the trouble of hauling you out of the ocean."

"I wouldn't have been in the ocean if it weren't for you, so don't tell me about your trouble!"

David sighed with pointed weariness. "If you want me out, Miss Anderson, you get out. And don't be ridiculous. I undressed you and got you in there." He turned around impatiently, grasped a towel, and dropped it next to the tub over his shoulder. "Are you happy now? You can wrap yourself up and I won't look."

"Thank you," she said stiffly.

But a second later he was whirling around again, alarm glinting in his eyes as he heard a plop. Her head was beneath the water. He knelt desperately by the tub and grabbed her arm. She came up, staring at him again with that ridiculously innocent and wide-eyed alarm.

"Damn!" he proclaimed anxiously. "I warned you—"

"I'm all right!" she gasped out. "I was just rinsing my hair."

"Your hair?" He released her arm.

"It was salty—"

"Oh, Lord!" David groaned, falling back to his haunches with relief.

"I'm sorry!"

"Think nothing of it," he muttered, rising and turning around again.

A second later she murmured, "I'm up."

He turned around again, just in time to see her wincing as she gingerly touched a spot on her scalp behind her ear.

"What is it?"

"Nothing," she began, but he was already next to her, pushing back her wet hair, frowning as he studied the bump.

"That must be the problem," he appraised quietly. His eyes met hers. "Nasty bump."

"I think I was thrown against one of the boulders," Susan murmured nervously. "I was almost back to the sand, and then . . ." She shook her head, then shrugged, trying not to jump away from his touch, trying not to tremble at it.

"I'll get an ice pack," he told her. But before he quit the bathroom, he paused at the door and warned her, "Don't come down the stairs without calling me."

"I'm fine. I'm really fine. It's just a little sore."

"You're not fine," David said impatiently. "You had enough water in you to fill a kiddie pool, and it took several minutes in a hot bath for you to come to. Call me."

He started out again.

"Mr. Lane!"

David paused and slowly turned around. He felt himself tempted to grin again. There she was, a towel clutched to her breasts, water dripping down the length of her legs, from her hair to her shoulders, and she was very primly addressing him as Mr. Lane.

"Yes?"

"You're drenched yourself, you know," she reminded him. Her lashes fell over her cheeks, as if she were sorry she

47

had spoken. "The water was cold. You'll catch something yourself if you don't change."

He did grin. "I intend to change, Miss Anderson. As soon as you're downstairs by the fire, and as soon as I've given Jerry a call back to tell him you're conscious with a lump on your head, and . . . as soon as you're out of my room."

"Oh," she murmured, realizing where she was and determining to leave.

She rushed past him, and he had to laugh. Although the towel quiet decently covered her front, it didn't do a thing for her back. And as soon as she had shot out of the bathroom to pass him in his bedroom, she seemed to realize it.

Surely his bemused, ironic laughter had something to do with that realization.

She muttered out some kind of an oath.

Feeling as if a strange and sudden void had swept through him, David found himself curiously following her.

She didn't run to the left, to his father's bedroom. Peter's old bedroom, he corrected himself painfully.

She ran to the right of the stairway, to the guest bedroom. It gave him an even stranger and more grave satisfaction. And then he wondered why.

He was well aware that people didn't have to sleep with each other to be very involved. To make love. What was he hoping for? he wondered. Who was he trying to kid? He'd been signing those checks made out to her for months. . . .

He clenched his teeth together and started out of his room to the stairway. He'd stoke up a fire, put on some tea, call Jerry, see her situated, and then shower and change. He hadn't been in the beach house in more than a year, but he knew his things would be in the closet just as he had left them.

Peter wouldn't have disturbed them. He had always expected David to return to Maine, even when he knew that David had been making excuses and urging him to come into the city instead.

David clutched the banister for a minute, shaking with a quick resurgence of grief that took him unaware. Peter had lived a long and good life. Death was part of nature. The hard part was that he just knew he was going to miss Peter so damned much; a smile, a laugh, a word, a sparkle in the eyes. He was a grown man; he'd had Peter all through his youth; he had his memories.

Memories. That was it; that was part of the present pain and confusion. He hadn't wanted anything from his father; he'd wanted Peter to enjoy the fruits of a life of labor— spend every damn cent that he could. Only the beach house had meant anything to him, because it was a home filled with memories.

And Peter had left it tied up in joint ownership with *her!*

The door to Susan's room opened suddenly. She was dressed in a long white terry robe that fell to her feet and belted at the waist. Even completely covered, she was incredibly sensual-looking. Wet hair slicked back from her face, only her tanned collarbones visible at the *V* of the robe.

And her emerald-sea eyes were on him so strangely, with that touch of innocence that was so disconcerting.

Such a lie! he thought, warning himself. And yet he paused as she did, staring at her, because he had no choice.

At last she spoke, stiltedly, a little hoarsely, "I want you to know this at least, Mr. Lane. I—I was at least five feet away from your father when he died." A flush covered her visible flesh, but she didn't flinch or blink. "I don't know exactly what you suspected, but having met you, I can imagine. We were out on a small launch. Peter was fishing from the bow." She hesitated, swallowing, then added softly, "He died very peacefully."

David didn't say anything. He just stared at her.

"I wasn't near him!" she repeated, almost desperately.

He smiled. "What a pity," he said as quietly. "I kind of hoped he'd gotten to go out with a bang."

49

She looked as if she were ready to hit him again, whether he had saved her life or not.

"You—"

He held up a hand. "I'm sorry! I didn't mean anything against you. Really. I believe you. Are you ready to go down?" He reached out a hand to her. She stared at it, and he knew that she was thinking about stepping back into the room and slamming the door in his face.

He clutched her fingers, raising their hands between them. "Truce," he said softly. "We're cut off here; you might very well have a concussion. I don't want you hurt—honestly— and I don't want you to hurt yourself because of me. Honestly."

She didn't bolt, but she still stared at their fingers, held high and laced together.

"We can discuss the weather, politics, recent movies— nothing else."

"I don't think I can discuss anything with you," she said with a sudden flash of anger. "Not after—"

"Truce!" he said, reminding her sternly. He'd be damned if he was going to apologize for any of the obvious truths he had stated earlier. He didn't wait for her answer but tightened his fingers around hers and started down the stairs. "Come on."

She tugged back with little success and found herself following him down the stairway. "Why should I?" she said, protesting irritably. "Because I'm supposed to be so damned grateful that you saved my life when the whole thing was your fault to begin with?"

He stopped so suddenly that she crashed into his back. He steadied her and smiled rigidly into her eyes.

"Not because I saved your life. Because I'm not giving you any damned choice! Last chance—truce?"

Everything about her went rigid. "Truce," she snapped back.

It didn't sound like a truce at all.

CHAPTER THREE

Outside, the storm continued to rage. Rain and wind smacked ferociously against the windowpanes. It was dark beyond them, the whirling darkness of a tempestuous nightfall.

Inside, there was gentle light. The fire burned brightly, and a candle glowed before Susan on the table.

The electricity had failed the moment they had gotten downstairs.

And Susan had to admit that although David Lane was, indeed, the most arrogant and high-handed man she had ever had the ill fortune to meet, when he determined to be responsible for someone, he was that to that letter. Darkness had been no difficulty for him. With a mild sigh and a "That's to be expected, I guess," he had gotten her to the couch in the parlor, gotten a fire going with little fuss or effort, disappeared to produce tea made with water boiled on a camp stove, then warned her to sit still before disappearing again.

And so far they hadn't argued again, but that was because she hadn't opened her mouth at all.

She shivered a little, then drew her bare feet beneath her, covering them with the long skirt of her terry robe. She should have worn her slippers, she thought idly, but dismissed the idea of running back up the stairs for them. She didn't want to risk a surprise meeting with David Lane in the darkness. Not when he'd told her to sit still.

Not that she was accustomed to obeying orders in such a fashion. It was just that she knew a few things about him. She knew what he thought of her, and she had discovered that there were no holds to be had on him. She'd slapped him—poor judgment on her part—and wound up on the floor. Not hurt, albeit, but forced against her will by greater strength. And she had no doubt whatsoever that he wouldn't blink before using that same strength again. Against her, at any rate.

Was that what he was always like? she wondered wistfully as she nursed her tea and stared into the flames. No, she had seen hints of someone else, of a different man. One who could be gentle . . .

Could be! What was the matter with her? If she had the least bit of self-respect, she would manage to be as cold as he. She wouldn't lose her temper. She would wait out the storm because there wasn't any choice, then she would turn her back on him—give him her half of the beach house and forget that he existed.

She sighed softly and took another sip of her tea. Let him think the worst. She wasn't going to tell him anything else, not that his father had been dying and knew it long before the merciful heart attack took him. Of course, that fact would be the stab that could really cut him, but she wouldn't ever use it, not when she'd heard his words, seen his face when she first came in.

And as far as other things went, the hell with it. Anger still burned deeply within her. He had instantly jumped to conclusions without meeting her, without even wanting to meet her. Fine, she vowed, she'd be glad to help his warped little mind right along. Whatever he said from here on out, she'd manage to smile and agree.

And yet, as she stared into the fire in the darkened room, she shivered again slightly but not with cold. Whether closing her eyes or watching the flame, she kept seeing his face. His deep, crystal-blue eyes that were so like Peter's! The curve of his mouth, the lean structure of his cheeks, the set of his jaw. He was an arresting man. The type that anyone might turn to watch. His handsome features had a slightly elusive quality, and his indifference, the coolness with which he had totally ignored her in his office, could change so quickly to passion. He would always be like that, so quiet until, without warning, the sudden explosion of heat broke through.

"Oh!" she cried out as she was suddenly touched by a flicker of that heat. She hadn't heard him; he had come up behind her and set his knuckles against her throat.

"Sorry. I didn't mean to startle you. You're cool, and your pulse seems to be just great."

"I'm fine."

David walked around the couch to the fire and bent on one knee to toss another log onto it. "Did you keep the ice on the bump at all?" he asked dryly, his back to her.

She looked a little guiltily at the bowl set before her on the floor with melting ice cubes and a washcloth.

"I kept it on for a while. I'm telling you, I'm fine. I don't have a headache or even a sniffle."

He was still down on one knee, his elbow resting over the other as he gazed into the flames. He'd showered, she noted, and changed into very worn jeans and a burgundy sweater. He'd looked so elegant and sophisticated on that day she'd gone to his office—or at least what she had seen of him had been. Now he looked more relaxed, more approachable.

"I was just talking to Jerry again," he said, poking at the

53

fire. "The way you blacked out, you're not in the clear. You should be in a hospital."

"Oh, for God's sake! I've cracked my head before."

He stood, rubbing his nape idly, then turned his attention from the fire to her. He picked up the tea he had left on the mantel and sat in the overstuffed Early American chair that faced the sofa, resting his bare feet on the oak coffee table between them.

Susan felt ridiculously like retreating from her corner of the sofa to the other—farther away from him. She stiffened, reminding herself that she wasn't going to crack a bit, and wondering a little painfully why she cared what this hateful man thought.

She didn't move. She sipped her tea carefully, eyeing him over the brim of the mug. "I really can't see why you're so concerned, Mr. Lane, the way you hate me."

His lashes fell over his eyes. He shrugged, then put his tea aside and laced his fingers behind his head, leaning back to make himself more comfortable. "I don't hate you, not personally. I hate what you did."

"Really?" Susan inquired politely. "And what did I do, Mr. Lane? I was here when you weren't. I helped your father. I listened to him and I respected him."

His eyes fell on hers with idle speculation. "And you made a hell of a lot of money off him, too, didn't you?"

She forced herself to smile sweetly. "I was paid for services rendered, Mr. Lane, if that's what you're getting at. But you pay all of your employees, don't you? Does that make them all whores?"

"There's a difference, Miss Anderson," he replied as cordially as she had spoken. "Most of them work hard, they're damned good at their jobs, and their salaries reflect those traits. They aren't paid for . . . your kind of services."

She managed to laugh softly. "Ah, but Mr. Lane! How could you know the full nature of my services? I assure you, I worked very hard, and I was . . . excellent at my job."

54

He lifted his teacup to her, smiling as his bitter survey ran over her form in the fire's glow. His reply was softly spoken. "I'll just bet you were, Miss Anderson."

She lowered her eyes, weary and sickened by her own pretense. "How long will we be stuck here?" she asked tersely.

"Depends on what the storm does. If it hovers, we're in trouble. If not . . ." He shrugged. "A day or two at most."

"A day or two!" She groaned.

He lifted a brow to her. "Well, I wasn't expecting to be hemmed in here, myself. And I sure as hell wasn't expecting to find you here."

"I certainly wasn't expecting you."

"You weren't? How curious. Logic alone should have told you I'd come here."

"Why? You never came before."

"May I remind you, Miss Anderson, that I spent my childhood summers here. It's my family home."

"If you would have written or phoned, Mr. Lane, I would have been happy to leave for those few moments you chose to walk down memory lane."

"It didn't occur to me, Miss Anderson, that you would still be here. I thought you would have had the decency to clear out."

The tone of their voices grew sharper and more cuttingly restrained with each retort.

"Decency!" It was an outraged whiplash. She quieted then, her green eyes narrowing and sparking like flint in the firelight. "Decency, Mr. Lane, is common civility. It's also caring; it's respecting a person's wishes and loving them whether you approve of their actions or not. You fell on your father like judge and jury. You condemned him and made him pay. I had no reason to clear out, Mr. Lane. I knew the house was being left in my name as well as yours. He worried about me, and I couldn't argue him out of it. I had assumed that I could merely refuse to inherit and toss it all back into your lap. But now, Mr. Lane, I've come to realize that I have more right to be here than you do."

It had been fun to watch the change in his face. Fun to strip away that look of scornful temperance. Very satisfying to watch the mocking curve around his mouth stretch out to a tight line.

But she didn't like it at all when he placed his feet on the floor, rose, and stalked behind her.

She twisted to watch him, too unnerved to have him at her back when she couldn't see him.

His head was slightly lowered so that she could not see his features. His hands were in his pockets as he idly, slowly paced the distance of the couch behind her.

"Did you ever study much history, Miss Anderson?" he inquired politely.

"What are you getting at, Lane?"

"Oh"—he paused, very close to her, looking down at her to smile, a blue iciness in his eyes that belied his pleasant words—"I was just thinking about Charles II of England. Have you heard of him? He was a man famous for his mistresses. And on his deathbed one of his favorites came to him—they're not sure whether she bothered to say good-bye or not—and wrenched a jeweled ring off his finger. You see, she knew her days were numbered."

Keep your temper! Susan thought, warning herself. She returned his chilling smile. She even chuckled softly. "I could hardly 'wrench' the beach house off your father's person, Mr. Lane."

"Yes, well, it's still the same, isn't it?"

"Is it?"

The mask slipped from him. He looked hard and determined. Almost ruthless.

"Whatever you want for your half, I'll pay it, Miss Anderson."

"Will you really? Even an outrageous sum?"

"Name your price."

56

Susan unwound her legs and stood, smiling as she faced him. "You couldn't come up with my price, Mr. Lane," she said sweetly. She picked the candle up from the coffee table and sailed through the hallway to the kitchen, setting the candle back down on the counter with fingers that trembled with both triumph and anger.

The sense of triumph left her as she heard his soft tread behind her. She spun around, bracing herself against the counter.

He didn't come near her; he paused across the large room, leaning against the hardwood breakfast table. "Did you really manage to be left in such a comfortable position that money doesn't matter to you?" he asked in a manner that sounded ridiculously conversational.

She answered evenly. "It's none of your business. But if I were starving, Mr. Lane, I wouldn't sell you my interest in this house."

She didn't realize how tightly her hands were braced against the counter until he started to approach her, looming too tall and powerful in the dark shadows of the kitchen.

"Don't touch me!" she exclaimed, forgetting for the moment her determination to play it entirely cool. "I swear I'll call the police and get a warrant against you!"

He laughed, walking past her to the sink. "I wasn't planning on touching you, Miss Anderson." He grimaced, still a little too pleasant, then raised his hands to her, looking at them himself. "I'm well aware that it isn't at all logical," he murmured, and to Susan's annoyance she discovered that she stared at his hands, barely hearing his words. They were large and long-fingered—just as Peter's must have been once. Short-clipped, clean nails. He wore a sports watch and one ring, on his right hand, a garnet.

"But I'm afraid I'd feel a little tainted," he continued pleasantly.

"What?"

She stared into his eyes, the blood draining from her face.

His pleasant, searching smile brought home the import of his words, and the raging desire to tear into him again was almost more than she could bear.

She pushed away from the counter, lifting her chin as she strode past him in the shadows.

"Miss Anderson?"

She ignored him and walked back to the parlor. He followed her but didn't touch her. He blocked the stairway, leaning idly against the banister.

"I think it only decent to warn you: I'm afraid you can't call the police. We lost the phone wires while I was talking to Jerry."

He was staring at her very curiously. She wondered what he could see. Here—away from the glow of the fire—it was very dark. She could see little herself, except for the casual stance of his form and the glint in his eyes.

"Would you excuse me, please, Mr. Lane?" she said politely.

"Why?"

"I'd like to go up to my room."

"I'm sorry. You can't."

"Why on earth not?" she exploded.

"Because he said not to let you sleep for several hours."

"Oh, good God!" He still didn't move, and Susan was sure that he wouldn't. Even in the shadows she could see—or perhaps sense—something else about him that was heart-wrenchingly like his father. He had a certain twist to his jaw, a determined jut that meant neither hell nor high water would move him.

She turned around again and strode back to the kitchen. He followed her.

Back by the refrigerator she spun to face him. "Have a heart, Mr. Lane. Some semblance of one, at least! I will not pass out again. I will not drop dead and disturb your conscience. Please—let me be someplace where you aren't!"

"I wish I could," he whispered softly.

58

Returning his gaze, she found herself momentarily tongue-tied. Mesmerized for the passage of countless seconds. The way he looked at her . . . there was a real sense of sorrow, almost wistfulness, in his eyes. And more. A certain scrutiny that made her feel hot inside. Nervous and uneasy . . . and breathless, her heart pounding too hard within her chest.

He walked over to the refrigerator and pulled it open. Darkness greeted him, and he emitted a soft groan, turned to get a candle, then returned with it to study the contents. "In regard to your earlier comment," he muttered, "I'm starving at the moment. What have you got in here?"

"If you're starving," she said tartly, "you should be grateful that I was around or else there wouldn't have been a thing to eat."

"Ah, but if you weren't here, I could have merely taken the brandy bottle up to bed."

"You're quite welcome to do so."

"What's this stuff in the tinfoil?"

"Chicken."

"Cooked?"

"Yes."

"Dynamite." He picked up the bowl and held it out for her to retrieve. She hesitated. "Take the damn thing!"

With a sigh Susan took it and set it on the table. With everything else it seemed absurd to make a stand against a bowl of chicken.

"Anything else in here that's good cold?" he asked.

"Potato salad," she replied. "Lettuce. Tomatoes."

"A feast," he muttered.

Susan remained by the table. She watched him as he found the items she had mentioned, set the candle on the counter, and began to wash the lettuce. She didn't move as he deftly prepared a salad.

When he was done, he turned to her with a certain annoyance. "You could have set the table."

59

"I'm not hungry," she replied.

"That's a bad sign," he muttered, shaking his head. "Maybe you should lie down with the ice on your head for a while—"

He broke off as she moved, flushing despite herself, afraid that he might come over and run his fingers through her scalp once more.

Her fingers were shaking again as she pulled out the silverware drawer, and she hoped he couldn't see them. It had occurred to her then that, although she might have "tainted" his righteous fingers, he had undressed her. He wasn't just a stranger; he was the arrogant bastard who had jumped to conclusions, wronged her—and despised her. He'd not only seen her completely naked—he'd also made her that way.

And to her horror she was afraid of his touch in more ways than one. In some dark and fascinating way, even as he stalked and baited her, he beguiled her. Dear Lord! How she wanted to get away from him. . . .

As serenely as possible she set the table. David placed the candle between them.

"What's there to drink?"

"There's a bottle of white wine—"

"I wouldn't dream of drinking without you."

"I'd love a glass of wine."

"I don't think you should."

Well, that sounded absolute enough. "Pity," she murmured, "it might have made you bearably palatable."

"What's nonalcoholic?"

"The brown pitcher is iced tea."

"It's hard to tell what's brown. . . ."

Not thinking, she brushed past him. He was solid and warm, and she could sense the muscle structure beneath the sleeves of his sweater.

"This is brown," she said quickly, thrusting the pitcher into his hands, then sweeping to the table. It was a square table with small Early American chairs, little diamonds carved out of their backs, and cheery cushions tied to the seats. Susan sat.

He poured the tea and joined her. The table was too small. Her knee brushed his.

She folded her legs in the other direction.

He started to reach for the chicken, then frowned and reached beneath him, pulling a slim book from the chair. Susan felt her heart catch. She couldn't help but watch him as his eyes narrowed and he studied the book in the flickering light.

"*Night of a Thousand Storms,* by S. C. de Chance," he murmured. He studied the cover, then shrugged with little interest, placing it by the candle. His eyes fell on hers.

"Science fiction?"

"Yes."

He grinned. "The new romantic kind?"

"Yes."

"Full of sex scenes?"

"A few."

"Yours, I assume," he said politely. "My father was never big on romance."

A breath escaped her. She wondered why she had been so nervous; there was nothing to give her away. And if he did know, what of it?

She stared at her plate, pushing potato salad around with her fork. It did matter. She was still consumed with that furious urge to taunt him with his own despicable misconceptions.

"Yes, it's mine," she said curtly. Then she smiled at him winningly. "But you are wrong, you know. Your father read everything. He always said that—"

"Good writing was good writing; it didn't matter the topic, the category, or the style."

"Precisely." She pushed more potato salad around. "Do you write, Mr. Lane?"

"Not a word, Miss Anderson. I love the business, but I'm hopeless at the quest myself. You're not eating."

"I told you," she murmured uneasily, "I'm really not hungry." And before he could press her, she quickly asked, "How long am I supposed to stay awake?"

David was busy pulling apart a piece of cold chicken. "I'm not really sure. The line went dead when we were in the middle of that conversation. I guess midnight would be all right."

Midnight. How far away was that? She tried unobtrusively to lean over and look at his watch. He noticed her effort and offered up his wrist.

"Eight P.M., Miss Anderson."

Four more hours in his company. They stretched out like an eternity. She'd rather be in a hospital!

"You'd get a few minutes reprieve if you ate," he told her.

Startled, she noted that there was a teasing gleam around his eyes, as if he did have a sense of humor. A pleasant sense of humor—quite possibly—if she were anyone else in the world.

"Then I'll have a piece of chicken," she muttered, and he laughed.

There was silence for a moment, then to her surprise he pushed back his chair a bit, and she gazed up, aware that he was watching her. "I want to apologize—"

"You're going to apologize to me?" she said incredulously, and couldn't help but add a sweet, "Will wonders never cease!"

She should have left it alone. His mouth stretched out tightly, taking on a grim, white hue.

"Not for my opinion of the situation—or anything I said to you about it, or yourself. I'm apologizing because I called a truce for the evening and broke it. If we're going to survive it, though, the truce needs be put back in place."

"Why the hell don't you just let me go to bed?"

He shook his head. "I really can't. Jerry was insistent that I watch you."

"For what? If I did fall over, there would be nothing to do, anyway!"

"Yes, there would. I've got a list of instructions."

"This really is ridiculous."

"Maybe, Miss Anderson, but you're right about one thing: I really don't want your injury on my conscience. So that's the way it is."

Her jaw was solidly locked; her eyes snapped with more fire than the candle's flame. He laughed.

"Poor, poor Miss Anderson! It really is a hell of a situation, isn't it? You're accustomed to calling the shots, ruling the old manor. It's unthinkable for you to be trapped into taking orders. And there's not a damned thing you can do about it. No police to call, no way out."

"I'm sure there will be a way eventually," she said pleasantly. "I'll just get past you and lock myself up somewhere!"

He laughed, and she sensed that humor in his eyes again. "But you won't do that, will you? Because, of course, I'd just come after you and haul you back."

"Oh, but, Mr. Lane!" she proclaimed, her eyes very wide and sweetly naive, "You wouldn't want to do that! You'd have to touch me and you might get your elegant little fingers tainted and grimy."

"My fingers are neither elegant nor little, and sometimes I like to play in the mud, Miss Anderson."

"I'm quite sure, Mr. Lane, that you've played in truckloads of it!"

To her surprise he chuckled softly again, then lifted his tea glass to her, eyes studying her in an appraising fashion. "Perhaps, Miss Anderson, I should have made your acquaintance earlier. I might have been more understanding. You've got an angel's beauty and a devil's wit. I can see how you managed to garner his heart and soul—and his mind."

"I did love his mind," Susan replied pleasantly. "And his

soul and his heart and just . . . every little thing about him."

"I'm glad to hear it," David muttered. He pushed back his chair and picked up his plate, methodically scraping chicken bones into the trash, then filling the sink with dish detergent. "Do you play Scrabble?" he asked over his shoulder.

"I do. But I'm not sure I care to play with you."

"Don't you think it would be better than baiting one another for the next four hours?"

"I think it would be better if you let me go to bed."

He hesitated. "You're not going anywhere alone."

"I'll get the Scrabble board."

She stood, delved into a side drawer for another candle, lit it from the first, and returned to the parlor.

The board didn't fit on the coffee table. She set it up before the fire and brought two of the throw pillows down from the couch for seats. She glanced at the setup a little uneasily. It looked very intimate and cozy. Maybe she should have taken it back to the kitchen.

"Want some hot chocolate out there?" he called suddenly.

"Ah—I guess."

Susan grimaced, looking out at the storm. She was in an intolerable position, and it seemed as if the weather were laughing at her on top of everything else. The rain hadn't abated at all. With a sigh she sank down to her pillow and began turning all the letters over in the box.

Bringing the hot chocolate out on a small silver tray, David paused involuntarily in the doorway. His fingers tightened around the tray; his muscles seemed to quiver, then contract.

Yes, he could see so clearly how she could seduce and lay claim to a man. Her head was slightly lowered as she sat there, and the fire touched her hair, making glittering gems of the red highlights. It had dried now; it streamed over her shoulders like a satin cloak, contrasting beautifully with the

64

white terry robe. She looked so soft, so feminine, her long elegant fingers with their red nails moving over the letters in the box. Very feminine . . . the *V* of that robe not at all too low but falling just a shadowed half inch from her flesh as she moved. Maybe the shadows were so alluring to him because he knew what lay beneath. And maybe, if he'd never seen her before, he would be every bit as beguiled.

More so. If he didn't know her, he would be compelled to go to her, to touch her, to talk to her and whisper gentle words. He would want her, want to seduce her, to feel the brush of her hair against his shoulders, the slim length of her thighs against his own.

He closed his eyes and a new image rose before him: this woman, with her deep russet hair, standing slowly, shedding the robe. Stretching like a cat before the sultry flames, her breasts rising high and taut, the smooth line of her stomach flattening even further, enhancing the narrow curve of her waist, the flare of her hips. . . . She would smile, that slow, taunting smile, and a man would step forward. His hand would slide along her bare side to her hip and rest there, pulling her against him. . . .

A man. He gritted his teeth and opened his eyes, fighting dizziness. The man had been his father, and her sensuous smiles and liquid beauty and talent had been for sale.

He gave himself a little shake. What the hell was the matter with him? He wasn't exactly starved. He was no kid dragged out of a jungle after months of abstinence. Sexual play was easy to come by these days. Maybe too easy. He didn't remember what it was like to want a woman and not find her equally enthused. Or to be wanted himself and smile and play the game. Only the kid he had once been felt like he did now; so entranced, so shaky, so hot and on fire, as if having her were the most important thing on earth.

Ass! He thought self-accusingly. Just like he had been that one fool time when he had learned how badly it could hurt and destroy to fall in love.

She had been his father's mistress. She hadn't tried once to defend her mercenary position. She had bled Peter, and she was still here, gloating over her earnings.

Why the hell didn't he just let her go lock herself away? She was all right, he was certain of it. Precautionary measures weren't really necessary. She'd bumped her head and passed out. She'd been waterlogged and frozen, but now she was dry and warm, and her eyes were bright and her pulse was strong.

He stepped into the room, setting the chocolate on the coffee table. He got down on the floor on his own side of the Scrabble board, leaning on an elbow, his legs stretched out beyond him.

"Pick your letters," she told him.

He did. They played in silence for a while, the game moving swiftly. Her prowess with words surprised him a little, then he wondered why it should. She was obviously very smart. Bright, challenging, mocking. He could tell by the tilt of her head, the glint of her eyes, that she had decided to do battle with him. She would never cringe or apologize for her actions; she would flaunt them in his face. Taunt him, bait him . . .

It was his turn. He formed a word.

"What are you planning on doing now?" he asked, offering a crooked grin.

"What do you mean?"

"Well, you are off the payroll. We only pay for services while they're still being rendered. And you have been living with champagne tastes. What will you do for money?"

He saw her tighten; her fingers twitched, as if she longed to set them around his throat. But she spelled out her word, commenting that it was a triple score, then smiled directly at him.

"I'm quite sure I'll get by," she purred.

"I'm sure you will. You could get by a little better if you sold me your half of the beach house."

"I have other things to sell, Mr. Lane."

He chuckled a little too harshly. "Is that an offer, Miss Anderson? Maintain the status quo? You keep up the beach house and I keep writing out payroll checks. You just transfer the services to a different Lane?"

One of the little wooden letters went snapping out of her fingers, but she managed to smile at him. "I don't think so, Mr. Lane." Her eyes moved over his reclined length in an unimpressed assessment. "You just don't . . ." She hesitated, as if she were trying desperately to speak gently. Then she shrugged, as if it were useless. "You just don't compare, Mr. Lane."

Somehow he managed to laugh. "Ah, but what if it meant a tremendous increase in salary?"

"You couldn't pay me enough. Besides," she reminded him very nicely, "you condemned both your father and me for what you're now offering yourself. You consider me more grating than the sand on the beach. Why on earth would you want to suggest such a thing?"

"Curiosity," he told her very quietly.

Susan found her eyes drawn to his, although she was trying very hard to maintain control over her temper and return his humiliating taunts with digs guaranteed to draw blood from his male ego.

She couldn't help but stare at him and quiver inside. Curiosity. It was his word, but despite her rational mind, all her good sense—and her absolute fury—she felt it too. Something, something about him . . . His eyes, so blue. His ironic smile. His hands . . .

Something inside her ached. It had nothing to do with thought, the natural assessment she gave any person in regard to becoming friends—much less lovers. Some small part of her, some instinct, wanted him. Wanted to know how his hands would feel on her, how his mouth would touch hers in a kiss. The wanting swept over her like a tide made hot by the sun. Like a storm taking root inside of her, whirling into a reckless wind.

He's an insolent, dominating idiot, she reminded herself harshly. No self-respecting human being would ever forgive his words or treatment of her.

She picked up the letter she had dropped.

"Curiosity?" she returned idly.

"Curiosity," he said softly again, and though she didn't look at him, she could feel that strangely speculative look in his eyes. The crooked smile ruefully turning up his lips. For all the violence he had shown her, she could imagine that he could be gentle. That he would stroke her cheek, would stoke passion slowly, tenderly, until it was returned with ecstatic splendor, and then it would fly on silver wings to . . .

"I can't help but wonder," he said a little huskily, "what it is about you, what you do, that made you worth everything in life. Are you really that good?"

She snapped a letter into place, having no idea if she had spelled a word or not. She stared at him coolly.

"I'm absolutely the best, Mr. Lane. But you'll never know."

He chuckled. "I wasn't really making the offer, Miss Anderson. I just wanted to hear your reply." She froze; he sounded a little disappointed, as if he'd expected some protest of innocence.

She owed him no explanations, she reminded herself. He'd made them all up for himself.

"I suppose," he said dryly, "that you do have other—assets—to sell too. There's the sable, of course. That coat should draw a small fortune in itself."

So he had looked at her that day. At her back, anyway. Of course, the water in his face had forced him to look up.

She smiled. "Your father just loved me in fur," she told him in her best, most sensual drawl.

The board jiggled as his hand moved convulsively, knocking it. "You didn't spell a word," he said. *"Xet* is not in the English language."

Susan stared at the letters. David went ahead and moved them for her, tossing the *T* back to her and attaching the *E* and *X* to an *S* already on the board.

He whistled softly. "Found you a triple-letter score on that *X,* Miss Anderson. 'Sex.' I'm amazed that you didn't find that one yourself."

Susan stood up, unwinding gracefully. "Good night, Mr. Lane. It's surely midnight or close to it by now."

He didn't move, but his eyes were on her. She wondered why they could hold her with such force, why they still seemed to pin her there.

"I believe it is," he said, his lips curling ever so slightly, so that he might have been laughing at her inside.

"Good night."

"Take the candle up the stairs."

"I will."

"Make sure you put it out."

"I will."

"And say a prayer, will you please?"

"A prayer for what?"

He unwound and stood, keeping his distance from her, his hands on his hips.

Shadows played against his face, but there was something there in his taut features, something that might have been a form of anguish, as if he were a man pulled roughly in two directions.

"Pray that the storm breaks," he said simply, and then he turned away, disappearing through the kitchen door.

CHAPTER FOUR

Saturday dawned dark. Susan awoke lethargically, aware that although the rain had ceased for a while, it would come again. That meant that the road would still be flooded, that the phone and electricity lines would still be down, and that David Lane would remain in the house.

It seemed rather senseless to bother to rise.

Susan rolled over, casting her eye on her alarm, a little relieved to discover that she had slept through the morning and that it was almost noon. There would be another afternoon, and an evening, but surely by tomorrow the rains would cease and Mr. Lane would be on his way.

She sighed softly, hugging her pillow. She'd had a right to sleep so late. She had tossed all night long in a realm of nightmares. The water had been coming over her again, the tide so strong that she couldn't resist it. She'd seen her brother Carl's face in her dreams, heard his voice pleading, "My hand, Susan, take my hand. . . ."

And she'd seen David Lane in those nightmares, too, his

eyes condemning her. She'd even felt his hands on her shoulders, shaking her . . . on her naked body, carrying her into the tub . . .

Thank God the night was over!

She stretched and settled back into her pillow, staring through her window to the ominous gray day beyond it. She mused that the day was really rather apropos; David Lane was just like it. Even when the storm wasn't raging, it simmered and brewed. And one always had to be wary because the calm would cease and the wind would rail once again.

She started, chills racing instantly down her spine, when a tap sounded at the door. She didn't answer, and it came more insistently.

"Miss Anderson, are you all right?"

There was a touch of anxiety to his voice, and impatience. If she didn't answer, he would probably knock the door down.

"I'm fine!" she rasped out quickly.

There was a slight pause, then, "Sorry I disturbed you. I was concerned."

She heard a soft tread of footsteps as he moved away, and she wondered irritably why her heart continued to pound with such a nervous fervor.

He meant nothing to her. Nothing. He was dangerously presumptuous, concerned for her life, perhaps, but little more. She'd learned the hard way that he didn't intend to tolerate her temper, yet he was adept at igniting it with ease. She knew exactly what he thought of her and she hated him for it.

And she was still nervous around him. Amazed that when he chose to be pleasant, he could be arrestingly so. Attractive and compelling; a little too beguiling by candlelight.

Ah, and why not? He was Peter's son. With his father's dark Gaelic looks and crystal-blue eyes. Sharp as a tack, young, a handsome man. He was a disturbing presence, and he would have been no matter when or how she had met him. If he were to enter a crowded room, he would be noticed right away.

She should just stay locked in here all day, she thought, but even as she did so, she rolled off the bed. It was impossible to lie there any longer. She was too restless, too confined. If the rain stopped at all, she was going to get outside.

Susan dressed in jeans and a red cardigan and came down the stairs. David was in the parlor, clad in a mackintosh, straightening a new supply of logs by the fire. Apparently he'd been out in the shed to bring in more wood.

He gazed up at her entrance, his eyes roaming lightly over her, a slight smile curving his lips.

"Good morning, Miss Anderson."

"It's not really, is it?"

He chuckled softly, dusting off his hands and standing. "No, it's not. The radio says this is some kind of major squall. There's no chance of it breaking before tomorrow."

"Wonderful," Susan murmured, her lashes falling over her eyes.

David Lane shed the mackintosh. He was wearing black, form-fitting jeans and an old blue football jersey. "Don't sound so bleak, Miss Anderson. It's possible for us to spend the day being polite to one another."

"Mr. Lane, I was never rude," she said in bitter reminder.

He shrugged, apparently believing that he could dispute her but didn't intend to bother. "There's coffee in the kitchen on the camp stove. And a plate of pancakes if you're interested. They might be a little rubbery now; they were made a long time ago."

She couldn't help but frown curiously. "You made pancakes on a camp stove?"

"Mmm."

"You cook?"

He grinned at her in return. "Obviously, Miss Anderson. I've been on my own quite some time now, and one tends to become fairly proficient that way." He plopped down on the

72

sofa with a book. Susan walked on by behind him, holding her breath a little when she was right behind his dark head.

"Bring me some coffee when you finish and are on your way back through, will you?"

Like hell, she thought, but then she released her breath, and at the sink her fingers tightly gripped the edge of the counter. Now she was getting ridiculous. He'd had the consideration to make the coffee and breakfast. It would be rather childish to refuse to do something so simple in return.

She hadn't touched much at dinner last night, so she wasn't terribly surprised to be ravenous. And his pancakes were delicious. It was a little irritating that he had managed them so well on a small stove, but Susan tried to shrug off all her nasty feelings. After all, she had gone out of her way to reverse his knife thrusts and convince him that she was exactly what he thought she was. Their war was being waged on a grand scale—and she was surely the victor, simply because he was so damnably, arrogantly wrong!

She brought him a cup of coffee from the kitchen and then realized with a little chill of horror that he was reading her romantic science fiction book.

His eyes came to hers as she handed him the cup, and he smiled with just a trace of cynicism. "You don't mind, do you?"

"I wouldn't think that you'd enjoy it, Mr. Lane," she said smoothly, despite her pounding heart. "There's a full library just—"

"Oh, I was interested," he said, interrupting her.

"In?"

"In your reading taste, Miss Anderson."

There was a flush rising to her face despite herself. And despite herself, she reached down and tried to take the book. But his fingers held the spine tightly, and she came too close to him in her efforts to snatch the book away. Too close! She was leaning over him, touching him, and all the while his sharp blue eyes were watching her speculatively.

73

"It's only a book, Miss Anderson," he reminded her softly, his words a warm whisper against her cheek.

She held still for a minute, realizing that she was never going to wrest the book from him. And the longer she tried, the deeper his mocking smile was going to grow—and the more curious he would become.

She released her hold on the book and quickly steadied herself. "It seems rather absurd to read a book you don't like!" she snapped.

He arched his brow. "I never said I didn't like it. I can enjoy reading anything—if it's competently written and offers an intriguing plot."

Susan moved over to the window and stared out at the beach, empty beneath the gray sky.

"And is it competently written?" she asked.

She heard him rise behind her and wished she hadn't trapped herself by the window. Arms crossed over his chest, he joined her perusal of the great outdoors.

"Yes, actually, I think it is."

She didn't dare look at him. "I think I'm going to get a little fresh air," she murmured quickly.

"Spicy, though, isn't it?"

"What?"

"The book." He smiled pleasantly, but he seemed exceptionally tall and broad to her right then, like a powerful demon toying with some cornered soul. Very warm, well muscled, too male.

"Spicy?" she repeated a little vaguely.

He laughed. "Sexual . . . sensual. Almost enough to make one feel like taking a cold shower. Tell me, does this kind of reading help you in your chosen life-style, Miss Anderson?"

Her blood seemed to grow cold. She stared at him, some deep sense of self-preservation warning her not to slap him, then spun quickly around.

"I definitely need some fresh air!"

She didn't bother to dig into the closet for a mackintosh, but slammed out the front door. It did feel good to be outside. Her cheeks were flushed, and she was in a tempest of fury all over again. There was absolutely no trusting him; he might speak as politely as a political orator, but he just wasn't able to keep his barbs to himself. Oh! She usually loved being here in this forlorn little outcrop, so wild and beautiful. Independent . . .

But right now she wished Peter had chosen to hide away almost anywhere else—as long as there was more than one road that washed away with every storm leading to it.

She started to the water, then drew back. With her luck David Lane would see her and rush out to keep her from throwing herself back into the ocean.

She started toward the rise of pines instead, berating herself for having gotten out of bed, for drinking his coffee and eating his pancakes, for not spending the night in the sand rather than beneath the same roof.

She paused in her thoughts suddenly, aware of a low moaning sound. Frowning, she pushed through the scraggly brush and past a weatherworn slab of granite, then paused again.

It was whimpering sound, full of pain.

She kept walking, pausing to listen now and then. Seconds later she passed another of the boulders and found the source of the cries beyond.

"Sam!" she cried, falling to her knees beside the massive Irish wolfhound. He was just lying there, whining pathetically.

"What is it, boy?" He whimpered again, and then she saw the problem and realized why she had missed it at first. Quills were embedded alongside the dark whiskers that grew all along his homely silver nose.

"Oh, Sam!" When she moved to touch him, he growled at her and she sat back, unnerved and at a loss what to do. Sam belonged to Dr. Harley Richmond's father, a widowed retiree who lived about half a mile into the pines. Susan had known Harley for years but hadn't met his father until she had met Peter. Sam had never growled at her; she had always thought that the dog cared about her.

"There you are!"

She glanced up, startled to see David Lane coming toward her, a look of naked relief on his face. He seemed exceptionally competent in the stark woodland environment.

"What are you doing?" he asked impatiently, and she realized that he couldn't see the dog behind the slab of rock.

"It's Sam," she murmured, too concerned about the dog to inform him that she wasn't suicidal, that he certainly didn't disturb her that much, and that she didn't appreciate being followed.

"I was worried," he said briefly, stepping past her. "Why, it *is* old Sam!" David, too, fell to his knees, studying the animal. "What did you do, boy, get into a tussle with a porcupine?"

The dog whimpered.

"He—he snapped at me," Susan offered.

"He's in pain, that's why," David said. Then he started talking to the dog. "Take it easy, Sam, it's me, David. Yeah, I know it's been a while, but I'm going to help you, okay?"

He glanced at Susan. "Those porcupine quills are just like fishhooks," he murmured. "We've got to get him back to the house. I'm going to need a good strong clamp to get them out."

Susan nodded a little hesitantly. Sam weighed over a hundred pounds, and the usually gentle creature had teeth that now seemed exceptionally large.

David didn't seem concerned. "Go ahead of me, will you? Get a big towel and find a clamp." He grinned. "We'll perform surgery in the kitchen."

She hesitated. "You know Sam?"

"Sure." He gazed at her, his smile a little rueful. "I grew

76

up here, remember? I remember when Jud Richmond bought Sam."

Susan swallowed uneasily. "You're friends with—with Jud Richmond?"

He gazed at her briefly, as if he considered the question strange. It probably was.

"Of course I know him."

He turned his attention back to the dog, speaking very softly. "It's going to be okay, Sam." The dog growled again. David didn't pull back, he just waited. Sam went silent, then whimpered. David brought his knuckles closer to the dog's nostrils, still whispering soft and assuring words. "I've got to pick you up, boy. You've got to trust me. . . ."

David got his hand on the dog and started stroking his neck. Sam kept whimpering. Then David braced himself and slipped his arms beneath Sam's body. Sam made no protest, and David rose, staggering a little.

He gazed at Susan, grimacing. "Miss Anderson, I'd really appreciate it if you could at least get the door!"

Susan flushed, turned, and raced ahead of him. She waited at the door until he was through it with his burden, then hurried upstairs to get a towel, down to the basement to dig through the tools for a clamp, then back to the kitchen. David already had Sam situated on the floor in front of a bowl of water. He'd talked the dog into dipping his nose in it to ease the sting of the quills.

He glanced up briefly at Susan and muttered his thanks, then took the clamp and indicated that she should wrap Sam in the towel. She did so nervously, remembering that Sam had growled at her. David caught her hand.

"I've got him. He can't reach you."

She realized then that his legs were locked around the dog's shoulders and that Sam's haunches were caught beneath the kitchen chair on which David sat. She nodded and wrapped Sam's damp and sand-coated body more closely.

She noted that David's lip tightened a little grimly as he

caught the wolfhound's lower jaw with one hand and took the clamp to the first quill. David started talking to the dog again, soothing him, and Sam started and bared his teeth, then yelped as the first quill was pulled from his nose. He shuddered and whimpered. David took a breath and went back to work.

In time the quills were out. Seventeen of them in all. David doused the dog's nose again, then released him. "That's it, Sam!"

Sam barked joyously; his tail began to thump the floor furiously, then he rose on his hind legs, planted his forepaws on David's shoulders, and slurped his face.

"Sam!" David protested, stumbling backward. He was tall, but the dog stood on a par with him.

Susan couldn't help but laugh. David shot her a quick glare but then started laughing too.

"Get down, you pest!" David commanded, and in a moment the dog complied. "You're filthy. What did you do, get caught out in the storm?" David sobered suddenly, glancing at Susan. He winced. "We need to get him home. Old Jud will be sick with worry."

She froze, not wanting to see Jud with David. She'd never discussed Peter with Jud, but the two men had been good friends. She even doubted that Peter had told Jud about his illness; the problem was that Jud was Harley's father, and Harley had treated Peter at the hospital. And Jud, of course, knew all about her.

Knew about her in a way, she thought bitterly. Jud knew where she had met Peter, knew about her past, and about her work. But it occurred to Susan that no matter what anyone else thought, David Lane would probably think them naive. He had already condemned her, and his opinion would not change easily.

"The storm is going to break again," she said quickly. "If it's going to clear tomorrow, I can take Sam back up—"

"You don't have to come with me. I'll probably get

drenched, but that dog is like a child to Jud. He's his best friend. And Jud is too old to get himself worried sick over a dog."

Susan winced, wondering how a man who could be so brutally crude could also be so damned sensitive. But, she reflected, he was also probably right. Jud would be worried sick about the pet he so adored.

"I'll get the mackintoshes," she muttered.

"Maybe you shouldn't go," David said, halting her. "There's no reason for us both to get soaked."

She didn't want him alone with Jud! "I don't mind getting wet!" she blurted quickly, then raced through the parlor to the foyer and the closet.

Sam appeared ridiculously happy for a dog who had so recently been in so much pain. He bounded ahead of them as they walked through the brush and pines, then came running back.

"Damn rascal would probably get along just fine without either of us!" David commented disgustedly as Sam came back to him once in a flying leap, almost knocking him over.

Susan chuckled and taunted, "My, my, Mr. Lane, you do seem to have an affinity with canines!"

He cast her a dry glare, then returned her cool smile. "And you, Miss Anderson, seem to have an affinity for aging men."

"I do, don't I?" she replied briefly, then rushed ahead to catch up with Sam.

Twenty minutes of rugged, uphill walking brought them to the small hunter's lodge where Jud Richmond enjoyed his retirement. They found Jud—a man who resembled a true hermit, if ever there was one—standing outside the door of his rough log home, hand shielding his eyes as he searched the field and trees. Sam let out a joyous bark, then raced toward his master. With the finely tuned inner sense of an animal he did not jump on the older man as he had done to

David. He approached Jud on his belly, whining and thumping his tail.

"Why, you old tramp!" Jud said, admonishing the dog and bending down, gnarled fingers shaking as he patted Sam. "If my hair weren't gray already—what did you do to your nose, boy?" At that Jud looked up, then waved as he narrowed his eyes and saw Susan and David. "Susan!" he called.

She reached him and gave him a little hug. "You okay up here in the storm, Jud? I found Sam by the pines—"

"He run off on me last night, fool creature!" Jud said. "I was in a dither, I can tell you that, young lady. Now who's this—David? David Lane! Well, I haven't seen you in a month of Sundays, boy!" As Jud embraced David, Susan found herself watching the two critically. If David hurt old Jud in any way, she'd be ready to go to battle all over again.

David didn't. He returned the greeting with sincerity, smiling and tolerating being called boy with an easy smile.

"Sorry about your pop, son," Jud told him, his rheumy eyes sad. "He was the best of them, you know."

"Yeah, I know," David said huskily, then quickly changed the subject. "How are you doing, Jud?"

"Good, good—now that you two have brought me my friend back. What did the fool dog do?"

"Tangled with a porcupine," David told him.

Jud shook his bearded head wearily. "Fool dog!" he muttered affectionately, patting the wolfhound's head. "Well, maybe you learned your lesson! Maybe you won't hightail it out on me again when the rain starts next time." He looked up to the sky. "And it's going to start again soon!" He peered at Susan. "You want to come in for a drink, missy? Something to warm your bones before you start back?"

Susan didn't get a chance to speak. David answered for her. "Thanks, no, Jud. Miss Anderson got a bit of a whack on the head yesterday—wind got her and a boulder at the same time. She's sticking to the nonalcoholic stuff today. And the rain is going to start. We'd better head back."

Jud nodded. He peered at Susan again. "You okay?"

"I'm fine, Jud," she said, flashing David Lane a quick glance to convey her irritation.

"Anything you need with the road washed out?" he asked.

"I don't think so."

"I've got a batch of the best New England clam chowder you're ever going to taste. If you won't come in, why don't you take some back?" Jud suggested.

"Now that sounds great," David said, brushing a windblown thatch of dark hair from his forehead. "I haven't had anything as good as your clam chowder since . . ." He grimaced, then laughed. "Since the last time I had your clam chowder."

"Just hold on one second, then." Jud hurried into the log house. Susan knelt down to pat the dog on the head, feeling ridiculously alone again—alone with David Lane.

But Jud was true to his word; he was right back, a large covered kettle in his hand. "You can hang it right over the fire in the parlor," he assured them. His voice cracked a little. "I sure do thank you both for old Sam, here."

"It's nothing, Jud," David said.

"I hope I get to see a little more of you, David." Jud nodded toward Susan. "Nice to see you together. Your father sure did want the two of you to meet."

David smiled pleasantly; only Susan heard the edge of bitterness to his voice. "Yes, well, we've met now."

Jud shook his head. "Pity Peter ain't here. But then, that's one of the problems with life, huh? Seems like things just happen too late sometimes. You just can't put things off. Got to do them when the time is right."

"Yes, I guess you do," David said, still pleasantly, but he looked up to the sky. "That rain is going to start. We'd better start back."

Susan didn't want to start back. She suddenly wanted to

plead with Jud to let her stay with him until David went back to New York. But the words died in her throat because Jud was talking again. "Harley was asking about you, Susan. He was worried, what with Peter gone and all. About how you were bearing up and all."

"I'm really fine," she said, forcing a smile to her lips. "Uh, tell Harley that I'm . . . fine."

"You gonna go by and see him soon?"

"Yes, soon," she promised. David Lane had her arm now. He was pulling at it with his customary firm force.

"Jud, take care. It's a twenty-minute walk back, and the sky is getting darker and darker."

Jud waved. Sam barked and thumped his tail against the ground. Susan was barely able to wave with David quickly leading her back to the trail through the pines.

He was silent at first as they hurried along. A long streak of lightning rent the sky, followed by a tremendous clap of thunder. "Can you run?" he asked brusquely.

"Of course."

His hand still clutched her arm. Long bronzed fingers wound around her wrist. They started to run: he, surely; she a little bit breathlessly.

They broke onto the beach and saw the house just as the heavens let loose. David quickened the pace. Seconds later they were in the foyer, shedding the soaked mackintoshes.

"Take this, please," David said, passing her his as he carried the soup kettle over to the mantel. Down on his knees, he hooked in a spit over the fire and set the chowder over it to heat.

Susan hung up the coats uneasily, wondering why she wasn't still at Jud's. What a solution that would have been! What had brought her back?

David's grip on her arm, she reminded herself uneasily.

He stood, his shirt damp and plastered to his chest, outlining the fine tone of muscle beneath. He gazed at her with his crystal-blue eyes, more enigmatic than usual, and said coolly, "I'm going to grab a shower and dry clothes. I suggest you do the same."

He passed her and proceeded up the stairway. She heard the door to his room close, and she shivered, wondering if the sensation that rippled along her spine came from the wet rain or from David Lane.

She hated to follow any suggestion he made. But she was wet and cold, and a hot shower and dry clothes were needed.

She walked up the stairs slowly, wondering how the man could be so decent to an Irish wolfhound and so rigidly cool to her.

"Oh, I hope he rots!" she muttered aloud, slamming her own door and hurrying into her shower to quickly strip and suds herself beneath the hot water.

She should get out, she told herself. Give him his half of the damned beach house and get out of his life quickly. After all, she had intended to give up her half immediately; she hadn't wanted the inheritance. But then she had come up against his attitude and decided that hell could freeze over before she did one blessed thing for him.

Susan stepped out of the shower and wrapped herself quickly in a towel, pressing it against her cheeks. Darkness had fallen along with the rain. It was night, a stormy night again. She had survived the afternoon, and in places it had been strangely absorbing, disturbing . . . watching him with the dog, helping him, collecting the quills as they came from Sam's nose one by one. Watching his hands, so gentle on the animal, so powerful in their hold . . .

Hearing his innuendos! she reminded herself sharply.

But despite herself, she was remembering her last stint in a bathroom. Realizing that she was naked, that he had made her so, that he had touched her and cared for her and was still doing so.

"Argh!" she exclaimed aloud, and rose. She dressed in a nightgown and covered it with her full-length terry robe, securely belted, then brushed out her damp hair and walked resolutely down the stairs.

David was already down there, sitting on the sofa and sipping a glass of wine. The clam chowder was on the coffee table; bowls and crackers were set around it. The scene was pleasantly inviting. Too much so, Susan decided. The fire's glow touched the room. It seemed so comfortable, a cozy haven that lovers should share.

Susan paused in the foyer; he hadn't seen her yet. His eyes were on the flames, reflective and far away. She wondered what was going through his mind; she quivered a little bit inside because he was such an arresting man: a curious character etched into his features, his eyes such a haunting, brooding blue.

If she didn't hate him, she thought, she would be drawn to him. She would want to know him, to laugh with him, to—

No! The word was an outraged shout in her mind. And she might well have laughed then, at herself.

She moved into the room. All she had to do was survive one more night—and pray that the roads would clear.

His gaze fell on her; she walked straight to the fire, stretching out her hands to warm them. "I do have to hand one thing to you," she murmured. "You do all the work."

He didn't reply. She turned around at last and found that his brooding gaze was on her; his lashes fell, and the gaze was gone.

"You can serve," he told her.

She sat down in front of the coffee table and dished out the chowder. "You could get me a glass of the wine," she said, hinting dryly.

He shook his head.

"Well, really—"

"Give it one more night," he said very softly, and to her amazement she didn't argue with him. He disappeared into the kitchen and returned with an iced tea for her.

Jud's chowder was delicious, filling, and perfect for such a night with the rain streaming and the fire burning. They both commented on it, and on Sam, and on how sad he had looked with all the quills in his nose. In fact, the conversation began so nicely that Susan relaxed and had to admit that she was enjoying herself.

But then it came time for coffee, which David had preplanned with his usual efficiency, and they were both on their opposite sides of the sofa, sipping it, staring at the flames.

"Harley Richmond is married, isn't he?" David asked suddenly, and she felt a cold chill seep through her.

"Yes. Why?" He didn't answer, and she hesitated and asked a little breathlessly, "You know Jud so well. Do you know Harley?"

"No, I don't," he said, stretching out to cross his ankles over the coffee table. "Jud moved up here about ten years ago. His son had a practice in Philadelphia then; we never happened to be here at the same time." His eyes fell on her speculatively. "I was just curious as to how you knew him."

"None of your damn business!" she snapped, furious at his insinuation. Apparently she bled old men and had affairs with married ones in between!

Of course, she could have told him then. Told him that she had met Harley through the hospice center; that she had worked for Harley at times; that his father had been dying of cancer. . . .

She still couldn't be that cruel.

She sighed, wondering whether to bother or not, then offered an explanation, her tone clearly informing him that she didn't care whether he believed her or not.

"I've never had an affair with Harley Richmond, Mr. Lane, if that's what you're insinuating."

"I wasn't insinuating a thing," he told her. He stood and collected the dishes from the table.

"I'll wash them," Susan heard herself say.

He shook his head. "Why don't we go back to Scrabble? That was fairly safe, and it went along all right for a while."

He disappeared into the kitchen. Like the night before, Susan set up the game. He had been right; it had been safe enough for a while.

He returned from the kitchen in a matter of minutes, then took his same position, just as he had the night before.

And it did go well—for a while. They even laughed at the words they claimed each other was inventing; David pulled out his father's dictionaries.

But the night ended frightfully like the one before it. David set out all his letters, attaching them to an *S* on the board. The fire flickered and Susan couldn't make out the word. "Is it another one you're making up?" she demanded, leaning over to see.

And that's when she discovered that nothing had changed at all, that his eyes could still proclaim all the loathing and contempt he felt for her and burn into her like searing blue lasers.

"Mistress, Miss Anderson. It's a word with which you should be extremely familiar. There are a few others, of course, that would fit, but this is probably the most civil."

Susan stood, dropping the dictionary dangerously near his head. "Good night, Mr. Lane. I will definitely say my prayers for the rain to stop."

She stalked to the stairs, only to pause on the first step again as he called her back. His voice was soft, husky, very curiously so.

"Miss Anderson, I must apologize again for a total lack of manners."

She turned back to him, speaking coolly. "And not for a gutter-bound mind, Mr. Lane?"

His hands were on his hips; his legs were apart and firmly on the floor. A shock of dark hair eased over his forehead, and his eyes were touched by the glint of the fire.

"My apologies, Miss Anderson. Good night."

CHAPTER FIVE

Susan alternately awoke and dozed, forever aware of the relentless rain that streamed against the window, sometimes easing to a drizzle, then streaming down again.

She thought about David Lane a lot, feeling heat creep over her body, then tossing around to really burn, exasperated and totally disgusted with herself. She would determine not to think of him and doze again, only to enter restless, disjointed dreams.

And peculiarly, they did not center on David Lane. Nor, for that matter, did they have anything to do with Peter.

They swept her back further in time, and she was sitting in Carl's last hospital room, fighting the tears for her brother's sake, incredulous at his serene conversation.

"The Muslims believe that Mohammed was invited to come close to God. And what Mohammed was able to see was light. Fierce, penetrating light. The feeling was to go to that light. That the light was comfort and peace. And you know, Sue, that's what they all say. The people who have 'died and come back.' They say it's light. That they're going to it, trying to reach it. And that it's very, very hard to pull away from it. Oh, Sue, don't cry. Please, don't cry. We all forget that everyone is mortal. We're all going to die. The day will come when you have to face the light, and I'll be there. I'll reach out and touch your hand. I'll be there, against any darkness, to reach out—"

A tremendous shattering sound crashed into her dream, making Carl's image fade as a horrible, wrenching scream tore from her throat.

It was so dark. Dark and wet and cold. The rain seemed to have come inside, spattering her, driven by the frigid wind.

She shook her head to clear her mind and fight off the terror, then realized what had happened. The wind had risen again, and a branch on the tree outside had been torn off and slammed against the window, breaking it.

"Damn," she muttered, wishing she'd had the sense to keep a flashlight in the room. The candle and matches were on the bedside table beneath the window and surely were soaked by now. She could barely make out the shape of the bed, barely see the curtain flying in with the wind.

She sat up and put her feet to the floor, swearing softly again as both her thumb and big toe caught pieces of glass at the same time.

"Susan!"

Suddenly there was light. Her bedroom door—previously locked—burst in with a force equal to that of the wind. She raised a hand to her eyes against the brash glare of the huge flashlight aimed at her. Beyond the glare she could just make out David's form.

"I'm . . . I'm all right." She laughed a little nervously. "I'm sorry I screamed like that. It was just the window. A branch slammed against it."

He didn't reply. He strode across the room, checking the damage quickly, then gazed at her. With the glow from his flashlight she could see that she was surrounded by shards of glass.

"Damned lucky you weren't any closer," he muttered. Then he stepped forward and quickly lifted her from the sea of glass. She didn't have time to think about it or protest; it was something he just did in his no-nonsense, determined way. She was clinging to his neck with little choice, noting that he smelled very clean, that he had thrown on one of his dad's brocade smoking jackets, and that the hair on his chest just below his collarbone tickled her nose. She also noted that he was very warm when she had been so cold, that he held her with a complete sense of confidence, that the strength in his arms seemed incredibly secure.

In the hallway he paused, balancing her so that he could throw the flashlight's beam around. "You can't sleep in there tonight. I can board up the window, but the bed is already drenched."

"I guess I can take your father's room," she murmured, lowering her head and wincing the moment the words were out; he had stiffened like ice.

"Yes, I suppose you'll be comfortable there, won't you?" he asked almost lightly.

He started walking again, quickly, as if he were truly loath to be touching her now.

He knew his way around and set her down in the center of Peter's firm bed and quickly stepped back. "Is there anything you want from your room? That gown of yours is all wet."

She stared down at herself uncomfortably in the yellow glare of the flashlight. The sleeveless silk gown she had put on with so little interest earlier was indeed drenched—and clinging to her skin so closely that not only were her chilled nipples clearly delineated, but the dusky color around them showed almost as plainly as if she'd been naked.

Her eyes rose to his with a start as she automatically shivered and hugged her arms around herself. There was a grin on his face now, but it seemed to be a bitter one.

He didn't comment on her appearance, but the air between them seemed riddled with what he could have said.

"Would you—" Her voice caught, and she straightened, instinctively striving for dignity. "Would you mind grabbing my robe? It should be on the peg by the door."

He nodded, then started to turn away, but paused. A frown creased his brow. "You're bleeding."

"What?"

He bent on a knee before her, a determined rather than a humble gesture, and his fingers gently caught the damp material at her thigh as he inspected the bloodstain there. "Where are you hurt?"

"I'm not—oh, it's just my thumb, see? I must have brushed it against my gown." She showed him the cut on her thumb, then automatically brought her thumb to her lips, sucking on the small cut. He stared at her for a long, strange moment, as he had done before. She couldn't understand the look on his face. It wasn't really tenderness—certainly not tenderness—and yet there was something . . . gentle, yet something that wasn't really gentle at all in his eyes. It sent the whirling sensation in motion inside of her and made her feel as if a touch of velvet stroked along the length of her spine.

"I'll get your robe," he said briskly. He stood and left.

"Watch your feet against the glass!" she called. He didn't answer. She sat in the darkness, awaiting his return, remembering that his feet had been bare, that he had really nice calves, which were tightly muscled and riddled with dark, crisp, masculine hair. Nice kneecaps too. The hem of the smoking jacket had been just above them. He wore the smoking jacket well, she decided. He looked made for it; the executive, the man in power, in nonchalant control. The black lapels and hem against the Chinese brocade made it a very elegant garment.

Then she found herself wondering what he was wearing beneath the smoking jacket he had so hastily thrown on. And then she hated herself for the thought.

The approaching beam of the flashlight warned her that he was coming back. She hugged her arms more tightly around her.

He tossed the robe on the foot on his father's bed. "If by some strange chance you're not aware of it, there's a flashlight in my father's top drawer."

She nodded, loath to stand and go for the flashlight. But he kept staring at her—not intending to get it himself, quite obviously.

She dropped her arms and stood serenely, walking across the room to procure the light. He was still standing there.

"Why didn't you share the same room?" he asked suddenly.

She didn't turn around; she was tempted to scream out the truth at him, but the truth was something he didn't deserve, she reminded herself sternly.

It was quite likely that he wouldn't believe her, anyway.

"Oh," she said as lightly as she could manage, "we both preferred to sleep alone."

She thought that he was going to slam the door and leave. He didn't, and she was compelled to turn at last and find him frowning as he watched her, his eyes on her feet.

"What?"

"Your toe."

"What about it?"

"It's left a trail of blood across the floor." He moved the flashlight beam to prove his point.

"Oh, it's nothing," she began uselessly. He was beside her again, beaming the light on her foot, swearing softly, then fitting his hands beneath her arms to sweep her quickly back to the bed. "It isn't nothing, the glass is still in it!"

He used the hem of her gown to stanch the blood, then

carefully extracted the surprisingly long sliver of glass she hadn't even realized was in her foot.

"Thanks," Susan murmured uneasily. And to her surprise she discovered him looking at her again, his brow slightly arched, his smile one of pleasant amusement.

"Damn, but you're a mess!" he told her. "Is your life always like this? It seems like the wind itself is out to get you. First you're in the ocean, next you're swimming in a sea of glass, then bleeding all over the place."

She flushed. "No. My life isn't usually like this."

"Fate is trying to warn you to mend your wicked ways!" he said. Susan gazed at him sharply but discovered that he was still teasing her.

"I think fate is warning me that you're the dangerous one," Susan retorted dryly. "My life was never like this until you entered it!"

"Well," he murmured, rising and returning to the door, "I'm going to put a board up on that window. Clean that cut out and stick a bandage on it before you go to sleep."

Susan nodded. He left the room, closing the door behind him.

For several seconds she sat there, shivering in the darkness, then she thought to flick on the flashlight. The room still seemed hollow and empty, filled with haunting shadows. It was Peter's room and Peter was gone. She had known how to let him go, but she still missed him terribly. Especially here. His pipes were on the dresser; piles of books were everywhere. His porcelain statue of the barefoot boy fishing was next to the bed lamp with its powerful reading light. His clothing was in the closets and drawers; she could smell the old-fashioned shaving lotion that he had liked so much.

With a little cry she stood up and quickly shed the wet gown for her terry robe. She had loved Peter; he was too close here.

She could hear a pounding sound from her bedroom.

92

David had already found some kind of a board to seal over her bedroom window.

Susan walked quietly down the stairs, through the parlor, and into the kitchen. She wanted something, but she wasn't sure what. Maybe the soothing glass of wine David had denied her at dinner. She set her flashlight on the counter and opened the refrigerator to start groping through it. Just as her fingers closed around it a husky voice right behind her startled and challenged her.

"What are you doing?"

The wine bottle slipped through her fingers and shattered on the floor.

"Damn! You are a disaster," David muttered, already stooping to collect the large pieces of glass. "Get some towels and the broom, will you? And watch your feet."

Sighing, her heart pounding too quickly, Susan went for the broom and a roll of paper towels.

"Smells like we just adopted five winos," he muttered lightly, taking the towels to mop up the liquid. Then he stared at her with a curious light in his eyes. "How did anyone manage to live with you?"

"I seldom drop things!" Susan protested. "And I can't be blamed if a storm chose to break my window. Besides, this was your fault—you startled me. I didn't hear you come in. For that matter, I wanted that wine!"

"Need a drink that badly, huh?" She couldn't quite fathom his meaning. He brushed the last of the glass on a dustpan and dumped it into the trash. "You're lucky you didn't break your toes this time." He paused, his eyes on her feet. "And you're still bleeding all over the place!" he said impatiently.

Susan looked at her toe. "I—I really can't feel it. I forgot."

She started for the cabinet over the sink where there were bandages and peroxide. She didn't get there. She felt his hands around her waist, lifting her to the counter. She opened her mouth to protest, but he'd already spun her around so that her foot was beneath the tap. He let water run over it while he hunted out the peroxide, poured some over the cut, then managed to dry it with remarkable sensitivity before carefully winding a bandage around her toe.

"You should live," he told her.

"I rather thought so myself."

"And you didn't need the wine."

"What I don't need is a watchdog!" she snapped. "If something dire were going to come of the lump on my head, it would have been here by now!"

He shrugged. "Maybe you're right." Then he did what she had been afraid of earlier: He clutched her chin in his hand and twisted her head to probe the scalp behind her ear. When he released her, he shrugged again. "I guess you're right. The swelling is gone."

"So is the wine," she murmured.

"Are you that much of a lush?"

"No! I'd just give my eyeteeth to be able to go to sleep, and I don't think I can right now."

"There's brandy," he offered flatly, hands on his hips as he studied her.

"I hate brandy."

"Ah ha!" He arched a brow in a rather devastating fashion, almost like a playful buccaneer. "Not the way I can fix brandy, Miss Anderson!"

He set her on the floor with a flourish. Even after he released her she could feel where his hands had been on her waist, as if the terry of her robe had been nonexistent.

He lit the small stove and set the kettle on it, then glanced over his shoulder at her, his eyes a bright, rakish blue. "The fire is still burning low in the parlor. If you want to go out and wait, Miss Anderson, I promise to produce brandy that you will love."

Susan hugged her arms around herself and shrugged, then hurried out to the parlor. The Scrabble game had been put

94

away. The fire was burning, and the warmth seemed wonderful. She added some wood, then sat before it, bringing her knees to her chest and resting her cheek on her arms there. She wasn't so sure she liked this pleasant side of him, and she wasn't sure she should be here at all.

She just didn't seem to be able to pick herself up and go elsewhere. Susan found herself wondering about him again. When he chose, he could be entirely charismatic—gallant and supportive and reckless and . . . fun. She could well imagine him on a date with a woman. He would be easy to be with, willing to try anything. Surely he wouldn't be pushed around; but maybe he would send flowers on the spur of the moment, and if he planned to lure that woman, he might just be ready with iced champagne by the pillows. . . .

And the only problem would be that, in the morning, he would don his suit, run out to battle the business world, eyes ice-blue and shrewd, and forget all about the woman.

Unless he loved her. And then he would stand like an oak, he would demand, he would dominate, he would hold her and force her to love him in return with the sheer force of his will.

But David Lane didn't fall in love. He . . .

She felt like laughing at herself. She didn't know David Lane. She didn't know anything about him. But that wasn't exactly true. She knew all the things that Peter had told her. And that he didn't fall in love was one of them. Peter would shake his head in bafflement. "Don't know what's with the lad. He's had some bloody lovely lady friends, he has. And I could tell by their eyes that they'd all be willing to give me a grandson or two to toss on the old knees. David just won't marry one and give her the chance!"

After she had seen David Lane—the top of his head, at least—and heard his voice, she had been certain that she did understand. He felt that he was composed of superior rock!

"Miss Anderson? Watch out, the glass is hot."

She looked up quickly, then reached for the snifter being offered her, wrapped in a napkin. He sat before her cross-legged, the smoking jacket falling just right to keep him decent.

Susan sniffed at the liquid. She could smell the brandy, and something else, and see that a shot of cream had been added to the hot concoction.

"What is it?"

"I'm not sure what they call it. Kind of like a White Russian, except that it's brandy instead of vodka, you add a little hot water and sugar, and you drink it hot."

She took a sip. It was sweet but very good, and it seemed the perfect thing to sip in front of a fire when a storm still raged outside.

She glanced at David. He was staring into the fire, his thoughts far away.

"It's . . . nice," she said. "Thanks."

He didn't turn to her. His eyes maintained their look of seeing a distant world. He smiled slightly.

"My father taught me to make them." He took a sip of his own and set it on the brick of the hearth, then shifted to rest his elbows on his kneecaps as he idly played with a twig. "I was up here about three years ago for Christmas, and the weather was just like this. Dad loved it. He always said that next to a good book, there was nothing like—"

"A good storm," Susan finished.

He glanced her way, a little startled. Then, as he was so prone to do, he picked up his drink and studied her thoughtfully over the rim of the glass.

He lifted the snifter to her slightly. "So, Miss Anderson, where did my father find a science-fiction-reading twenty-five-year-old?"

"I'm not twenty-five."

"How old are you?"

"It's none of your business."

"Twenty-four?"

"Twenty-six, Mr. Lane," Susan retorted, draining more of her brandy. It was nice; it gave her back some of her confidence, false though it was, and most of all, it relaxed her. She could have said then, "I met your father at the hospital, Mr. Lane. My brother was in his last stages of dying when your father was in the first." But she didn't say it. It would shock him; oh, yes, it would shock him.

But for all that he had said and done to her, she knew that he had loved Peter. And the longer the night wore on, the less she was hating him—no matter how she tried to hold on to that hate. If they just could have parted ways, she would have been fine. But they hadn't parted. The fickle winds beyond the cozy circle of the fire had decreed that they would know one another. He was an autocrat, used to snapping his fingers and being obeyed, but the hours had forced her to see other sides of him. Concern, capability, responsibility. A gentle touch, a winning smile, a dash of humor and adventure.

She lowered her head, smiling a little. "I met your father on the beach. I was an orphaned alien, dropped down from above. Peter came by and offered me shelter, and here I am."

He chuckled softly, and she couldn't help but look at him, savoring the warm amusement in his eyes, the crinkle of laughter around his mouth that etched lines more deeply into his features.

"A twenty-six-year-old alien, dropped in from Venus, no doubt," he returned. "Tell me, have you parents anywhere?"

"Mr. Lane," she said, drawling with mock humor, "surely you don't think that I was actually born, do you? Women of my type are most obviously hatched!"

Susan could see the humor leaving him, and she was suddenly desperate to get it back. She reached out with little thought, her hand resting on his bare knee. "Sorry. I did have parents, of course. I don't remember them, though. They'd gone over to Bonn for a second honeymoon when I was about three and were killed when two trains collided."

"I'm sorry," he murmured softly. She realized that her hand was still on his knee and drew it away quickly, determined to be light.

She shrugged and sipped more brandy. "As I said, I don't remember them at all. Carl did, of course. He was older—"

"Who's Carl?"

She glanced at him, realizing that she had gone farther with pleasant honesty than she had intended. "My brother," she said briefly, then she smiled with cheerful charm and raised her snifter to him. "Could I have another one of these things?"

She wasn't sure if she wanted another and she certainly didn't need it, but she had to change the conversation.

He gave her a rather odd look, then rose slowly, stooping for her glass. His eyes met hers. "Sure."

She stared at the fire, lost in thought, as he left her. She started when something fell on her—it was the feather comforter kept on the end of the couch.

"You're shivering," David said simply.

"I'm really not—"

"You are. Get comfortable and I'll hand you your drink."

Susan groaned softly, but the temptation to curl up in the soft feather ticking was strong. He tossed her one of the throw pillows to lean against the coffee table. She hesitated, then took the pillow, rested her back against it, and drew the comforter to her waist.

He handed her the drink she had almost forgotten and sat before her again, his back to the fire this time.

"Well, you've quizzed me long enough, I think," Susan said beneath his direct, intrigued stare. "I think I'm due a few returns."

"Well," he murmured, "let's see. I'm not an alien, I'm not twenty-five, and I have no siblings. That about covers what you've told me."

Susan smiled, lowering her head. "You'll be thirty-five on November second. Your middle name is Daniel, you were an incorrigible child, you graduated from Columbia, you spent three years in the Air Force. You've been president and major stockholder of Lane Publications for the past seven years, and you despise artichokes and anchovies. You were an absolutely adorable child on a bearskin rug once, though what happened to that cute little kid, I'll never know."

He watched her, neither smiling nor scowling, while she went on with her recital. Then he shrugged. "I'm rather at a disadvantage, aren't I? My, my, Miss Anderson, you are a veritable encyclopedia on my life."

Only the brandy could have brought out her next taunting words. "Not really. I told you, I listened to your father, to anything that he had to say. But, of course, your father didn't know everything. He seemed to have thought that there was some trauma in your life that he missed out on. Something, somewhere, that turned you against natural feeling. Love, in his opinion—consideration in mine. Was there a trauma, Mr. Lane? Haven't you ever been in love?"

He seemed very relaxed. She didn't see his fingers clench around the stem of his snifter.

"Trauma?" He arched a brow pleasantly. "Sorry, I don't recall any great trauma. And, yes, I've been in love. At least a dozen times. Hasn't everyone?"

She lowered her head, feeling a little guilty. It wasn't the response she had wanted—it was a light, polite response that left her feeling as if she had been disciplined for getting too personal.

She looked up, sensing his movements. He had stood up and was now standing over her. He lowered slowly, down on a knee, and tilted her chin with his knuckle, drawing her eyes to his. "Hasn't everyone, Miss Anderson?" he whispered in a husky refrain.

"I wouldn't know," she murmured in return.

She should have jerked from him then and reminded him that she didn't want him touching her, that he had already labeled her as everything bad beneath the sun.

99

She didn't. Later she would never understand why. She didn't even know exactly why she didn't at the moment.

But that was exactly it, really. The moment. The moment was everything; the fire burning in the grate, creating mysterious shadows and beautiful glows; the storm raging outside; the intimate comfort that their sheltered haven provided.

It was the man touching her, searching out her eyes, his own so strange, as if he were mystified himself.

And he was, of course. He had just been sitting there, watching her. Watching the firelight play against her hair, the way her eyes glimmered like emeralds in the night. He was mesmerized by the beautiful, delicate contours of her face, the length of her fingers curling around her glass. The storm outside had come in; it played havoc, sending vengeful winds through him, and he knew he had to touch her. . . .

And none of the words said meant anything. He forgot who she was, why they were together. He remembered only the sweet innocence in her face each time she saw that he was truly concerned and she assured him that she was really all right.

And now . . . now he plucked the brandy glass from her fingers and absently placed it on the table. He looked into her eyes and became as hopelessly entangled there as she had become in the sea.

She was for sale, he tried to remind himself, and not even that to him—or so she claimed.

Not even that mattered.

"You are," he told her, "the most beautiful woman I have ever seen. Heaven help me or the devil take me."

And that was it. He kissed her.

From the moment that his lips touched hers Susan knew that it was going to be no light play. His mouth was everything that she had imagined: gentle, coercive, firm . . . so undeniable. The stroke of his tongue was a liquid fire that engulfed her, probed her, demanded, and so subtly took everything that she was barely aware she had been seduced to surrender before the battle had begun. Her breathing grew ragged and her heart stopped, then raced ahead recklessly as it sent blood pounding through her veins.

And still, still she had a chance to run. His lips parted from hers; his eyes, cobalt now, questioned her. She might have been hypnotized. She couldn't even shake her head. She couldn't begin to voice the no that raged, ignored, in the depths of her soul.

He stroked her cheek softly and then again; it was all over for her. She was swept down into the comforter, and his arms were around her, his knee wedged between hers, the slit in the robe falling away easily.

He was kissing her again. Hungrily his fingers twined through her hair, his lips moving restlessly now and then to touch her forehead, her cheeks, the corners of her mouth. His hand was on her throat, stroking it. . . .

Her arms had slipped around his neck. There was no excuse for it, would never be. She wanted him. He had awakened yearnings she thought she had left behind to voyage out into a sea of pain, always the strong one, the one to be there, serene . . .

She was anything but serene. She was alive, and he was masculinely beautiful, seducing everything within her. The wanting wasn't shy, though she trembled. It was fierce, showing her that she was alive, on fire, a part of the tempest outside, a part of the blaze burning in the grate. Oh, God, yes, there was something about his touch, about the lightest graze of his fingers. It wasn't so much tenderness, it was cherishing; it touched her as if he loved to do so, as if he truly needed her.

It had been years since she had been touched, needed, loved, but never, never like this. Never had the feeling, the ache of desire, started from a distance, from a look in the eyes, from the softest touch against her flesh.

There would be consequences. Even knowing what she wanted with a desperate desire, she recognized somewhere that there would be consequences. This was David Lane. David Lane . . .

His body shifted against hers. She felt the hardness of his thighs and his desire, but his movement was both ardent and slow, as if he would never rush her. Each slight ripple of muscle, each movement, each breath, made love to her.

She would bear the consequences, she thought in silent anguish. Whatever they were, she would bear the consequences.

Her fingers raked through his hair as his kiss consumed and enflamed her. His lips brushed against her ear with a whisper, lowered down her throat again. His hand moved into the vee neck of the robe, parting it, freeing her breast, caressing the weight, stroking it, the heart of his palm moving slowly over her nipple until she moaned, twisting to bury her head against his neck. The robe continued to part, the belt giving away easily. His touch moved with bold possession over her hip, to her waist, to the shadows of her belly.

She cried out softly when his mouth possessed her nipple, his tongue laving it, his teeth taunting it. Instinct decreed that she arch to him, and of its own accord, her body began to writhe. Her nails moved over the brocade fabric that stretched tightly over his shoulders; she felt his warmth beneath her fingers, the wave and ripple of muscle, the wonder of his strength.

And all around her, it seemed, the fire burned and the wind raged. His kisses moved over her stomach; his hand moved to her thigh, stroking gentle, light caresses that made her turn to him again, to force him to stop . . . to continue.

He moved away from her. She opened her eyes to see him shrugging from the jacket, and and she remembered vaguely how she had wondered earlier what he wore beneath it. Nothing.

She started to shake again at the sight of him. Given a moment longer, she might well have realized just what she was doing, thought of the consequences. He was built magnificently, tall and lean and solid.

She did not have a moment. She saw the hunger in his eyes, the fascination, the desire. She had never known anyone like him. He drew her to him, slid his hands to her shoulders, and shed the terry fabric from her.

Firelight . . . firelight played all over her. It touched her eyes, her hair; it glimmered and shone over the rise of her breasts; it created shadows of intrigue and silk over the endless length of her limbs.

He took her face between his hands. "You are . . . beautiful," he murmured, and when he pulled her to him, his voice was ragged. "Susan, touch me. . . ."

And she did. Moaning softly, she stroked him with her fingers, making love to his body with hers. It was natural, easy, all that she could do. It was the call of his sensuality to her own, rising like a rosebud touched by an awakening sun. Knowing him . . . the tautness of his muscles, the smoothness of his flesh. So masculine, so perfect. The only flaw on him was a long scar that ran along the left side of his back. An old scar, turned white with time. Vaguely she wondered if he had been injured in the service. And the wondering made her long to know him more, to know all about him, his touch, his life, his mind, his soul. . . .

His hand found hers, closed it around his hardness, and then she sank down, down into the softness of the comforter, thrilled with the heavy weight of his body bearing down over hers. She gasped at his entry, biting into his shoulder, her body raked by shivers at the ecstasy that raced through her. He moved so slowly. Drawing her, taking her, seducing her all over again. She felt as if she died a thousand tiny deaths of wonder.

And when she thought that she had received all the wonder that she could, the tempo changed. Like a lulling rain that pattered only to become more powerful as the deluge began, he changed. An utter brilliance flared between them.

103

She was saying things that made no sense, crying, whispering, fitting to him more and more tightly, adoring his body within hers, embracing it, meeting his hunger with a sinuous and soaring grace. Reaching for the rainbow that lurked past the storm, for the gold there, glittering like a heaven full of stars.

They burst over her with shattering and wondrous force, and she wondered if she did black out a moment, so violent and sweet was the sensation. One that lingered, then exhausted, then left her drifting slowly, slowly down from the heavens to the feathers of the comforter that cradled her body.

The feathers were a reality, as was the man lying beside her, his muscled flesh covered with a sheen of sweat, his breathing still ragged. He had an arm cast over his forehead; the other still rested above her head, catching her hair.

The man . . . the consequences.

He looked grave, thoughtful. He sensed her eyes upon him and turned to her, a gentle smile curving his lips. He looked wonderful, tousled dark hair falling over his forehead, eyes so strangely tender.

He stroked her cheek. She returned his smile with a little shiver and closed her eyes. Everything was going to be all right.

In moments she fell asleep. There were no dreams to trouble her, and outside, the rain at last ceased.

Sometime near dawn she awoke from a sense of movement. He was carrying her up the stairs. Idly she ran a finger over the hair on his chest. He smiled down at her. "You're awake."

"Not really," she murmured drowsily.

She wasn't even sure of where they went. He laid her on a bed, and it felt cool and clean and luxurious.

And then his body was against hers, more luxurious still, creating the wonder and ecstasy again, teaching her that the feelings had not been a dream, that they could come again and again. . . .

"I have to tell you . . ." she murmured once, relenting completely, determined to tell him all the little truths except for that fact that Peter had known he was dying. It was possible to forgive him; the situation probably had appeared bad, and she had done everything to taunt him. . . . She had been so bitter since that day she had first heard his voice.

Before that, she had been a little bit in love with an image. The man in the photographs, the son Peter had always talked about with such pride and joy. Oh, not really in love, just whimsically so. Nor was she in love now. She was . . . a captive of the moment, of the man. The emptiness that had echoed so hollowly within her was gone now, that desperate need to feel cherished fulfilled. But nothing so natural and compelling had to be right. She owed herself no excuses. For all that she had suffered and lost, she deserved this reckless abandon with a man who was young and strong and touched her with such magic.

But she had to clear herself with him so that he could apologize, know his fault . . .

"I have to—"

"Love me, touch me . . ." And from there his whispers became more erotic, and she knew that anything she had to say could wait for the morning.

It was so wonderful to be held all through the night. To fall asleep in his arms.

The thought was with him again when he awoke, the sun glaring through the windows, the storm a thing of the past.

She was the most beautiful woman he had ever seen.

But daylight quickly changed the magic to a groan, a shudder, and incredulous self-reproach.

Wincing, pressing his temples between his palms, David berated himself in silence. Ass! He had scorned and despised

Peter's sordid payoff, and in a matter of hours she had seduced him too. All she had to do was sit there, look at him, laugh, and say a few words, and he fell like a green kid with his first case of puppy love!

Him—of all damned people!

He grated his teeth together, remembering one set of her softly purred words: "Peter loved me in furs. . . ."

With a little oath he rose, intending to dress and finding that he was gazing at her again.

This morning, sound asleep, she could still touch him! So sleek and long, curved so sweetly, lying so innocently on his bed, a gentle smile just touching her lips.

A smile. She had earned her amusement. He had crashed like a felled oak.

David felt horrible, churning. He had taken something of his father's, invaded something personal and private with Peter dead and buried.

"Oh, God!" he muttered aloud.

He tossed the sheets over her nakedness. It didn't really help. He couldn't toss them over her face, and it was the fine quality of her features that haunted him as much as anything else.

He felt betrayed—as he hadn't allowed himself to be in over a decade—tricked, seduced. The bigger they come, the harder they fall! he thought, taunting himself bitterly, and along with all that was still the amazement that she had made him forget everything but his desperation to touch her.

He dressed quickly and quietly, clenching his jaw tightly. He could imagine her laughing victoriously. You mocked your father, David Lane, and look at you. . . .

He gave himself a shake. What the hell had it been?

He didn't know, but it wouldn't happen again.

Dressed, he stared down at her bitterly. Then he reached into his top drawer for a piece of paper, scribbled out a note, and then a check.

Staring at her one last time, he promised himself that she would never know that she had been the victor.

Susan awoke slowly, confused at first, certain then that he must have gone downstairs. The sun was shining brightly through the windows. It was going to be a beautiful day.

She stretched deliciously. It was David's room, she realized, filled with the memories of his youth, things a man would have thrown away, things his father would not: trophies, banners, baseball bat, bowling ball, an assortment of unused after-shaves on the dresser.

And a note attached to the mirror.

Susan frowned and walked quickly to it. She snatched at it so hard that the envelope ripped, then she stared, numbed, as a check fell to the dresser. She saw her name on it, and an amount twenty dollars higher than the weekly salary she'd drawn from the separate company holdings.

"All debts paid—account closed."

She sank back to the bed, so stunned that her heart and mind froze. "Oh, God!" she whispered with horror.

The consequences . . . How she despised herself! She had known, she had known. . . .

But she had fallen just a little bit in love with the night, with the man, with longing to be held.

Susan stared into the mirror. She saw a very pale woman there, eyes wide and torn with misery.

"David Lane, if I ever get the chance, I will rip you into a thousand shreds!" she swore.

She had learned not to cry years ago; stupid tears trickled down her cheeks, anyway. What had possessed her? She had been so determined to force his own opinions right down his throat. . . .

Oh, she had certainly done that! But she had missed the main point; no matter what the magic, the call of the fire and the storm, she shouldn't have fallen into the man's arms after taunting him so.

107

She spun around and ran to the shower in her own room, turned on the cold water, and sudsed herself a dozen times. Each second that passed, she stiffened and straightened mentally. She had made a mistake. A horrible mistake. Well, it had happened, and it couldn't be undone. She would have to consider it a lesson in life. Bitter but part of it all. She *was* going to get her composure back—and her serenity. She would return the check with a letter and get on with her life.

Once dressed, she hurried downstairs. The fire was out. She lit it, then ripped up both the brocade smoking jacket and her own terry robe, throwing the pieces on the fire one by one.

She made coffee and drank a cup.

Then she sat down to write the letter with which she would return David Lane's check, wondering bleakly how long it would take to quit despising herself for the fool she had been.

Consequences . . .

She had been old enough to know that they had to be paid. She even had been aware, vaguely aware, through all the need and sensation that consequences were fated to arise.

She couldn't begin to suspect just how horrible they would be.

CHAPTER SIX

David walked into his office Monday morning feeling as if he had been through a meat grinder. Sleep had eluded him on the Sunday night he had returned to his apartment.

Erica had given him a disgustingly pleasant greeting when he walked through; he had barely sat down behind a stack of checks, contracts, cover art, and publicity releases before she followed him in, a cup of black coffee in her hands, a bright smile on her face.

"Thanks," he murmured, accepting the coffee and taking a moment to be grateful for his personable and ever efficient secretary. He offered her a dry smile. "What's up this morning?"

"Stacy says she has to see you—it's urgent. Gordon wants to go over the Gideon series covers. Rebecca thinks she has a good promotional idea for the fall sales meeting, but she has to have your okay before five o'clock. And"—Erica paused with a grimace—"Ms. Jameson called. You forgot to cancel your Saturday night theater date."

"Oh," David murmured with a wince.

"It's all right. You just sent her some lovely flowers and an apology."

David chuckled. "Good. Thanks, Erica. It's a cliché, but what would I do without you?"

"Get a slap in the face that you'd probably deserve!" Erica said, lightly chastising him. She appeared a little distracted, though. He sipped his coffee and studied her. She was a very pretty woman, dark-eyed and blond, slim, and prone to dress in a very businesslike manner. She'd worked for his father one year before David had taken over, and though she had been crazy about Peter, she had been just as pleased to work for David. Their relationship outside of the office was a sound friendship; nothing more and nothing less.

"What's on your mind?" he asked.

"Nothing."

"Yes, there is."

The anxious look left her features for a minute as she laughed. "I just hope you'll see Stacy right away. She's been after you to look at that manuscript for ages now, and you're still procrastinating!"

David shrugged, curious at her concern. "I have complete faith in Stacy's editorial decisions. I gave her my okay to make it a lead title next summer."

"Yes, but you haven't read it."

"So?"

"I brought it into the house!" Erica reminded him. She flushed. "I read it, and I maneuvered things a little unethically to get it here."

David leaned back in his chair, grinning as he watched his secretary. "So rumor is true? You're dating John Ketchem?"

Erica's coloring was very, very close to crimson. John Ketchem was a young but very promising literary agent. David liked him; he knew his business, when to go to bat for his clients, and when nothing would be accomplished by endless hours of haggling.

"I—uh—see him now and then, yes."

"See him?" David couldn't help raising his brows to her and allowing a wicked, knowing grin to creep into his features.

"Stop that!" Erica pleaded.

He stood up, chuckling, and walked around his desk to brush her cheek affectionately with his knuckles. "Just don't go 'maneuvering' too far in the pursuit of business, okay?"

"It wasn't anything like that!" Erica protested. "But I did get him to send the manuscript here first. And Stacy moved like lightning to get the contract out." She hesitated, and he realized that she was nervous about the book itself. "David, you won't understand until you read it!"

He shook his head. "Understand what? Stacy told me the gist of it: Irish immigrant making it in the New World. She said it was great, and I believe her. I will read it. I read everything. It's just that lately . . ."

His voice trailed away as he shrugged, and Erica instantly looked sad and contrite. "Your dad. I know, David, and I'm sorry. But that's exactly why I'm so anxious! You've got to read it, because it should be rushed. And if you'd just read the damn thing, you'd understand! David—"

"Good morning!"

They both started as a pleasant drawl sounded from the door that Erica had left ajar. David looked over his secretary's shoulder to see Vickie Jameson standing there, serene, confident, and lovely in a new fall outfit, a beige off-the-shoulder sweater and a calf-length tweed skirt that contrasted nicely with her silver-blond hair.

"Good morning, Ms. Jameson!" Erica reacted quickly. Vickie was always charming to Erica; Vickie was just the type of stylish woman that instantly commanded respect.

"Vickie," David murmured, surprised that his lids fell to cover his eyes a little uneasily. He should have felt something—sorry that he had neglected to call her, sorry that he didn't feel like embracing her . . . that he didn't really feel anything at all because all of his emotions were still bitterly entangled with another woman. His father's mistress.

He forced himself to look up with a smile. "Vick, I'm sorry about the other night. Want some coffee?" He gave Erica a glance, quickly understood. "I got . . . tangled up in Maine."

"There was that horrible storm!" Erica said innocently. "All the power and phones were out."

"Mmm," Vickie murmured dryly, casting off her kidskin gloves as she moved into the office. "Erica, thanks so much for the flowers. They were absolutely lovely."

Erica flushed and looked at David a little helplessly, at which point he laughed. One of the things he liked about Vickie Jameson was her blunt and rational view of life; she wasn't annoyed, merely resigned. She held no ties on him, and because of it they had enjoyed a long relationship. He didn't owe her excuses because of his absence; he did owe her an excuse for his rudeness.

"I'll get some coffee," Erica murmured. She paused in the doorway, clearing her throat. "Da—Mr. Lane, please don't forget the manuscript. It's on your desk."

"I won't forget it, Erica. Give Stacy a buzz and tell her to come up at ten."

The door closed. Vickie moved into the room, smiling as she stood on tiptoe to give him a light kiss on the cheek. David smiled back and left her to sit in one of the conference chairs in front of his desk while he walked around to take his chair behind it.

Her kiss, her touch, her scent . . . all left him ridiculously unmoved. He couldn't forget the way a pair of emerald eyes had stared into his; how the grazing of long red nails moving down his back had created a path of fire. . . .

"You louse!" Vickie laughed, eyeing him with reproach and amusement. "Do you know what I went through to get those tickets? I actually stood in line in the rain to get them!"

He shook his head. "I should have called you on Friday morning when I decided to go up to Maine. I didn't mean to stay. I got there late, and then the storm broke. I'm sorry."

Erica buzzed. David hit the button on the interoffice phone. "Yes?"

"I've Ms. Jameson's coffee."

"Bring it in," David said a little impatiently. She should have known she didn't need to buzz; his office was a place of business, and if a secretary didn't know it, of all people . . .

Erica brought in the coffee. Vickie murmured her thanks and complimented Erica on her hairstyle. David barely heard the exchange.

His thoughts were just a little bit of a lie. If she were before him . . . Susan Anderson . . . in that white robe, with that soft smile and that streaming firelit hair flowing over her shoulders, he would be just as mesmerized, just as enchanted as he had been while the storm raged in Maine.

He ground his teeth together, realizing that Erica was almost out of the room. "Erica!" He called her back a little sharply.

"Yes?"

"Get the attorney's office for me, will you? I need to see someone today."

Erica nodded and closed the door.

"My, my, what a sudden temper!" Vickie commented. "What's up?"

"Just a little hitch in my father's estate."

Vickie frowned. "I assumed everything but a few small bequests would have been left to you. I can't imagine you begrudging anything to anyone, David. For that matter, I thought you hadn't even seen the attorneys yet."

"I haven't. I'm just expecting a little flaw," David said smoothly. He frowned suddenly as his eyes were caught by words on the manuscript in front of him. There was no title page on it; it began with page one, and the author's name

113

was in the upper left-hand corner. The name rang a bell: S. C. de Chance. The title was *The Promised Place*.

Vickie was talking, saying something about dinner, but he wasn't really aware of her words. He had started to read.

Jem didn't see the fire or the smoking ruins. He couldn't hear the shots in the background or the torn and anguished cries of women. He saw only the girl, Amy, who had loved him so dearly against family and heritage, blood, and the wrath of the Catholic God.

Amy was tied to the post behind her. Black tar covered her beauty; feathers flew about her. There were tears in her eyes as she turned to look at him, tears and love and regret, but no anger, no resentment. . . .

There was a roaring sensation in David's ears. He saw nothing but mist.

It was Peter! In those few words he knew it. Jem was Peter, and Amy was his mother, Mary Lane.

"Who the hell is S. C. de Chance?" he thundered.

"What?" Vickie stared at his face, dark and gaunt and stormy.

David's thoughts seemed to come back into focus. "Oh, uh—"

"You're not paying the slightest bit of attention to me," Vickie murmured ruefully as she rose. "My fault. I should have known better than to come here."

She moved around to the back of his desk, touched his broad, suited shoulders, and lightly brushed the top of his dark head with a kiss. "I'm leaving, Mr. Lane—before you toss me out. Are you coming to dinner or not?"

"When?"

"David, I just told you! Tomorrow night."

He stared down at the manuscript again. The words were blurring before him. He didn't want to go to dinner. He didn't want to laugh and enjoy Vickie's fun-loving form of seduction.

All he wanted to do was go back and find an emerald-eyed redhead; hold her, shake her, demand to know what it was that gave her such incredible power that he couldn't think or reason, behave rationally, or forget her! To know how, and why, he had managed to lose all passion and interest in anyone else . . .

"Sure, dinner sounds fine." He stood up and distractedly kissed her. He forced himself to smile, swearing inwardly that he would forget Susan Anderson, sweep her from his mind and soul with all the scorn she deserved.

He walked Vickie to the door. "Dinner tomorrow. I won't forget."

"I'll call. I don't think you're with me at all, David."

"I'll be there!"

"I'll have the champagne iced for eight o'clock."

"Wonderful."

"Hmm," Vickie murmured, appraising him. "Heaven knows why I chase you so, David! You're a lost cause. You're never going to marry me. Don't—" She held up a hand when he would have said something. "You're not, and I know it. It's all right because I'm having a hell of a good time. And I have beaten out the competition so far, hmm?"

David winced, feeling very guilty. He pulled her quickly into his arms. "Vickie, you beat the competition hands down."

"Thanks. You're just too good-looking and too damn sexy, David. But watch it, son!" she warned him. "Someday some guy who does want to get married will come along." She studied him critically, then chuckled. "The worst of it is that you'll probably wish me all the luck in the world."

"Vick—"

"I'm going, I'm going! I know that impatient, tough Mr. Businessman look. One last word of warning, Mr. Lane: Someday you're going to fall in love. I mean, really in love, David. And I actually hope I'm around to see it. David

Lane, rugged ice, tied up in a tempest! I hope she gives you your walking papers—nothing cruel intended."

"Vickie, come on!" He groaned.

She chuckled, collecting her gloves. "In the meantime I'll settle on dinner—and a night at a time."

Blowing him a kiss, she departed. Before the door closed, David was striding back to his desk and hitting his buzzer. "Erica, get Stacy up here—now!"

He sat down at his desk and started leafing quickly through the manuscript.

It was there, it was all there: his Protestant father's flight from Ireland with his Catholic mother during the Irish Free States' battle for independence; his first sight of the Statue of Liberty; his confusion as a penniless immigrant. The days when he had sold apples on the streets, three for a dime. World War II. The boom that followed; his first job in a publishing company.

David noted that there were two children born to the immigrants in the manuscript rather than one; the one who went into the service was killed. The boy, the son. The one who quarreled with the father . . . himself.

Almost as if the writer thought that he should have been knocked off!

A cold outrage settled over him, even as his objective knowledge told him that the manuscript was good. It had pathos and struggle, laughter and tears. It also had miniseries written all over it. And Peter Lane had been a fairly famous man. Written up in *Time* and *Life,* respected, honored. Many people would recognize his life; it was perfect for publication—publication right away.

He started flipping to the end, his face set in a grim mask. Someone had really known Peter. Dug deeply into his life. Thank God, David thought, that he owned the book! He wanted to see how it ended, see if all the dignity and pride and quiet character that had been his father had been retained throughout.

Or had the author tarnished it all at the end? Known to put a finale to an epic life that would include an October to September affair, an old man, lonely and broken, seduced and bled by a mercenary witch who knew she had only to bide her time to reap an income?

He exhaled. There was no such ending. No mention of the woman who had overwhelmed his life as it ebbed away.

Who the hell had written it? Who the hell had known Peter well enough to be privy to so many family secrets, to write in what might well have been his father's own words, riddled with his father's own feelings?

His buzzer sounded. "Stacy's here—" Erica began.

David didn't let her finish. He was on his feet, pulling open his door, and dragging his salt-and-pepper-haired, shrewd editor-in-chief into his office.

"Who is S. C. de Chance?"

Stacy Leigh looked at him over the clear rims of her bifocals. "Really, David! I've been asking you to—"

"Who is it?" David demanded.

"I know who it is, but not much more than that, David. Have you read the book yet?"

He strode back to his desk, tapping a pencil furiously over the opening page. "Enough!"

Stacy hesitated, a little uncomfortable. Then she frowned and walked over to take a seat. "It's a wonderful book," she said a little stonily.

David leaned over his desk, staring at her to acquire her attention and force her eyes to his.

"Stacy, this is my father's life!"

"Yes, I, uh, rather thought so," Stacy murmured, then her smoky eyes seemed to flash with irritation. "David, I've been after you to read it for three weeks! Before your father died."

"You didn't tell me why!" David exploded.

"Well, I couldn't!" Stacy said, defending herself. "First you were at the West Coast conference, then Peter . . . passed away, and when the funeral was over and it seemed

117

that things were settling down, you suddenly flew off to Maine! I've been trying to tell you—"

"Who is S. C. de Chance?"

"David, if you'd give me a chance . . . Oh! I got a pun in there. Chance—de Chance . . . you see?" He was smiling. She cleared her throat and smoothed a pleat in her skirt. "She's done a number of science fiction books for one of our dearest competitors; it's a pseudonym, of course. And really a bit of a pun, if I heard the story right. Apparently she started writing as part of a team. She and her brother. The S. C. de Chance was just that—we'll take the chance. At writing, that is. The brother passed away about a year ago, and Susan kept writing, maintaining the pseudonym out of sentimentality, I imagine. That's what I learned from John Ketchem. I've only spoken with her once, but she seems to be a lovely person."

"Susan who?" David thundered.

Stacy frowned, inadvertently sinking a little into her chair. She was one of the best at what she did, and she knew it. She had been in publishing for decades. She also loved working at Lane, for David, in particular. When he gave her free rein, he meant it. He trusted her judgment. He paid her highly to keep the larger houses from snatching her away, but she would never want to leave, anyway, because she cherished his respect for her judgment more than she did her salary. In the years she had worked for David she had learned to respect him greatly in return. He could snap out orders in a meeting, and when something went wrong, he found out where and why. He would peg an employee to the wall and demand better performance, but he'd be the first to remember that same employee's birthday or anniversary. He could give brusque orders one minute, then wish you a pleasant night in the next and really mean it.

Stacy had known David for ten years. She had never, never seen him look like this, as if he could pick up his desk and crush it between his hands.

"Her name is Susan Anderson."

"Susan Anderson!"

"David," Stacy mumbled, nervous and distressed. "What's the matter? You're scaring me to death!"

His fingers unclenched slowly. He straightened, relaxing his shoulders as he did.

"Sorry, Stacy."

"What on earth is wrong?"

David picked up his coffee cup and walked over to view the river far below his windows. "You don't know who she is?" He asked quietly.

"Do you? You know her?"

"Yes," he said simply, and he realized ironically that naturally Stacy would not know Susan or anything about her. Susan's "salary" had come out of the private account. Peter had never come into the office with her. The one time she had come in alone, Erica had been the only one to really see her, and that had been only as a vague Miss Anderson who had been there for all of thirty seconds—and left him in an explosive temper all day.

"She was a friend of your father's?" Stacy breathed. "Oh, I knew it! I called Peter and told him about the book and he seemed so smug. No wonder!"

"Oh, yes," David commented, staring out beyond the windows. "She was a friend of his. And my father knew about the book, you say? I'll be damned."

"Well, he wouldn't say anything," Stacy told David. "When I said I could have sworn I was holding his life story in my hands, he just said that America was well populated with Irish immigrants. I laughed and said that maybe I should be careful; I joked about his suing his own company. He told me he was quite certain that the author was very careful to assure that no legal action could be taken against her."

"Oh, I'll bet she was," David murmured.

"Do you know, though, David," Stacy mused, absently

tucking her pencil behind her ear, "Peter did seem a little surprised. He knew about the book but seemed startled that I had it."

David turned around to glance at her. "What do you mean?"

"He asked me if we bought it under the Lane imprint. I told him no, that it was going out under the Puma imprint."

David turned back to the window, frowning. He had been thinking that Susan Anderson must have been truly enjoying herself the other night, aware that he would eventually be signing different checks to her—royalty checks.

And his father hadn't even told him! But Peter must have loved the whole situation. He loved secrets and surprises. Maybe he'd intended to tell both David and Susan about the delightful turn of events when David went up for Labor Day.

David started to laugh dryly, bitterly. Oh, God! The joke certainly was on him.

"David," Stacy said a little hesitantly. "I—I realize that it must hurt you. We all loved Peter. But it's really a wonderful book! It's Peter, and it shows all the strengths and frailties and greatness that were Peter; why we loved him. I wasn't so adamant that you see this to hurt you. I thought that . . ."

David tightened his fists; relaxed them. Then he turned to Stacy with a pleasant smile. "Stacy, I haven't read it through yet, but I'm certain that it tells my father's story beautifully."

Stacy swallowed. "We're going to publish it? There's really no reason for us to renege on the contract."

"I wouldn't think of letting anyone have this book. We're most definitely going to publish it. As soon as possible."

"Well, next June—"

"Is much too late. Three months from now."

"Three months!" Stacy gasped. "David, we can't do it! I have the art sketches, but—"

David chuckled softly, his emotions under tight rein.

"Stacy, don't be ridiculous. Anything is possible. We got out the book on that new fighter the day he took the championship."

"But we were prepared."

"We've got the complete manuscript, and you said we've got an art sketch. I'll call sales and promotional meetings this afternoon. I want it to be a January title. We won't bump anyone from the present lineup; we'll put this out as a special release."

"David . . ." Stacy shook her head.

He sat down at his desk and looked at her with eyebrows raised a little autocratically. "Is there a problem, Stacy? Do you feel there are numerous revisions?"

"No, no," Stacy murmured. "It looks almost as if it were edited before it got here."

"Then get to the line work today. Anyone who wants to see you for the next two days can see me instead. We can get it to the copy editors tomorrow night. Chris is great with the language on this kind of thing. Give it to him."

Stacy nodded slowly, rising. "But the publicity, David. Publicity takes time to line up—"

"Leave that to me, Stacy, okay?"

His imperturbable editor-in-chief was still sitting there.

"Stacy!" he said softly. "Is there anything else?"

"No, no." She shook her head and rose, still dazed. David followed her quietly to close his doors behind her. She stood in front of Erica's desk.

"I couldn't even get him to read the damn thing!" she wailed softly, "and now he wants to have it out in January!"

"Is he upset?" Erica asked nervously.

"Darned if I know!" Stacy murmured. "I thought he was going to strangle me for a minute. Now he's all calm efficiency and determination again. Erica, if I were you, I'd go to lunch early."

David silently closed his doors and leaned against them. He didn't know whether to laugh again, slam his head

121

against the wall, or fly back to Maine and shake the life out of S. C. de Chance.

He walked over to his desk and called the contracts department. Charlie Haines, head of the department, answered.

"Charlie, get John Ketchem on the phone. Tell him we're putting a rush on Susan Anderson's book, that it will be out in January. Tell him that it will be a special release and we'll go all out on publicity and support. But tell him I want an amendment to the contract. I don't want a pseudonym used. I want her real name on the cover."

Charlie agreed to do David's bidding and hung up. David sat staring straight ahead of himself, seeing nothing.

It was going to be his book, all right. It was his father's life, and by God, he'd do everything in his power to give the story justice—even if it was going to be Susan Anderson who would reap the rewards. It seemed the greatest irony to him, but he'd see that it was all done right. He'd keep his hand on it every step of the way.

And he'd see that Miss Anderson's involvement with his father was kept from the pages of the book and from the press. He'd help her hide from the public. But not from herself. Her name—her real name—was going on the cover.

David called Erica in and dictated a memo about the book to all departments, calling meetings to get it all rolling. Erica quickly informed him that the attorney would meet him for lunch, that Gordon would bring cover art by for his approval at one; they could schedule the first meeting for two, if that met with his approval.

"Perfectly," he told her, then, when she would have hurried out to start on it, he called her back.

"Get Vickie Jameson on the phone for me, please."

"Yes, David." She stood there, staring at him miserably.

"What is it?"

"David, are you upset with me? I didn't mean to do anything wrong. I just got a chance to see the manuscript and I

122

knew it had something really substantial to it, so I started assuring John that under the Puma imprint we could do just as much with it as any of the big publishers could do. I did it because I thought it was good. I thought it was warm, and—"

"Erica," he said, interrupting her, "it's a wonderful book. You did good, kid, really good."

She still stared at him, uncertain.

"Erica! You did great. Now do me a favor and wake up—it's going to be a long day."

She nodded and left, quietly closing the doors.

A second later she buzzed him. Vickie was on the phone.

"Vick, listen, can you give me a rain check on dinner? Next Tuesday instead of this one?"

She sulked a moment, quizzing him. He told her he was just awfully busy and really tense; she promised that she could relax him but acquiesced pleasantly at last.

"I'm sorry, Vickie," he murmured, hanging up on her. He was sorry, but he wasn't going to inflict her with his temperament. Not until he toned it down. Not until he could get Susan Anderson out of his mind.

The longing to rush back to Maine and strangle her . . .

The longing to rush back to Maine and hold her again, touch her. Stare into her eyes and discover why she was so damned special, so different . . .

"I will get her out of my system!" he swore aloud, slamming his fist against the manuscript.

She had been Peter's mistress. A woman who had seduced an old man and done well by it, used him in his final days.

David should be able to turn his back on her with no thought at all. He closed his eyes. He would, by God, he would! He would will himself to think of her as no more than a nuisance.

The buzzer sounded.

"Yes, Erica?" he asked pleasantly.

"Is Checker's okay for lunch, David? Noon?"

"Perfect," he replied. He glanced at his watch. Fifteen minutes from now. He stood and left his office, determined to give his secretary an assuring smile and behave in such a casual manner that she couldn't possibly wonder anymore about his volatile reaction to a book.

"Oh, David!" She had been smiling back at him, relieved, when she suddenly seemed to remember something important. She hopped quickly to her feet, running over to him with an express courier package.

"What's this?" he asked.

"It just arrived, marked 'personal and urgent.' "

"Thanks."

There was no return address or name on the envelope; the postmark was from Maine.

Something warned David to step back inside his office before he opened the envelope. Erica went back to her desk, humming softly as she returned to her typing.

David closed his doors and ripped the envelope open.

And then he was glad he had come back and closed his doors. A soft but furious oath escaped him as his own check fluttered to the floor and he read the brief, unsigned note that had been sent along with it.

"No account payment necessary; I told you—you could never pay enough for me. Consider it a charity case."

There was a tap on his door, followed by Erica's anxious, "David? Is something wrong?"

He crumpled the note in his hand.

"Everything is just fine, Erica. Just fine."

He stared out his windows, fighting to regain his equilibrium. "I'll throttle her if I ever see her again!" he murmured softly.

He turned his back to the windows, looking grim. He didn't want to see her again; he didn't want to throttle her. He was going to find a way to get her out of his beach house.

Outside the building on the street, he started to laugh at himself. What irony. He was about to make her famous!

124

CHAPTER SEVEN

The hallway loomed before them. A miasma of decay filled the senses and Lenora was overcome by fear.

"We can't go on," she whispered. "Don't you see, Raoul? They want us to panic and—" In terror she started to choke on her words. "To fall straight into the tentacles of those horrible creatures. They've planned this, Raoul!"

"Lenora, we can't stay here," Raoul told her, his hand winding tightly around hers. "We've got to get away."

"We could wait for it to be light!" she pleaded. The comfort of the cave was behind them; a comfort and security they could so easily go back to.

Go back . . . together . . . alone. With so many recriminations between them. Oh, what did it matter? she asked herself. Daylight would give them a fighting chance against the terrors ahead, more so than the flames of the tapers they carried. By day, light would fall through the cracks in the earth high above them, but he didn't seem to realize the advantages of that.

In the flickering glow of the tapers she saw his face. His rude half smile taunted her, as did the gleam in his eyes. "You want to spend the night with me, Lenora?"

She couldn't answer. His smile faded; his hand, still scarred from the battle with the dray beast, came to her cheek. And she knew it was not just the light she craved; she longed for one more time to touch him and hold him before she had to face the darkness.

His dark eyes were suddenly gentle shadows. "Lenora!" he whispered, and the cry was a plea.

She fell against him, delighting in the strong feel of his body. She looked up at him. "Yes, Raoul, I want to spend the night with you."

"Oh, Lenora, you ass!"

Disgusted, Susan drew her hands from her typewriter, as if the keys had burned her fingers. "Tell the man that he's a pompous jerk and that he can sit on his side of the cave while you sit on yours!"

Susan pressed her fingers over her temples, closing her eyes. She had to remember that Commander Raoul Tierson was her own creation, that he was—beneath his granite facade—totally captivated by Lenora. Sex with her had been the next best thing to the invention of the microwave.

She felt a warm flush of color come to her cheeks as she realized—in a moment of objectivity—that this would be the absolute best time in the world for her to write a sensual love scene. She would be able to describe it all, capturing that feeling of it all being so perfect that there just had to be something there. Not love eternal, maybe, not the kind of love you'd willingly die for, but the tenderness that made it begin. . . .

Susan stood, switching off the machine. Lenora was intelligent. She was a navigator who had been with the Interga-

126

lactic Shuttle Agency for almost a decade. She'd had her spats with Raoul, but he'd been good to her too. He'd been gentle at times. He'd been there to defend her when she'd been under attack by the ship's lecherous second mate.

"Just because I acted like an idiot," Susan told the typewriter and Lenora, "there's no reason for me to turn you into a fool." She sighed, wondering with pure malice of heart if David Lane had received his check yet. And if he had been at all wounded by her proclamation that he was a charity case.

"I will not—I will *not* think about that man!" she swore, then mentally told herself that she was talking to herself and that she wasn't going to do that, either. But two seconds later she was staring at the typewriter again. "Lenora, you are going to have a fabulous night. Raoul is going to get on his knees and beg you to forgive him for everything. As soon as I've made a cup of tea, you're going to have the most fabulous evening of your life. And, oh, Raoul! You poor, sorry SOB. You're going to feel yourself falling apart, body and soul, for her love. But she's going to put her lovely little nose in the air and—"

Susan paused, frowning. Raoul was going to ask Lenora to marry him, and Lenora was going to say yes. They were going to brave the tentacles of the creatures together and live happily ever after. That was the book, dammit!

With a little oath of self-disgust Susan went into the kitchen to set the kettle on, still arguing with herself.

Everyone made mistakes. It was part of living, part of aging, part of maturing. Surely every soul who had ever lived had been made an idiot and a fool at least once!

Yes, but she was too old for the type of mistake she had made. As a high-school senior, as a college coed, she had behaved with far more sense and wisdom.

Maybe she should have made a few mistakes back then. She would have been in better shape to deal with a practiced seducer like Mr. Lane.

The kettle whistled. Susan plopped a tea bag into her cup and watched while it steeped in the water. Just like getting too close to him, she thought. He had touched her in that incredibly gentle way, and the feeling had warmed through her body, coloring it with fever just as the tea filtered through the water.

She dropped the tea bag, added cool water from the spigot, and decided that she had a horrendous headache and the tea wasn't going to help unless she swallowed an aspirin too.

Just as she swallowed the aspirin the phone began to ring. Back into service at last, she thought, and then her heart started to beat loud and hard in her chest.

It was him. It was David Lane. He had received her note, and he . . . he what? What could one reply to such a thing?

It was David Lane, calling to say that he needed to see her urgently; he didn't know how on earth he could ever beg her pardon, but he wanted to do so—he knew that he had been wrong. Would she ever, ever consent to see him again, give him a chance to apologize, to say how grateful he was for the care she had given his father? Would she consider giving her a chance to take her to dinner, to convince her that he had been upset and in a bit of a turmoil and so enamored by her that he hadn't been able to think straight?

The phone shrilled again, and Susan laughed out loud at herself. It wasn't going to be David Lane; he would never believe that he was wrong, never apologize. And she didn't want him to; she just wanted to get him out of her life.

Then why was she still in the beach house?

Because Peter had seen fit to leave half of it in her name. And, by God, she did deserve it more than Peter's willful and judgmental son!

Another shrill jangling of the phone set her into motion. Susan ran back to pick it up in the library, panting a little.

"Susan? Are you all right?"

For some ridiculous reason her heart seemed to career to

128

the pit of her stomach. It wasn't David Lane. She had to learn to leave her fantasizing to paper.

"Hi, John. How are you?" Usually she was thrilled to hear from her agent. When news was bad or problematic, he wrote letters. When news was good, he called.

"Fine, thanks. How are you?"

"Fine," she replied, a little inanely. Well, why not? It was what people said. Not, "Just like hell, John. I mean, I'm in the pits!"

"How's the sci-fi going? I need it up here next week, you know."

"Uh, it's going all right. Well, actually, it's going a little slow."

John hesitated a minute. "I know you've had a bit of a bad time lately, Susan. Want me to get an extension for you?"

She bit lightly into her lower lip, thinking. She knew that Joan Railey at Klayton wouldn't mind if she asked for more time; she just didn't like to do it.

"No. I plan to do nothing but work for the rest of the week. I don't like to change things."

"It wouldn't matter—"

"I just don't like to do it."

"Okay, it's up to you. Hey, I read about your storm. Bad one, huh?"

"Yes, it was something, all right," she replied lightly. "What's up? You didn't call to make sure I didn't get washed away, did you?"

John chuckled softly. "Actually I was a little concerned. But I did call for business." His voice suddenly went very low and husky with excitement. "Susan, big things are happening with that book at Puma. There's a rush on it; there's going to be a truckload of publicity for it. I knew from the beginning that we were dealing with a hot property, but I wasn't sure it would go this far. There's just a minor amendment they want to put on your contract. I need your okay."

Susan hesitated, still feeling John's excitement spill into her.

"What is it?" she asked quickly.

"You haven't got anything against using your own name, have you?"

Again she paused, reflecting. A while ago she might have felt tears prick her eyes, and she might very well have said yes. The pseudonym had been a way to hold on to Carl. But that was one of the nice things that Peter had taught her; she didn't have to have crutches to hang on to. She would always hold on in her heart.

"No, I guess not. But why the change? It might not be anything tremendous, but the S. C. de Chance name does have a bit of a following."

"In select circles, but you're shooting beyond that. I don't know exactly why; neither did the contracts department. Susan, it's such a little thing for the windfall that's coming! The boss man wants it, apparently."

"The boss man?"

She heard his sigh of exasperation and quickly swallowed. "David Lane is in on it now."

"David Lane!" She knew she shouted the word; she almost dropped the phone, and then she was screaming again. "How can David Lane have anything to do with it? This is Puma Publications!"

There was a silence at the other end; obviously John was shocked to hear her violent charge of emotion.

"Susan, Puma is a subsidiary of Lane Publications. Didn't you read your contract? You signed it."

She closed her eyes, winding her fingers around the phone wire, feeling a little sick and definitely dazed.

"Susan?"

"I . . ." She paused. She hadn't read the contract. Peter had read it; Peter had been delighted with it. In fact, remembering back, he had been almost as ecstatic as a kid.

When she had agreed rather nervously to attempt to write

it for him, she had insisted that they go through all the normal channels, that they do it completely as a work of fiction and he use none of his influence in getting it published. No wonder Peter had found it all such a delightful joke—his own company had picked it up at the best price.

"No," she murmured weakly. "I guess I didn't read it. I always trust you—"

"Susan! Don't ever just trust me!" he warned her. "I'm an agent—you're the author, and it's your work!"

"I'll remember that in the future," she murmured, then added quickly, "John, can I get it back? Couldn't we offer it elsewhere?"

"Susan, are you all right?"

"Yes!"

He sighed again, letting her hear his aggravation. "Susan, I don't even know what your problem is. You have no just cause. What's the problem? Have you got an enemy at Lane? I thought you talked to Stacy already; I thought the two of you got along just great."

That was before she knew Puma was Lane, Susan thought.

"Stacy seems lovely," she murmured aloud.

John sighed again. "Susan, I'm your agent. I can't make your decisions for you; I can only advise you. They're putting all their faith—everything—behind this book." She remained silent. "Susan, I have to have an answer on this. Don't be an idiot. Don't mess this up! It means wonderful things for your career!"

Susan sank into Peter's chair, staring at her typewriter. "You said that David Lane insisted on the name change."

"Yes."

So he knew. David Lane owned her book. She was certain he hadn't known a thing about it when he was here, but now he seemed to know. Well, now she knew that Puma was Lane!

"Susan . . ."

131

"Do whatever you want, David. Say anything, sign anything."

"Why the hell do you sound like such a martyr?"

"Do I? Sorry, I didn't mean to." So David was holding the book, a book he knew she had written. And he was planning on doing all kinds of things with it, no matter what he felt toward her.

Why?

Because he's capable of being more professional, she thought. No—because the book was his father's life.

"Listen, Susan, can you get down here anytime soon? I promised the publicity department that I'd get you here."

"New York?"

"No, Susan," John said with waning patience, "we've moved the business hub of the country out to galaxy twelve in the Centurian region. Of course, New York!"

"Ha ha."

"Susan, you do not sound well."

"I've got to finish this book for Joan, David."

"And it's due next week. Finish it and bring it to me. Let me know when you're going to come in. I'll even get you at the airport and we'll go swanky for dinner, on the agency, okay? Susan, this is a celebration, not a funeral. You're getting me really worried. Are you coming?"

"I—"

"Susan! You're worried about making waves over a few days on a due date, yet here you are with suddenly very wet feet about what could be the most important opportunity in your life! This thing is different! Think of the years you've been working away on cult books. You could sell more of this one book than you have of everything else you've ever written combined! Come on, pay attention here! You come into the city."

New York. David Lane lived in New York. So did millions of other people. She wouldn't go over to Lane; she'd make sure she got to meet whoever it was she had to meet some-where else.

"I'll be up at the end of next week, John. When I've made a flight reservation, I'll let you know."

"That's better." He laughed, apparently relieved, as he should have been. Poor John! He must have thought he had a client dangerously close to going over the edge.

"Get back to your sexy corners of the universe! I'll talk to you soon."

Susan knew he said good-bye and that she made some kind of appropriate reply. Then she sat there with the receiver still in her hand.

David Lane was holding her book. Peter had known it, but he hadn't told her, and he hadn't told David. She and David had finally really met—just like Peter had wanted—but the whole thing had been a ridiculous travesty. And now . . .

She gave herself a little shake. She'd been working with Joan for more than six years, and she didn't know more than three people in that office of hundreds. She didn't even know the names of the publisher or the art director or any of the others. There was no reason to assume that she would have anything to do with David Lane.

And if she really wanted to make sure she didn't see him again, she'd move out of the beach house. No. She'd never do that. Not after the way he'd behaved. She couldn't help it. He'd condemned her: her and Peter. She wanted to hurt him back, and the only way to hurt him was to hold on to her rights in the house. Her home. She had lived here for the past year. In all that time he hadn't been near it.

Suddenly her eyes fell on Peter's corncob pipe. She picked it up, then brushed away the moisture that formed in her eyes. "Oh, Peter! What were you thinking of? Why didn't you set that son of yours straight a year ago? And why, in heaven's name, did you tie this house up between us? Why didn't you warn me about the book?"

She set the pipe down. "Well, you were right about one thing. . . . I think I would have liked him if I'd met him under different circumstances."

But she hadn't.

The phone started to ring again, causing her heart rate to rise. Would it be David? Calling to tell her that even if she was a blankety-blank, he would see that the book received fair treatment? In his father's memory, of course.

"Yes?"

It was Jerry, calling from a break at the emergency station. "It's good to hear your voice," he told her, adding a little anxiously, "You are all right, aren't you?"

"Fine, Jerry. Thanks for calling to ask."

"Well, it sounded as if you'd be okay, but you should always take care with a head injury. You should get to a doctor and have a checkup, you know."

"I'm okay, really, Jerry."

"Where's David?"

"David left early yesterday morning."

"He left?" Jerry sounded surprised. "Doesn't sound like David."

"Why not?"

"Leaving you after an injury and all—"

"Jerry! Please listen carefully: I'm fine, I swear it."

"How'd you wind up in the water like that, anyway? Thank God he was there! You might have—well, you know. Susan, with Peter gone now, you really shouldn't stay there alone. Every time a storm whips up, the house is cut off. And it's so lonely out there."

"I like it, Jerry."

He was a dear friend, but he was about to launch into a lecture, so she decided to tactfully cut him off at the pass. "I'll think about moving out," she promised. "I've got some work to get done this next week, though, and then I've got to run down to New York. Afterward I'll start thinking about my future."

"You really should," Jerry cautioned her. He hesitated. "You're a young woman, Susan, and you've spent so much time with age and death," he said softly. "I understand how attached you got to Peter. He was a great guy—the greatest. I understand you having to care for your grandparents, and then your brother, but, Sue, you've got to live—"

"I know, Jerry. I intend to. Really. And I do appreciate your concern."

He laughed. "But you're busy! Okay, okay, I get the message. How about drinks with the crowd Friday night? Think you can squeeze us in?"

"I'm not sure yet." She chuckled softly. "I honestly have to get back to this galaxy this week. But I'll call you tomorrow, okay?"

"Okay. Take care. Oh! I forgot to ask you. How did you get along with David?"

"Like fire and wind," Susan replied sweetly.

"You're kidding!"

"No, I'm not. Why should I be?"

"Oh, I don't know. I spent summers with David. Everyone liked David." Jerry chuckled, and she could imagine his homely but oh so pleasant grin. "I did, too, except during my flights of jealousy. You know, he had the greatest parents —Mary was like the perfect Kool-Ade mom. All the kids were always welcome. And David just eased through everything—the best grades, basketball star, baseball, soccer, tennis, you name it. And then he was so damned good-looking, too! But he always shared—and smoothly. Managed to get one of his dates for his friends all the time. Of course, I haven't seen a lot of him lately, but it didn't seem like he'd changed any. I went to New York once and gave him a call and he treated me just like royalty. Peter was like that. No matter how big he got, how rich, how influential, he was just the same."

"That's nice," Susan murmured, her fingers wound so tightly around the receiver, she thought she would snap it.

135

For heaven's sake, why hadn't she just said that she had gotten along just fine with the great Mr. Lane? If there was anything she did not want at the moment, it was a glowing testimonial in his behalf!

"Jerry, I've really got to go. Say hi to Mindy for me, and I'll probably see you all Friday night. Oh, and Jerry, I've got a broken window upstairs. It's boarded, but I need new panes. Can you check into it for me?"

"Sure thing. Take care. And you should see a doctor, Susan. Bumps on the head—"

"Are nothing to fool with." Susan laughed. At last she hung up and sat staring at the phone, daring it to ring again.

It didn't. She retrieved her tea, stared at the phone several seconds longer, then convinced herself that she had to get back to Raoul and Lenora. The going was difficult at first. She stared at the page for at least five minutes, but then she forced herself to concentrate. And she was still so mad at herself that she managed to be coldly objective, drawing upon her own recent experience to give her characters a really wonderful night. At least she salvaged something out of that catastrophe!

It had started to grow dark outside by the time she finished with her pages, made herself another cup of tea, and carried the papers to the parlor, curling up on the sofa to reread, scratching in a correction here and there. She had done it! She had actually concentrated and was pleased and comfortable with the results. All she had to do was add in a word here—

It was then that the phone started ringing again, shrilling so fiercely into her absorption with her work that she spilled tea over her pages. Letting out a soft oath, she ran back into the library, not thinking until her hand was on the phone, then getting furious with herself when her heart started pounding again. Was it fear? Loathing? Anticipation? She didn't know, but it was ridiculous. She wasn't going through this every time the phone rang.

136

"Yes?" she said rather crisply.

"Miss Anderson?"

It was him. Her blood began to race through her system, hot and cold, hot and cold. She clutched the phone wire like a life-support system.

"What do you want, Mr. Lane?" she demanded coolly.

"I'll give you two hundred thousand for your half of the house, Miss Anderson," he replied smoothly. As smoothly and remotely cordial as if they had never met face-to-face. "It isn't worth a quarter of that sum."

She started to laugh. "Talked to the attorneys again, have you, Mr. Lane?"

"Yes, actually, I have. Well?"

"No, Mr. Lane."

He was quiet for a moment. When he spoke again, his voice was a husky drawl that seemed to touch her physically. "Miss Anderson, think about it. Two hundred thousand dollars is a lot of money. An awful lot of selling, you know."

She hesitated, desperately trying to create a bored and disinterested sound. "Mr. Lane, surely you're aware that I have an income."

"Ah, yes! S. C. de Chance."

"And Susan Anderson, apparently at your insistence."

"I do call a spade a spade, Miss Anderson."

"Call it like you see it, right?"

"Something like that."

"Well, Mr. Lane, I do believe you're reaching the age for bifocals."

"Meaning, Miss Anderson?"

"Not a thing, Mr. Lane." She made a pretense of yawning. "Is there anything else? I'm not selling my interest in the house."

"What if I chose to move into it, Miss Anderson?"

Susan laughed softly. "You're not going to leave New York, Mr. Lane, and you know it. However, I am able to admit that the property is half yours. Anytime you wish to use it, you have only to let me know, and I will vacate the premises while you're here."

"Miss Anderson, I never know when I might get the time to get away. If you stay there, you do so at your own risk."

"Risk of what?"

"Being disturbed."

"Oh, you don't disturb me, Mr. Lane. You only imagine that you do."

"Perhaps that will put things to the test, Miss Anderson. You might wish to reconsider. Two hundred thousand dollars is a ridiculously high sum of money."

"Is that a threat? You forget, Mr. Lane," Susan said carefully, very slowly and sweetly, "that I considered you a charity case."

"I don't threaten things, I do them. And I haven't forgotten a thing, Miss Anderson. Not a thing. Not even a moment. Think about it, will you? You might find it to your advantage to bend early."

"Why is that?"

"Because I promise that I can be disturbing when I so choose."

"I'll just bet you can, Mr. Lane. But you—" She broke off, suddenly chilled. "Are you planning on destroying the book?"

"What?" He sounded puzzled, actually lost by her quick change of tone.

"The book." She tried to breathe evenly, tried not to care, but a year of her life had gone into it, Peter's last year had gone into it, and it was just too damn important.

"What are you talking about?" he asked. "Your book is going to get royal treatment. Surely you suspected as much. I'd hardly let anything go wrong with something that so obviously traces my father's life." He hesitated, and she wondered if he was testing her in some way. "If you had any worries about the book, why didn't you voice them during the weekend?"

"I didn't think the damn thing had anything to do with you during the weekend!" she snapped back, then bit her lip. He had been baiting her, and she had fallen right into his trap. "If I had suspected Puma was part of Lane, I promise you—"

"That I wouldn't have it, Miss Anderson? That's rather childish, isn't it? Publishers don't meet all their authors, usually only the best-selling ones. And even then the contact between them is minimal." Except in our case, David added silently.

"I really don't understand why you want—"

"It's a good book," he interrupted curtly.

"That's big of you to say."

"No, Miss Anderson. It isn't really. I say it with bitterness. You really bled my father right to the end."

"He wanted it written!" Susan exclaimed. "It was his idea, and when he found out I was a writer, he—" She stopped abruptly, wondering why she was defending herself, why she was so ridiculously close to tears. "I'm busy. Is there anything else?"

"That's it, Miss Anderson. Take care."

Susan heard the click of the phone, and still she gripped the receiver. "I'd like to bat him over the head with a brick!" she muttered. "I'd like to . . ." she paused, closing her eyes tightly, bracing herself. It was a pity that she couldn't cast David Lane into the pit with the monsters in her latest book.

Her mouth curled in a grimace of sudden pain. Jerry's words came home to her with a cutting resolve. She needed to piece her life back together. She had been living for others as they prepared for death. If she could go back, she wouldn't change a moment of it; she had gained too much. But she had loved and lost, and even learned to deal with loss. She was going to get out and live again. Forget the past pains and the past mistakes, the great mistake—David Lane.

She dialed Jerry's home number. Mindy answered, a little breathlessly, making Susan hope she hadn't interrupted anything. Mindy assured Susan that she was thrilled to hear from her, that she had been worried all weekend.

"Except that you were with David. And you couldn't have been in better hands. Unless Jerry had been there, of course," Mindy added loyally.

Susan didn't want to hear about David. "I just wanted to say that I would be glad to go out with you all on Friday," she told Mindy.

"Great! Hang on, Jerry's saying something. . . . Oh, we'll pick you up, okay?"

"Why don't I just meet you in town? There's no reason for someone to have to drive out here."

"Yes, there is. Mrs. Hennessy's house was broken into today. A guy with a mask shoved her around quite a bit."

"Is she hurt?" Susan asked anxiously. A frown tightened her brow. Crime was unheard of in this tiny northern town.

"She's going to be okay. Bruises, scratches, a lump on the head, but Jerry doesn't want you coming in alone late at night. Okay?"

There was a plea in her friend's voice. "Sure, that's nice of you both. I'll see you Friday night, then."

"Eight o'clock?"

"Eight sounds fine."

Susan hung up. She was going to go out with her friends and have a good time. She would work—totally professional at all times!—and when she wasn't working, she wasn't going to worry about anything. Especially not David Lane.

Especially not David Lane, dammit!

140

CHAPTER EIGHT

The crowd, as Jerry called the group of friends, consisted of himself and Mindy, Lawrence Ewell and Carrie Smith—two more natives of the area—and Dr. Harley Richmond and his wife, Nora. Lawrence and Carrie had returned to Maine after painful divorces from separate spouses; Susan thought they would eventually leave again, that they only came home to lick their wounds. But, except for the Richmonds and herself, it was a group that had long known the ups and downs of friendship. They were warm and fun to be with. She didn't feel like a seventh wheel at all in their company.

They chose Badacini's for dinner, a fresh fish place on the water. The food was good, and after the meal they trekked upstairs where a trio played a bit of everything and the dancers ranged from ten years of age to eighty.

During the meal, during which they'd all passed their chosen entrées around the table for everyone to sample, Susan had been between Nora Richmond and Mindy. Nora had quoted humorous anecdotes about the things that came home from school in her children's lunch boxes; Mindy had laughed about her and Jerry's most recent attempts to begin a family themselves. The conversation had been pleasant and easy.

But upstairs, when they were all seated around the circular cocktail table, the conversation changed. Jerry mentioned that he was sorry he hadn't had a chance to see David Lane, and Carrie instantly picked up on it.

She was a pretty woman of about thirty-three with large, soulful brown eyes and sleek chestnut hair cut in a slant across her cheek, a pleasant angle to her heart-shaped face. She looked at Susan with curiosity and no rancor.

"David was here? Oh, what a pity! I'd have loved to have seen him myself."

"Rekindling old flames, eh?" Jerry teased, idly running his thumb along Mindy's cheek.

"Oh, you're just jealous!" Carrie said, flaunting back lightly. She gazed at Susan again, her eyes sparkling. "It's a good thing that Jerry cornered Mindy—and that she had a streak of kindness and pity in her! David had it all hands down when he was here! How is he?"

"He's . . . fine, I guess," Susan replied a little stiffly. "I barely know him; it would be hard for me to say."

"I'll bet he's aged well," Mindy murmured. Then she laughed. "Jerry's right; when I was a kid, I had a crush on him that wouldn't quit. What's he look like? Any distinguishing gray at the temples yet?"

"Ah, no. He's still dark," Susan murmured, playing with the lime in her gin rickey.

Jerry chuckled softly. "I didn't get the impression that Susan and David hit it off very well."

"You didn't?" Carrie persisted, astonished. "David is impossible to dislike!"

"Oh, no, he's not!" Susan snapped before she could prevent herself. She smiled quickly, wishing she could have kept her feelings to herself. She looked across the table at Mindy.

"Would you get your husband up on the dance floor with you, please? Then I won't feel guilty about trying to steal him for a dance later."

Mindy chuckled. "Sure." She and Jerry departed for the dance floor; the Richmonds followed them, and Lawrence charmingly assured Susan that he'd dance with her anytime she liked. And Carrie, too, of course.

As the numbers went on they all changed partners a half dozen times. Susan wound up on the floor with Harley, who gave her a look of concern. "How are you, Susan? I mean, really, how are you?"

She looked into his kind eyes with surprise. "I'm fine, Harley. Really fine. Why?"

He shrugged, stepping on her toe as he moved awkwardly to the music. "I'm just worried about you, that's all. I mean, you've had more than your share of it. Coming to the clinic with Carl, then working the hospice with him. Your home life was watching your brother die. Your professional life was helping other people die. And when you finally left it, it was to go and help Peter Lane die. Susan, Peter's gone now, and you've got to get on with living."

"Hey, Doc!" Susan protested, giving him a dazzling smile. "I was the psychology major, remember? The psychology major turned writer. I've been out of the hospice for a year now."

"You haven't been out of it. You were with Peter. And your own social life consisted of those characters in your novels."

"I loved Peter. Peter was there when I did crack, when Carl died. He was the healer on that one, Harley. If I'm not being social now, warn me and I'll try harder!"

"Peter was the best," Harley said softly. He stopped moving to the music and just looked down at her with the concern of an old friend. "That's just it; you did love him. You were involved again. Susan, a person can only take so much. Of course you're being social, but I meant that you should be a whole lot more social with someone than you could ever be with any of us! You need a good man, Susan—one who's under forty! Please, Susan, tell me you're not going to come back to work now!"

She laughed reassuringly. "Harley, I guess I haven't had a chance to tell you yet, have I?" She tried to keep the edge of bitterness out of her voice. "I'm going to be a rich and famous author. It turns out that I sold Peter's life story to Peter's son, and if he's on the up and up, David Lane intends to create a best-seller."

He frowned at her when Susan thought he should have smiled and congratulated her. "Did you ever tell David the truth about his father?"

Susan lowered her eyes, shaking her head. "I never told David or anyone else. Peter wanted it that way." She hesitated. "I almost told David once." She looked back up at Harley, her bitterness shining brightly in her eyes. "I should have. I believe he thinks I excited his father to death!"

"So why didn't you tell him the truth?" Harley demanded, his eyes narrowing so protectively toward her that she wished she hadn't spoken.

"Harley, to what good sense could I correct the man now? He condemned us both. Let him stew in his own juice. Besides, Harley, I'd like to do some serious damage to the man, really I would, but it would just be too awful to make him realize that he avoided his father when Peter knew that it was the end."

"Oh, Sue," Harley murmured. He pulled her head against his chest. She felt a little like a child again, protected by an elder brother. It had been like this with Carl. Comfortable.

Not like being touched by David Lane. Touched and set afire with longing . . .

"I assume he resents Peter's terms regarding the beach house?" Harley murmured.

"You assume right."

144

"I thought you were going to give your interest in it over to David."

"I was—until I met David."

Harley didn't answer for a minute. He made a wide sweep to the music, which had changed; it had become a slower number.

Susan chuckled softly. "Harley, don't you think we ought to go back to the table now? I don't want Nora to start thinking the worst of me!"

"Nora never would," he replied absently. "Susan, I don't want you tangling with David Lane."

"Harley, you don't even know him!"

"But it seems to me that you're set on a dangerous course. Dad has known David for years, he likes him a lot, but he thinks he's tough as nails." Harley hesitated a minute, as if he were doing a little soul-searching before going on. "According to Dad, David was one of the most easygoing guys you'd ever want when he was in high school and college. He fought with Peter because Peter set impossible standards for him. But he'd do anything. Jerry almost got kicked off the summer baseball team once, but David pulled him through, doing extra practice with him. If a homely girl had a crush on him, he'd be nice and gentle. If someone laughed at her, he'd be all the more gallant. He had everything and it didn't affect him. And then . . ."

Susan stared at him wonderingly. "And then what?"

"He went away." Harley shrugged. "Dad says he could never put his finger on it but that something had happened to David. Something you couldn't see on the surface, but he had changed. Not that he wasn't still courteous. Just that there seemed to be a ruthless quality to him underneath the surface. As if you'd be a fool to underestimate him."

"I'm sure that's true," Susan murmured lightly. Oh, yes, there were numerous qualities to David Lane. She wouldn't put a damn thing past him. Not after their initial meeting. Not after she had found herself on the floor. . . .

145

But neither could she doubt the power of his charm, she thought bitterly. Not after she had felt the brush of his whisper, and then his kiss, and then fallen into his arms without a grain of sense, willing to forget everything in the heat of the desire he had so expertly kindled.

She stiffened, remembering the night. The utter sense of magic. And then the morning, finding the check.

She laughed and lifted her chin to Harley. "I don't give a damn about the man's past, Harley," she said coolly. "If he wages war against me, he's got a battle on his hands."

Harley shook his head dolefully. Lawrence tapped his shoulder, and Harley gave up his dance partner to go find his wife.

It was a good evening. Lawrence was a nice man, tall, well dressed, pleasant in appearance, and even more pleasant in manner. He was a nice, nice break after David Lane, complimentary and polite. He suggested that Susan go to a movie with him the next week, and she hesitated. She liked Lawrence, but there was simply no chemistry between them, and even if the movie was just a casual date, she didn't want to take chances with him, not when he was recuperating from a divorce.

She didn't want to hurt his feelings. She told him she had to catch up on some work and that maybe in a month or two they could get together.

It was about two A.M. when they finally decided to leave. Lawrence offered to drive both Susan and Carrie home, and because of it, Susan got to hear about David Lane all over again from Carrie—in glowing detail.

"I'll never forget what he did for me once," she said with a laugh. "It was the summer after our senior year. I'd realized by then that he wasn't going to wake up one morning and be madly in love with me. I had a date for one of the summer dances, but my date started by spending the evening trailing after one of the town beauties. David must have noticed, because he danced the night away with me. And consequently, of course, everyone else there thought I had to be magic if David thought so! I left that place the belle of the ball. It was great."

They'd reached the beach house. "Let's walk Susan in," Lawrence told Carrie. "It's so dark and deserted out here."

"Oh, yes, we should, shouldn't we?" Carrie murmured. She looked at Susan with an unhappy grimace. "Seems our new burglar was at it again. He broke into one of the cottages just south of here." She paused, not willing to go any farther.

Lawrence continued, apparently assuming that it was better for Susan to be frightened and careful than unfrightened and comfortable.

"Things got a little worse. A young college professor's wife was assaulted."

"Oh!" Susan said nervously. "Then thanks—I'll check out all the closets while you two are still here."

Carrie and Lawrence waited in the foyer while Susan gave the house a fleeting check. She looked into her own room, then Peter's, but the door to David's bedroom had been closed the morning he had left and not reentered since. Susan couldn't open it; the whole thing was actually silly, anyway. The front door hadn't been tampered with and neither had any of the windows. She was alone and a little gun-shy, that was all.

"Seems to be clear," she told the two in the foyer cheerfully. She gave them both friendly kisses on the cheek. "Thanks for a great evening."

"My pleasure," Lawrence told her. "I'll be looking forward to getting together again soon."

"Me too," Carrie said with a grin and a yawn. "Umm, I think I need to get home, too, my dear escort."

He shook his head, looking at Susan. "She's always been as bossy as all hell!"

"Oh, I am not!" Carrie protested.

Still grimacing, Lawrence prodded her out the door. "Lock up!" he called back to Susan.

"I will!" she promised, and she did, smiling and thinking that those two friends might be just what the other needed. Maybe after all the years, after separate paths, they just might discover each other.

She leaned against **the d**oor, reflecting that she had enjoyed the evening and that there would be many evenings ahead in her life to enjoy. On one of them the right man might come along, someone gentle and supportive and completely charming.

Someone who could touch her with the same fire as David Lane.

Someone who wasn't David Lane!

She pushed away from the door, flicked the foyer light off and the stairwell light on, and hurried up to her room, delightfully tired. Her feet even hurt. She hadn't danced so much in ages.

In her room she quickly changed into a nightgown and flounced onto her bed, certain that she would be sound asleep in minutes—so dead to the world that she couldn't possibly dream.

And she was drowsy, so much so that her eyes closed and she felt sleep begin to encompass her like a warm blanket. The wind was rustling gently and the waves were rolling onto the beach outside in a lulling cadence. Her sheets were cool and clean, and everything seemed to be deliciously comfortable.

Suddenly she bounded from her pillow, chills cascading along her spine. There had been a sound. Not the wind and not the waves, but something totally alien to the whispers and melodies of the night.

No, she thought, listening alertly, her heart thudding. How long she stayed there, barely daring to breathe, she didn't know. She tried to convince herself that she had imagined the sound in the parlor, and when nothing else came, she was almost certain that she had.

Mindy had asked her once if she didn't think that Peter would come back to haunt the place that he had loved so well. And she had laughed in return, assuring Mindy that if Peter could be a ghost, he would certainly be welcome back in his home and that he would never hurt her.

Maybe it was Peter settling into his library, lighting his pipe, she tried to muse whimsically.

She lay back down, but her heart continued to pound. Then she sat up, realizing that she would never sleep and that if she did sleep and someone was in the house, they could creep in on her.

Silently she reached into her closet for her umbrella—the best weapon she could think of. On bare feet she trod across the room, slowly cracked her door, and looked out. There was nothing, only the gentle glow of the night-light on the stairwell. Hurriedly she tiptoed down the stairs, crept down to the wall, and stared into the parlor. She gave herself a little shake, breathing more easily. She had imagined the sound.

Better make sure, she warned herself.

She crept across the parlor to the kitchen door, wondering what she was going to do if she surprised a thief. Maybe she should have gone the other way, into the library. She could have picked up the phone and dialed the police.

For what, goose? she charged herself. To tell them she heard bumps in the night?

She went on into the kitchen like a wraith, keeping close to the walls, almost chuckling aloud when she saw that the kitchen, too, was just as she'd left it.

She turned around, relieved and annoyed that her imaginings had destroyed what had promised to be a wonderful night's rest, something she hadn't enjoyed in a long, long time. Not since the day Peter had died.

Halfway back across the parlor she came to a dead halt, riddled with chills, goose bumps forming all over her body.

There *was* someone in the house. Someone who had been in the parlor. Someone who had been upstairs when she had been coming down. Someone who was now moving down the stairway.

At first she couldn't run. She couldn't even move. What had been imagination was now real.

And then she longed to run. With every fiber in her body she longed to make a mad dash for the door.

But she couldn't do that, didn't dare to. The footsteps were nearing the bottom of the stairway, and if she raced through the parlor to the foyer and the door, she would be caught, just like a trapped hare, desperately trying to undo the bolts she had so studiously fastened before going to bed.

How had the intruder gotten in? Oh, God! He hadn't, she realized. He had been there all the while, hiding in David's bedroom! And she was about to be assaulted because she'd been too disturbed to open that door while help had remained below.

All this passed through her mind in a flash while she prayed desperately for insight on what to do now. At the last possible second she flattened herself to the parlor wall, right next to the doorway. If she was lucky, the thief would have finished with the house. He would seek a way out.

And if she wasn't lucky . . . well, she was carrying her umbrella as a weapon. Her heart began to race afresh and then to sink.

The footsteps paused in the foyer, and then they turned, softly, stealthily, coming directly toward her.

Susan raised her umbrella, trembling. Again the footsteps paused, right outside the doorway. She was sure he heard the pounding of her heart, leading him straight to her.

Suddenly, too suddenly, he was inside. Looming tall and incredibly broad and competely shadowed in the darkness of the night.

Near tears, she restrained a cry of terror, stepping forward to lash out at the intruder with all her strength, bringing the umbrella down like a club over his head.

He ducked just in time but let out a cry of pain as the umbrella sliced over his shoulder. The umbrella was wrenched out of her hands by a ruthless power and sent soaring across the room, and before she could absorb that shock, powerful arms were around her, jerking her arm behind her back, sending her to the floor. She screamed then, loud and desperately.

"Susan!"

She was released so instantly that she sprawled down on the hardwood floor, face first. She didn't know whether to laugh or start screaming all over again.

Her "thief" was David Lane.

She rolled, blinking against the sudden harsh glare as he flicked on the overhead light.

David stared down at her, and for the thousandth time he wondered why he had come. What about her had been like a Circe's call, beckoning him back, to flounder upon the rocks?

His shoulder ached and he rubbed it absently, looking down at her incredulously. She had just clubbed him! But seeing her . . .

She was flat on her back. Her hair was spread around her like waves of flame, and her features were deathly pale. She was wearing a long white nightgown with slits up the sides that left almost the entire length of one long, tanned limb exposed. And as she returned his stare her lip started to tremble.

"David!"

"Who were you expecting?" he asked, still confused, but certain that she hadn't been attacking him personally. He reached a hand to her; she accepted it, dazed, and stood before him.

151

"There have been a couple of break-ins," she told him nervously. "I—I thought you were the prowler."

"Oh," he said simply, then frowned despite himself. "There's a prowler in the area and you're still determined to stay here alone?"

She spun around, hugging her arms across the low-cut décolletage of her nightgown. "If you're trying to get me out of here," she said bitterly, "forget it."

He caught her shoulder angrily. "I'm not trying to do anything of the kind! But what if I *had* been the prowler? You got your best shot at me. You missed and were at my mercy. And then what the hell would you have done way out here, alone?"

He realized then that she was still visibly shaken, and although he rationally thought she deserved a whole lot more, he relented, releasing her. Susan hurried to the sofa, sinking into it before her knees could buckle under her. She stared at her hands.

"What are you doing here?"

"Other than having you crack my shoulder?"

Her eyes were riveted to his, shimmering, moist and emerald. "I'd rather have cracked you with my palm across the face." She stiffened with regal poise. "I certainly didn't really mean to cause you injury."

"Well, you did, you know."

A little flicker of guilt and concern passed through her eyes. "Want some ice? A brandy or something?"

"Yes, as a matter of fact, I do," he told her, intrigued to see what she would be willing to do for him.

She stood and hurried into the kitchen. David pulled his knit shirt over his head and ruefully glanced at his shoulder. It was swelling up nicely. He sat down in the spot on the sofa she had just vacated. She came back into the room carrying an ice pack and a snifter.

"You've got a good batting arm," he said, teasing her.

She didn't smile but handed him the brandy and set the

ice pack on his shoulder, her brows knit in a frown as she did so.

"What are you doing here?" she asked, her eyes on her task. But she was close. So close that he could inhale the subtle scent of her perfume and remember; so close that he could have moved his hand and caressed her breast.

"I came to make you realize that it was uncomfortable to have to share a home," he told her, watching her. But her eyes didn't come to his. She finished adjusting the ice pack and straightened, and to his amazement she smiled.

"I see. You were trying to disturb me."

He grinned wickedly in return. "Yes—maybe I was."

Susan laughed, sailing across the room to the door, only turning back when she reached it. "I'm sorry, Mr. Lane. I'm not disturbed. I'm thrilled to death. You may be any number of things—which I'll restrain myself from vocalizing right now—but at least you are not a thief. I'm delighted with your appearance. I'll get a good night's sleep and you can tangle with the prowler if he should decide to show!"

"Miss Anderson!" he said, calling her back.

She paused, one brow delicately raised.

"You're not feeling . . . charitable this evening?"

"Oh, I only give to any cause once, Mr. Lane. Where you're concerned, I haven't a charitable bone left in my body!"

She disappeared up the stairway. David winced; his shoulder was throbbing.

Yet, he thought miserably, it didn't pulse with anything near the flame of desire that just seeing her brought to him.

Why the hell was he here? What had he thought he could prove? Ah, yes! He'd wanted her to know how uncomfortable it could be to share a house, to be surprised at any time.

And all he had achieved was a burning shoulder and something more than the misery of longing. Dear God! He wanted to believe in her! He wanted to pretend that there was no past, that the vulnerable beauty he had touched before was the truth.

He set his mouth into a grim line. There were things of his father's that he had a right to: memories, the house. There were things in the past that he had no right to—and she was at the top of that list.

David sighed and rose. He'd been waging a war—and waging it against himself. She'd never really wanted to fight him; some sense of outrage had simply forced him to drive her into a corner. The whole thing was insane. His best move would be to sue for peace, relent to what had been, after all, Peter's wishes. Maybe then he could get on with his life and forget her.

Upstairs, he threw open the windows, grateful for the cold night air. He lay down, lacing his fingers behind his head, staring into the darkness of night, but seeing things that lay in the past. His thoughts ebbed and flowed like a tide. They wouldn't allow him to sleep.

He started suddenly, tensing as his bedroom door opened. A glimmer of moonlight filled the room, enough so that he could see her. In her white nightgown she looked like a Grecian goddess, as virginal as an ancient maiden doomed to be sacrificed. She moved so lightly, like a wraith, like a nymph. . . .

Like a lover coming to him in the night in sweet secrecy. Sleek, shimmering white, passionate red, the flame of her hair catching the moonlight to cloak her with an innocent sensuality . . .

It wasn't true, of course. Fantasy—it was her business.

"David!" Her voice was anxious and hushed.

"What?" he answered, not moving. "Have you decided to be charitable after all?"

"David, stop!" she pleaded. "I think there really is someone downstairs!"

"What?" He bolted up. How could anyone be downstairs?

Since he'd been in the service, he'd learned to listen, to hear any unusual sound. "You're imagining things."

"No, I swear, I'm not!"

He threw his feet over the bed, mindless of his nudity. She stood silently aside, and whatever she was thinking was hidden from him in the darkness. He grabbed for his robe, then rummaged in his top desk drawer, finding his service revolver. "Stay here," he told her.

She shook her head vehemently, and in the muted light her eyes did indeed seem to glow like gems, making him ache all over again with the desire for things to be different. For her to be . . . his, in truth. He wanted to wrap her in his arms, assure her like a lover, swear to protect and defend . . .

"I'm not staying here!" she protested in a hushed but vehement whisper. "David . . ." There was the slightest plea to the words, and then she was nervously teasing, "Don't you ever watch horror movies? The heroine gets left behind —and then attacked! I'll be right behind you!"

"Behind!" he persisted gruffly.

"I'll stay where I'm supposed to," she promised. Her eyes fell on the revolver. "Is that thing real?"

"Of course, it's real," he whispered back impatiently.

He didn't touch her; he silently started out of his room, then down the stairway. In the light there he could see the front door; the locks and bolts were all still in place, and he frowned. It had been her imagination.

He didn't say so. He turned to her and motioned that he was going into the darkened parlor. She nodded and stood in the foyer, watching him.

There was nothing in the parlor. David went on in to the kitchen and began to smile to himself. She had been imagining things. Hearing about the prowler, convincing herself that he would surely come after her.

But then, just as his muscles relaxed and he exhaled a long

155

breath, he heard her scream. It was quick, sharp sound. Instantly cut off as if someone had—

"Susan!"

He had his gun out before him, his finger on the trigger. He drew up short, seeing her in the foyer, held in the powerful grasp of a man who seemed to be half monster. The guy was unshaven, muscle-bound and burly, and clad in jeans and a khaki jacket that added to his height and breadth.

His left arm was locked around Susan, his grimy fingers clamped over her mouth. In his right hand he carried a knife —one set closely against her rib cage.

David paused and swallowed, sickly aware that he couldn't show his fear. He spoke quietly. "Let her go."

The prowler laughed, showing yellow teeth. "No way, buddy. That thing's probably a kid's water pistol! Now you come over here and open the door for me—nicely. Throw the gun down and open the door, and as soon as I get into the woods, I'll let your little girlfriend go."

Like hell he'd let her go! God alone knew what he would do to her—David didn't dare think about it—but when he was through, it was more than possible that he'd slit her throat and leave her in the pines.

David shook his head slowly. "No way," he said very softly. "I assure you this isn't a water pistol. I had to shoot a lot of decent men who happened to be on the other side of the line with this thing. I wouldn't think twice about shooting garbage who preys on innocent women. And I promise you, the bullets fly fast from this baby. Real fast. I can aim right between your eyes or I can aim at your kneecap. There's nothing like a shattered kneecap for real pain."

Tension seemed to riddle the air like a tangible vapor. David felt as if he screamed inside, loud enough to be heard: *I'm not bluffing, buddy, I'm not bluffing. Touch her and I don't think I'll feel human anymore. . . .*

"Look, I don't want to kill you. I'll get off, but there will be all kinds of messy paperwork first, you know. But I will. Trust me, I'll do it."

The man didn't release her. David took careful aim at his eyes. At the last second he twisted his hand; his bullet sank into the door. The man jerked, shoving Susan down to her knees; a startled scream escaped from her.

"Don't shoot! Don't shoot again!" the thief pleaded.

"Susan, can you call the police?"

He was terrified that she would faint, that she would pass out on the floor.

Her head rose slowly. He saw her beautiful eyes, moist and brilliant against her pale cheeks, the waves of fiery red hair falling around them.

She nodded slowly.

"Move back!" David commanded the intruder, determined that Susan wouldn't have to brush by him to reach the phone. She crawled up from her knees and raced into the library. He heard her voice, trembling but coherent as she talked to the police.

"Open the bolts," he told the intruder. The man did so, eyeing David uncertainly all the while. "What are you going to do to me? Hey, you've called the cops—"

"Yeah, and I don't want you in the house while we're waiting for them to get here," David said flatly. "Get out. I'll be right behind you."

Susan came back into the foyer, anxiously watching him as he started to follow the thief.

"David?"

"Stay inside!" he snapped. "Lock the doors behind me!"

She closed the door, and then he sighed with relief. He could already hear the screech of sirens.

CHAPTER NINE

The thief's name was Harry Bloggs; he was thirty-nine, a drifter with a record who was last incarcerated in Massachusetts, which would surely please the northern Maine natives, since they felt they were too peaceful and civilized to produce criminals.

Sheriff Grodin asked David all kinds of questions, and then he asked Susan all kinds of questions, which David didn't mind, because Susan's nightgown was by then hidden beneath her forest-green floor-length robe; he idly wondered what had happened to the white one. Harry Bloggs was handcuffed in the back of the patrol wagon, and Ed Beaufort, the deputy sheriff, was staring at him.

Susan was very calm and seemingly unaffected by the incident, which pleased David. What hadn't pleased him had been a few of Bloggs's comments.

Once the sheriff had arrived, Bloggs had apparently decided that David wasn't going to shoot him—not in front of the law, at any rate. He'd come up with a vicious line of bravado.

"Hey, tough guy, they can't hold me. No one's ever gonna really hold me. And, buddy, when I get out this time, I'm coming back. You'd better watch out. You'd just better watch out." And then he'd smiled as if he could read David's mind. "And when I get my hands on her a second time—"

"There ain't gonna be no second time for you!" Sheriff Grodin had warned Bloggs curtly. "We're going to lock you up until you're so old, you wouldn't even be able to attack a baby!"

And Sheriff Grodin—a lawman with twenty years at his post—had assured David that it was true. Bloggs was a drifter with no money and no relatives willing to claim him. There would be no chance of his getting out on bail before his trial. He would go up for numerous accounts of armed robbery and assault, and the state would find little sympathy for such a man.

It was all over except for the paperwork, the hearing, and the trial. David assured Grodin that he would gladly come back to town if they needed him.

It was long past dawn by the time the sheriff left with his prisoner. Susan was sitting at the breakfast table, sipping coffee. David, having locked up again after showing the sheriff out, came back in to find her there, flushing a little as she glanced at him, staring at her coffee cup again.

"How are you?" he asked. Susan held her breath and swallowed as he came to her and lifted her chin, his thumb lightly stroking her throat.

"I'm fine," she said a little too huskily. He released her quickly.

David poured himself more coffee, leaned against the counter, and gazed at her. "You really shouldn't stay here, you know," he said softly.

159

He saw her color deepen further. "David, if that's another ruse—"

"Ruse? What would have happened if I hadn't been here?"

"Well, I wouldn't have gone downstairs. I would have hid in a closet. I would have been robbed, of course, but nothing else."

David emitted an inarticulate oath and pulled out the chair opposite hers. "Susan—"

"David, really. I could get mugged just as easily somewhere else."

"You might have gotten a hell of a lot more than mugged by Bloggs," he warned her sharply. "Unless, of course"—he paused, sipping his coffee and staring at her pointedly over the rim of the cup—"your charity extends to people such as Bloggs."

"Damn you!" Susan gasped.

He winced, raising a hand in the air. "Sorry. Really. But don't you get my point?"

She was still sitting very stiffly, but she lowered her eyes and spoke quietly. "I get your point, but I don't think you get mine. There's virtually no crime here. Bloggs was a freak incident for these parts. And he's been arrested. If this is another of your tricks to get me to leave—"

"No trick, Susan. I've decided that I haven't been terribly fair or moral or ethical—or something." He hesitated, alarmed again by his feelings when he was near her; aching to reach out and touch her and beg her to tell him that her previous existence was all a lie.

David pushed his chair back hard, jerking a chair leg so that it scratched over the floor like nails over a blackboard. "My father owned the house; he wanted you to have half of it. I'm never even here. You're welcome to it." A distance away from her, he grinned ruefully. "I'm warning you, though, that I'm going to have it wired for security. Bloggs apparently came in through the library window. We can pre-

160

vent something like that happening again if you're determined to stay here. You might want to think about it, though."

She gazed at him suspiciously. David noticed that her nail polish was different this week. It was a tawny color. He was tempted to look beneath the table at her toes. He was sure that they matched.

He smiled with his thoughts, and her eyes narrowed. "Why don't I trust you?" she murmured.

David chuckled, bowing his head courteously to her. "I haven't the faintest idea, Miss Anderson. If I do pat myself on the back a bit, I would claim to have been extremely beneficial to your health. Anyway, I'm not terribly worried at the moment. You can think about it while you're in New York."

Her head jerked to an even more suspicious angle. "And how do you know, Mr. Lane, that I'm going to New York?"

"Because you're meeting with my publicity department on Tuesday at noon, Miss Anderson."

She smiled rigidly. "And you told me, Mr. Lane, that writers rarely deal with publishers."

"You won't be dealing with me, you'll be dealing with publicity. But, as the publisher, I am aware of what is going on. And since you planned to be in the city by Monday afternoon, there's no real worry for the present, is there? You can fly back with me tomorrow."

"What? Wait! How do you know I was supposed to be in on Monday?"

"Your agent mentioned it, Miss Anderson."

"John? I don't believe he'd give away—"

David interrupted her with a laugh. "To mention the date that a client is coming into town is hardly comparable to divulging state secrets, Miss Anderson!"

He was mocking her, Susan thought furiously. She was angry, confused, exasperated—and ridiculously pleased.

If nothing else, he definitely didn't want to see her injured!

161

But so what? she thought, scolding herself. It was more than likely that he took care not to run over stray animals too!

She stood up, pushing in her chair impatiently. "I'll think about it, Mr. Lane. If you'll excuse me, I'm exhausted. I do suppose this means there's no hope of you leaving today?"

"I just got here!" He seemed to be laughing again. Why the hell shouldn't he? After the ridiculous culmination of the last hours they had spent together . . .

"Good night."

"Good night."

Susan squared her shoulders and tried to depart the kitchen regally. She tripped over the floorboard into the parlor, though, and was further irritated to hear his soft chuckle follow her.

But it seemed like a gentle laugh! she cried inwardly. Tinged with . . . affection. No! He was the one to consider the account paid in full! What in heaven's name was his game?

In the kitchen, David sat back down at the table, stared blankly at his coffee cup, and miserably wondered the same thing.

Susan awoke at three in the afternoon. The house was disturbingly silent as she dressed. Curiously she hurried downstairs, but David was nowhere to be seen. She made herself a ham and cheese sandwich and, generously, considering the circumstances, made him one, too, wrapped it, and set it on the refrigerator shelf. She'd been all set for her trip to New York before David's arrival, completely packed, but there had been one minor revision she'd been thinking of doing on her sci-fi manuscript. With him out of the house, it seemed a wonderful opportunity. Trying not to let thoughts of him plague her, she hurried into the library, pulled out the typewriter, and set to work.

It was only a matter of adding a few lines of dialogue, but she retyped three pages, and in rereading and repecking out her own words, she became absorbed in it. So much so that she gave a stunned little scream when he spoke to her from the doorway.

"It's me! The doors were locked—so were the windows. Or didn't you notice?"

Susan clenched her teeth and willed herself not to flush. He was wearing dark bathing trunks that displayed too much flesh and muscle to her way of thinking. He was still wet from the surf; his hair was slicked back, and his eyes were the color of the crest of a wave caught by the sun.

"What do you want?" Susan snapped irritably. The damn fool, she thought silently, only masochists swam in the Maine waters this late in the season.

He arched a brow and smiled like a subtle demon. "Merely to let you know I was back in the house."

"Oh, okay. I know you're back."

"Working?"

"Obviously!"

"Not feeling in the least charitable, I take it?"

"Not in the least."

"What a pity." He moved into the room, looking over her shoulder. Susan reflexively covered her manuscript, and he chuckled, bracing an arm against the chair to lean over her.

"You know, Miss Anderson, I made it a point last week to read all those lovely little novelettes by S. C. de Chance."

"Did you?" Susan muttered uneasily. "Whatever for?"

"Curiosity, of course. And to think that just last week I thought you were *reading* all those delightful scenes. Then I discovered that you wrote them."

"Well, that's just fascinating, Mr. Lane, but as we've discussed, I'm working. Do you mind?"

He smiled, pushed away from her, and slowly ambled back to the door. He turned to her, though, flashing one last, taunting smile her way. "You should consider being charitable again, Miss Anderson. After all, you won't be able to write on memory forever, you know."

There was a thesaurus beneath her hand. Quite naturally she threw it after him. He ducked, chuckling pleasantly.

"I'll keep your great words of wisdom in mind, Mr. Lane. Now get out of here!"

He left, not at all daunted. Susan was extremely grateful that she was retyping material. She wouldn't have been able to concentrate on writing.

He was back about an hour later, dressed in worn jeans that hugged his hips nicely and a tailored denim work shirt. Susan shot him a nasty glance as she covered her typewriter, but he didn't seem to notice. He bit into an apple, then suggested, "I think we should get out of here tonight. Really call it a truce and stay away from dangerous territory. There's an old Bela Lugosi classic at the movie theater in the village. We can stop by the lobster house for dinner, watch the flick, and have none of the evening left to irritate one another. What do you think?"

No—capitalized—is what she should have said. But he was right. Since they were both in residence, as it seemed, the most intelligent thing to do was get out of the house and avoid firelight, intimate meals . . . being alone, being too close.

"All right," Susan murmured. "What time is the movie?"

"Eight."

"What time is it now?"

"Six."

"We'll never make it! If we change—"

"The lobster house is casual, and no one here dresses for movies. You should have learned that. You're fine."

Well, she matched him, at least. Her jeans were worn and faded, and her shirt was an old one. Susan shrugged. "Let's go, then."

Outside, she offered to drive; David said that his rented Porsche would be more fun, but he didn't seem to pick up on Susan's soft sigh that should have indicated she would have loved to have driven. She wondered, settling in the deep bucket seat beside him, if he was the type who didn't like to sit in the passenger's seat or if he just didn't like to be chauffeured by a woman. They sped along, both seeming to enjoy their silence for the majority of the drive into town. Susan commented on the cold snap and asked David how he'd possibly decided on a swim. He'd flashed her one of his rare open smiles and laughed, reminding her that he had spent years swimming in cold water.

A pleasantly polite repartee was kept up until they were inside the rustic restaurant, until they'd both been served chilled white wine, until the waiter had taken their food order and moved away. And then, to her discomfort, Susan found that he was staring at her and that his eyes weren't mocking or taunting but dark blue and sharp with an emotion that seemed to be churning dangerously. He took a sip of wine, then asked quite suddenly, "What happened to your brother, Susan? The other half of S. C. de Chance?"

She stiffened, totally unprepared for the unwanted probing.

"He died."

"You were close?"

"Very."

"I'm sorry."

She smiled and said softly, "So was I." She quickly turned her attention to her drink.

"So you're all alone in the world now?"

The question was somehow intense, not at all casual. But there was nothing to discover from his penetrating crystal stare, and Susan smiled again, shaking her head. "Actually I'm not. I've a cousin with whom I'm quite close."

"Near here?"

"No. She and her husband live in Windsor, Canada."

"Well, at least there's someone," he murmured.

Susan sipped her wine, then raised it to him slightly.

"And what about you, David? You're actually quite alone, aren't you?"

He chuckled. "I suppose, if I went back to Ireland, I could find a number of relatives. Dad was one of eleven children. The name used to be McLane, as you must know. But when he first came over here, he wound up in Boston, and Boston was teeming with Irish. The thing to do in those days was to become Americanized as soon as possible. Dad was never big on beating his head against stone walls—he became a Lane and prospered."

Susan grinned. "Not completely. He never lost his brogue."

David grinned in return, then mimicked his father's accent so perfectly that it was chilling as he told her, "Ah, no, and he wouldn't be doin' that, now, would he? Appearances be one thing, and truth another."

Appearances and truth. David had just spoken the words without a thought, without a qualm. . . .

"That must have been very hard," he persisted, smoothly changing the subject back to her, "losing your brother after having been orphaned so young."

"I told you, I don't remember my parents. I was raised by my grandparents."

"I see," he murmured, as if she had just uncovered the final piece to some great puzzle.

"You see what?"

"Pardon?"

"You said, 'I see.' What did you just see, Mr. Lane?" Susan insisted, feeling her temper rise.

"Nothing," he began, but he saw the glittering persistence in her eyes and sighed. "All right, Susan. I think I understand a little better your . . . aptitude for dealing with an aging man."

"Aptitude?"

"Miss Anderson, everyone in the restaurant is looking at

us. If we're going to have a knock-down drag-out fight, maybe we should step outside."

She lowered her voice instantly but stripped none of her intensity from it. "Is that it, Mr. Lane? Aptitude? Well, then, hell yes, I've got it! I despise that attitude! My grandmother was sixty-eight when I was ten, but she was in there battling away at the PTA far more often than younger, busier working parents! My grandfather brought both Carl and I through too many seasons of Little League! And do you know what else, Mr. Lane? They were bright people. They helped us with our homework, and Carl and I both graduated at the top of our classes! They were just tops, too, when it came to American history—they'd lived a lot of it, you see. They were wonderful, wise, gentle, and kind, and I valued them—both of them—until the very end. And how you could ever consider your father less than a wonderful, wise, bright, gentle, noble man—no matter what his age—is beyond me."

He had gone white, very white beneath the bronzed tan of his features. And as Susan stared at him her eyes locked with his crystal-blue ones, the wineglass in his hand suddenly shattered. Susan gasped, and the horrible moment was at an end.

"Your hand!" she exclaimed, watching blood seep from his finger to ooze onto the tablecloth.

He snatched up his napkin and quickly wrapped his hand. "It's nothing," he muttered quickly, offering the waiter a pleasant smile and an apology as he came to clean up the mess. And when it was gone and a new glass of wine was set down to replace the old one, he was still staring at Susan with a cobalt gaze.

He started to say something, but then stopped, because their lobster was being served. Susan, very tense and nervous, picked up her cracker and started into a claw.

David leaned close to her. "Susan, I never thought of my

167

father as anything other than a great man. A very great man. I just want to say that . . ."

He paused. Tension seemed to mount in her ridiculously. What? she wondered. What? She gripped down on the cracker with all her might against the obstinate claw.

"That I'm sorry, really very sorry—"

"Oh!" The claw gave, shattering just as the glass had done. Pieces of shell went flying across the table and onto David's plate and his lap.

"Oh, Lord!" She moaned, ready to sink under the table as the anxious waiter came running back over to retrieve the bits and pieces of shell.

David apologized very graciously again. The waiter left them, and David smiled at her.

"Is he going to be glad to see us go!" Susan muttered.

David laughed. "Don't worry, we'll see that he's rewarded for his misery!"

She returned his smile across the table, then their smiles slowly faded, but their eyes remained locked together. A knot seemed to form in Susan's throat; she swallowed to clear it, and she saw something in his eyes beyond the laughter, beyond the war that had sprung instantly between them. A certain tenderness there. Wistfulness, almost pain. She wanted to tell him that he was wrong about her, but she couldn't.

When she did speak, her voice was soft and careful. "David, I . . . want you to know that Peter . . . Peter meant very, very much to me. That I—" Oh, she was floundering, making it worse. So much worse!

And yet, for once, he wasn't taking it that way. He reached across the table and his fingers entwined, strong and sure, with hers, and without mockery or malice he replied softly, "We're both going to miss him very much, aren't we?"

"Yes, we are."

And then she lowered her eyes and drew her hand away.

Nervously she picked up a claw. She was on such dangerous ground! She could never, never let him know that Peter had been dying, had known he had been dying. . . .

"I'd love some coffee. Do you think our waiter will dare come back to our table?" she queried lightly.

"Sure. Maybe he likes to live dangerously."

The waiter did come back. Susan wondered if she was chattering too much, about anything that came to mind. She wanted to steer away from shaky ground, yet she was also a little desperate, wanting to remember the few special seconds of tenderness that had passed between them, wanting to hold on to them for some reason.

At last David glanced at his watch. "We'll miss the show if we don't get going," he reminded her. He paid the check— tipping their waiter very well for his pains—then helped her into her coat, and his arm remained lightly around her shoulder as they strolled to the theater.

The movie was fun. They shared a large buttered popcorn and a lemonade and applauded Lugosi's *Dracula*. But Susan's mind often wandered while she stared at the screen; the entire situation was absurd. They had waged war like snarling cats, fallen into a night of intimacy and passion, and were just barely on the road to being acquaintances, much less friends.

She should have refused to speak to him, to be in any way cordial or agreeable after the note he had left her. Remembering that was enough to start her blood boiling all over again. But she was sitting in the movies with him and they had gone to dinner together. Of course, she hadn't expected to meet him a second time by thrashing him with an umbrella and finding herself on the floor. Nor had she suspected that Harry Bloggs would enter their lives, putting her life and safety once more into his hands. And so they were together, and she was enjoying herself, and the worst thing of all was that she did like him, and being with him. She liked the feel of his breath against her cheek when he bent to tell

169

her something, as if they were really together. Yet all the while she felt the fiercest of warnings inside—any further involvement with him would bring more disaster than she could imagine. He'd ignited his own flame of anger against her, and she'd done everything she could to fan that flame.

His hand was very lightly on her arm as they left the theater. He yawned once they were on the street, laughed, and excused himself, asking her if she wanted to stop for a nightcap, coffee, dessert, or any combination of the above.

Susan smiled, about to answer that she'd love tea somewhere, when another voice intruded instead.

"Susan! David!"

Looking over his shoulder, Susan was just in time to see Carrie hurrying toward them from the doorway of a restaurant down the street. Jerry, Lawrence, and Mindy were hurrying to keep pace with her, all smiling from ear to ear with pleasure.

"David!"

Carrie gave him an enthusiastic hug, which David returned, yet Susan sensed that he wasn't particularly happy to have been interrupted. Seconds later, though, the others were there, and David was shaking hands with the men and being hugged and kissed by Mindy this time.

Questions and comments seemed to shrill in a cacophony, all to David. He laughed and tried to answer them. But then Jerry mentioned that he had heard about the break-in at the beach house, and Susan was suddenly included in the conversation again.

"Weren't you just terrified?" Mindy asked.

"It must have been just awful!" Carrie added. "Are you really all right?"

"Yes."

"The sheriff was pleased as hell about the way you handled that guy, David." Jerry grinned. "Our hero, as usual."

"What hero?" David said, scoffing impatiently. "I had a

gun, he didn't." His gaze fell on Susan and he added softly, "The credit goes to Susan."

"Me?"

"Well, of course. If you had panicked or passed out, we would have been in a mess."

She returned his gaze, smiling, because what was passing between them just then was very nice. It spoke of a new start; it made her feel that a time might come when she could tell him she had lied, or at least abetted his misconceptions.

But just then Carrie laughed delightedly and innocently noted, "My, my, Susan! You do have a way with the Lane men! First the father, now the son!"

The smile faded from David's face. His change was subtle, but it was there and it was complete. Lawrence said something; David replied pleasantly, but he wasn't really with the group any longer, even if Susan was the only one to realize it.

"Hey, let's go somewhere for coffee, shall we?" Carrie suggested.

"I'm sorry," David said instantly. "I've got to get back to New York early tomorrow. But I promise, the next time I'm coming up, I'll plan in advance and see if we can't all get together then."

Susan didn't protest. She didn't want to prolong the misery that had come to the evening. They chatted on the sidewalk a few minutes longer, then David silently led her to the Porsche. He didn't speak on the drive back to the beach house; neither did she.

Inside, Susan tossed her purse on the parlor sofa while David bolted the door. She noticed that he went into the library and checked the windows. When he came into the parlor, he was still silent and remote. Susan wondered if she should run up to her room and slam and lock her door; she didn't much care for his brooding mood, and she certainly

171

didn't trust his temper. She had learned that it could be very explosive.

But she didn't race past him and up the stairs. In a voice she managed to keep deceptively steady she asked if he'd like a cup of tea.

"No thanks," he said briefly. "I'm going up. Are you coming with me in the morning or not?"

His hands were in his pockets, his eyes remarkably like blue ice. Susan didn't know if he was longing to reach out and shake her or reach out and hold her and demand she tell him that it was all a lie. . . .

But what was a lie? What he believed was truth—or what had happened between them?

"I don't really see how I can change my plans. I—uh—I'm not sure that I can get reservations."

"Miss Anderson, you certainly don't need reservations for my plane."

"Your plane? You fly?"

"Well, so they promised when I started doing so in the Air Force." A slight smile curled his lip. "I promise, Miss Anderson, I'm quite competent. Are you afraid?"

"No, of course not! I love the air, and you're—"

He laughed. "Still alive and well? Yes, I am. I'd like to be on the way to the airfield by nine. Does that suit you?"

Why was she going with him?

"Yes."

"Good night, then."

He turned around, and seconds later Susan heard his light tread on the stairs. Pensively she made her cup of tea, drank it, and crawled up the stairs herself.

It was a miserable night. She awoke constantly and was aware of one driving truth all night: He was there, not thirty feet away, sleeping, stretched out naked on his bed.

And she hated herself for her fantasies. But then, she mused, they weren't fantasies, were they? They were memories.

172

You can't write on memory forever, Miss Anderson!

The words came back to haunt her again and again during the night. Oh, God! What did the man really want?

In the morning, he was all business. From his three-piece suit to his brusque manner, he was business; proving, perhaps, that professionalism could be the name of the game.

He was reading the paper and drinking coffee when she came down to the kitchen. At the sight of her he rose, washed out his cup, and said that if her things were ready, he'd put them in the car. Susan said that her luggage was in the foyer, and he left her to retrieve it.

She quickly poured a cup of coffee, musing that she had expected to see him in some sort of old-fashioned aviator's costume. She'd worn a tawny jumpsuit herself, and next to him she felt frightfully underdressed. But she wasn't about to go change just to complement his attire.

She realized that he hadn't returned to the kitchen, so she quickly finished her coffee and rushed out. David was leaning against the Porsche.

She started to hurry out to the car. "The bolts!" he called to her, and with a sigh she hurried back to use her key to twist the top locks.

He had only one comment when she reached the car.

"I called Jerry this morning, and he's promised to get someone out to install an alarm system. It should be in when you get back; check with him."

She didn't try to tell him she thought it was ridiculous to install an alarm system when an incident like a break-in at the beach house would be like a sighting of Halley's comet— one that could only possibly occur every seventy-six years. After all, he did own half the house.

"Fine," she murmured, settling into the passenger's seat, wishing once again that she had the nerve to ask him if she could drive. She didn't know why she didn't, and that annoyed her too—so much so that she at last broke the uncomfortable silence between them, asking, "Why do you hate women, Mr. Lane?"

He gazed her way, obviously startled, then he frowned, shaking his head and returning his focus to the road. "I don't hate women, Miss Anderson. I'm rather fond of them in general, as a matter of fact. I'm rather decent for this day and age, I think. I send candy and flowers—"

Susan interrupted him with a laugh. "I'm willing to bet your secretary sends the flowers! And those, Mr. Lane, are nothing but appearance. I believe that you are not at all fond of women and that you automatically think the worst of us!"

His gaze flashed back to her quickly—too quickly to search for meaning in his sharp frosty eyes. "Hardly, Miss Anderson. I don't tend to 'think the worst.'"

"Like hell you don't," Susan muttered.

She didn't know if he heard her or not; he didn't reply. Moments later they were pulling the Porsche into a private airfield. The mechanic on duty apparently had the responsibility of returning the car; he took the keys, spoke casually about the weather being great, then assured David that his plane had been thoroughly maintenanced and that his flight plan was logged.

It was a small, sharp-looking Cessna that could seat six at most. Susan did love planes and the wonder of flying. She must have looked disappointed when David suggested that she sit in back, because, despite his formal coolness that morning, he relented and said that perhaps she would prefer sitting up front.

The flight took them two hours; two nice, peaceful hours. The weather was beautiful, and her enthusiasm was such that David Lane couldn't help but be the perfect host, pointing out landmarks, explaining the power of the wind on such a small craft. He stayed out over the water for most of the flight, yet she could see Manhattan to the west when he pointed it out to her. She saw Statue of Liberty and the great rise of the indomitable buildings against the horizon.

He landed in another private field in New Jersey. There was no rental car here but rather a chauffeur-driven limo awaiting them, one that was equipped with the works—phone, bar, stereo, even a small television.

Susan wished they'd taken the train or a bus, anything but the chauffeur-driven limousine. She found herself wondering about David Lane's use of the car. Was this where he entertained the women of whom he was fond? She felt terribly penned in with him; terribly aware of him. And painfully aware that the camaraderie they had shared in the plane was gone, erased, as if it had never been. He was polite, offering her a drink, asking if she was comfortable. That was all. They went from New Jersey to New York almost touching, yet they might as well have been miles away.

In the city, David tapped on the window to the front. "The St. Regis first, please, Julian. That's right, isn't it, Miss Anderson?"

She didn't bother to ask how he knew where her hotel reservations were—John had obviously mentioned the hotel, just as he had mentioned her other plans. And, of course, it was true—her whereabouts could hardly be considered a state secret.

"Yes, thank you," Susan said coolly, suddenly very exhausted. What difference did any of it make? If she held on to one iota of her pride, she would rightly despise him for his cold, ruthless judgment and his heated, deceptive passion.

But maybe that was the point. She just couldn't forget, and she still couldn't believe that anyone could be so tender and so temptuous and then . . . leave her a check.

Why not? He could wear any variety of masks. He was being civil; she was being civil. It was the most that could be hoped for, the most that she wanted. No! She didn't want anything. She wanted to forget that he existed, to get on with her own life.

"By the way, Miss Anderson," he said suddenly, glancing her way. "I'm curious. What was your major in college?"

"Psychology," Susan replied curtly.

He laughed. "That figures!"

"Why?"

"It explains your determination to find some elusive trauma in my past life."

"Was there one?"

"Everyone's life is filled with trauma, Miss Anderson. Isn't it?"

She smiled sweetly. "Some more than others."

"Did you ever use your training, Miss Anderson?"

She hesitated only briefly. "Yes. But you seem to be confused, Mr. Lane. I'm not a psychiatrist, just a student of behavioral sciences. Although I must say, you do make a fine specimen for such a study."

He arched a brow. "So do you, Miss Anderson, so do you." He twisted around. "We're here, the St. Regis."

Yes, they were. They had arrived. Julian opened the door, and David helped her from the car. A porter was there for her luggage.

"Well, thank you for getting me here," Susan murmured. He didn't reply but walked her through the small elegant lobby to the registration desk.

There he left her at last. "Have a pleasant stay in New York, Miss Anderson," he said, inclining his head slightly, then walking away.

And somehow, watching him leave, straight, broad-shouldered, completely casual, Susan did hate him all over again.

He was gone, out of her life at last! she thought. But it wasn't as comfortable a thought as it should have been. It left her shivering.

She should see the attorneys and turn the beach house over to him. Then he really would be out of her life.

But stubbornly she refused to do so. She checked into her room and took a long hot shower. Confused with the turmoil of her feelings, she tiredly curled up on her bed and stared up at the moldings on the ceiling.

Susan didn't understand any of it at all, but she was still determined that hell could freeze over before she gave David Lane anything.

CHAPTER TEN

On Sunday afternoon David picked up Vickie Jameson and they went to an early dinner. He commented on her clothing, asked her about work, and managed to look mildly interested while she chatted about the ups and downs of a model's life.

There was a musician playing on the street corner, and they stopped to listen. But when he had walked her to the door of her apartment and she asked him in, he knew he wasn't fooling himself, and he wondered if he was fooling her. He didn't want to go in.

"I've got an early morning—Monday, you know," he told her. "And I just flew back this morning. I'm beat."

She laughed softly, the warm, friendly woman she was naturally. "I can make it all better."

He took both her hands, kissed them, and stepped back, shaking his head. "Not tonight, Vick."

"How about a Tuesday dinner here?"

"I—oh, no. I've got a business appointment Tuesday that might run late. I'll see you on the weekend, okay?"

"Seems as if I don't have a choice," Vickie murmured, her eyes on him curiously. "Something has a hold on you, David. Something has a tight hold."

"Don't be silly. I'm just tired. See you soon, hmm?" He kissed her forehead and hurried away.

That night, lying awake in his spacious apartment, he thought about Vickie's words. He knew that it wasn't something that had a hold on him, but someone. He closed his eyes against the night, wincing as tension tightened his muscles with a cruelty that wouldn't let up. What was it? What was it about her that had wound around him, snared him and kept him from everything else?

Was it her eyes, was it her face? Was it the night they had spent together? Was it her voice? Just what was it that was so deadly fascinating to him . . . ?

And had been to his father too. "Ah, Dad!" he whispered to the room. She'd admitted to being little better than a well-kept prostitute, and still, he couldn't stop thinking about her. Seeing her in his mind's eye, again and again, naked, beside him, touching him, creating magic . . .

He opened his eyes and twisted, staring out the skylight. It was a full moon, and full moons were known to have their effect. Maybe that was it. And he had just left her this morning after two days and one full night in her company, seeing her imprisoned by that wretched Harry Bloggs, after a night in which they had talked, dined, enjoyed themselves.

Until he had been so curtly reminded that he was "dating" his deceased father's mistress.

"Leave it be; leave her be. Nothing can change that fact," he told the moon.

At length he fell asleep, and his dreams were of a far distant past. He was in the dreams, but he wasn't the man he was now. He saw the boy he had been at twenty, grown tall but thin, responsible, but still with that edge of youth. The

179

edge that allowed a man to be trusting, to care intensely. To fall in love.

She was a beautiful woman. Her hair wasn't chestnut and fire red, it was black. She was petite, large-breasted, slim-hipped. He could still remember watching her, thinking that he would gladly die in her arms. . . . And he had almost done so. He still had the scar on his back to remember her by. He saw her in his dream, coming to him, smiling.

And just before the blade touched his flesh, she changed. She was a redhead with shimmering green eyes, eyes filled with innocence and liquid beauty. Then he felt the searing pain of the knife.

He woke up shaking, drenched with perspiration. In a moment he knew that he was in his apartment, that Hong Kong was more than ten years behind him. David stretched out, tensing, relaxing, letting the air move over his burning flesh.

It seemed strange that the dream would come back to him after all these years, stranger still that Yvonne LaRue changed into Susan Anderson. A psychologist would have a heyday with it!

Susan Anderson was a psychologist.

He groaned, rolled over, and hugged his pillow around his head. Nothing brought sleep. Eventually the moon faded as the first streaks of dawn rose. Thank God. He could get up and go to work.

In the office he was careful to be charming. By ten, how-ever, he couldn't help asking Erica if Lena Sands in publicity was set for her meeting with Miss Anderson.

"Oh, yes. They're having a late lunch at the hotel."

He drummed his fingers against the desk. "We should have sent her flowers," he murmured.

"I'll take care of it," Erica told him.

"No." David stood up. "No, I'll take care of it myself. The florist we use is just downstairs, isn't he?"

"No, across the street."

"Okay, thanks."

He did it himself; a combination of a dozen red and a dozen white roses. He hesitated over the card, smiled a little grimly, then wrote: "Lane Publications welcomes you to New York. David Lane."

When he returned from a four o'clock meeting with the art department, Erica told him that Miss Anderson had called to thank him.

"Am I supposed to return her call?" he asked.

"No, I don't suppose so. She just said thank you."

David nodded and locked himself in his office.

He stayed in the office, working until almost ten. It was the one way he could guarantee that he wouldn't wander over to the St. Regis on one pretext or another. Before he left, he found himself staring out the window to the street, musing. He'd gone back to Maine in a fury to get her out of the house; his fury had done an about-face. It was true; he wanted nothing more than to leave her alone. And he could do it. It was all a matter of will, nothing more. She was haunting his days and nights, but that was a matter of time. All he had to do was let enough time pass by. . . .

Tuesday morning he had a racquetball session with B. J. Jones, a friend and competitor from Taryton Press. He played with rugged strength, taking out all his confusion and frustration on the ball. B. J. bought him a coffee after the game and told him he'd won because he wasn't married. "Sally spent all night harping at me to buy a house in Connecticut," B. J. said with a moan. "I don't think I slept two hours. Oh, to be free!"

David smiled and drained his coffee. "Sure. I get to sleep whenever I want," he murmured dryly.

The meeting that he'd been afraid would last into the night on Tuesday didn't last an hour. He had convinced himself to stop by Vickie's when Erica poked her nose in the door.

"I'm about to leave. Anything else you need?"

"No thanks, Erica." Then he frowned, wondering why she looked so nervous. "Come on in." He grinned at her. "What's the problem? I thought you had a date with John tonight."

Erica perched in the chair in front of his desk. "I did—I mean, I do. I'm not so sure I want to go."

"Why not?"

She hesitated. "I shouldn't say this. I mean, she is one of our authors."

"What are you talking about?" David asked, suddenly tense, his fingers winding around his pencil.

Erica flushed. "John. Susan Anderson is his client, you know. She's still in town . . . and John asked if I minded her coming along. Apparently they didn't have much time together on Monday, and . . . well, actually, he wanted to change our date. I told him that I was just thrilled to have Miss Anderson along. Which, of course, I'm not, really, because I hear that she's only about twenty-six and absolutely gorgeous."

"She is twenty-six, Erica," David said, trying to smile. "You've seen her."

"I have?"

"Yes, she was here last February. Remember? The hat, the sable coat?"

"Oh!" Erica looked even more miserable. "Oh, no! Our Miss Anderson is that Miss Anderson?"

Before he really knew what he was doing, David was on his feet. "Come on."

"Come on?"

"Yes, come on. I'll tag along for dinner and keep my arm around your gorgeous redhead all night, okay?"

"Oh, David, will you really? I just hate to ruin your evening."

The gratitude in her eyes made him feel horribly guilty. He grimaced. Susan Anderson had already ruined the ma-

182

jority of his evenings because he was incapable of forgetting just one.

"I'm sure I'll survive," he murmured. But then again, he wasn't really.

Susan and John were standing on the sidewalk far below his East Side office. The weather had turned suddenly cold during the day, and Susan was glad she had brought Carl's present, the sable, along.

"You don't mind about Erica, do you?" John asked, shivering and stamping his feet while they waited.

"Of course not. I hope she doesn't mind about me. I mean, really, John, this isn't necessary—"

"Of course, it is," he replied teasingly. "In case you get rich and famous, I want you to remember me as charming—and keep my ten percent coming my way!"

"I'll never forget you're charming, John," Susan promised, smiling. And he was. Medium in height and stature, he was young and energetic, with dark eyes and sandy, flyaway hair. Their relationship had been professional since Susan and Carl had found him in the phone book. He had been new then, and so had she. It had been nice. They were friends who were close but not too close. When Carl had died, John had shielded her from the world, work, and New York, until she had been ready to cope with it all again. When she had turned in the long manuscript, John had asked her curiously if she knew Peter Lane; she had said yes, and he had dropped it at that.

"So what's she like, John?" Susan quizzed, teasing him in return. "You haven't told me once about her body, which means that either she hasn't got a giant chest or that you're really in love."

He wrinkled his nose at her, then laughed. "Okay, okay, I've been kind of in love a lot! And maybe this is a little different, because she's got a beautiful body! And Susan, my dear, you should try falling in and out of love a few times. It's fun!"

"Is it?"

"Ah . . . but still waters run deep, don't they? Maybe you're running 'Susan's Pleasuredome' up in northern Maine. Gathering research for all that spicy sex!" He was looking over her shoulder at the traffic. "I'll be damned," he murmured. "The boss man is coming too!"

Startled, Susan turned around. The chauffeur-driven limo was pulling up to the curb. The door opened, and David Lane stepped out, meeting her eyes briefly before turning to help a woman from the car.

It was the receptionist who had been so horribly nervous on that long-ago day when Susan had decided to warn David about his father.

She wanted to melt into the pavement.

"Well, I'll be damned!" John said more loudly, grinning as he stepped up to shake David's hand enthusiastically. "What made you decide to join this humble party, David? Never mind—we won't look gift horses in the mouth." He set an arm around the receptionist and turned to Susan. "Susan, this is Erica Harris, the love of my life. Erica, Susan Anderson."

Susan extended her hand, trying very hard to appear gracious and pleased. "Erica and I have met," she said cheerfully. Lord, it suddenly seemed frigid outside.

"And this—but I get the impression that you two know each other, don't you?"

"Yes," David replied pleasantly, staring straight at Susan and smiling slowly. "Quite well, actually."

Susan wanted to stamp on his foot.

He turned back to John quickly. "Where are we going? The car is waiting."

John gave him the name of a Japanese restaurant downtown. David tapped on the window and spoke briefly to Julian. A second later his grip was firmly on her elbow, propelling her into the car, and she was seated almost on top of his lap despite the size of the car.

He asked her politely about her meeting with publicity; Erica, still nervous, told her loyally that she was working with wonderful people, and John cheerfully commented that he was certain the entire association was going to be wonderful.

"Of course, we've got to get Susan started working on some kind of similar material," John said. "We're anxious to get a good follow-up going."

Susan didn't at all like David's expression when he turned to her musingly. They had reached the restaurant then; John and Erica got out of the car, and David's hand was extended to her. His lip was curved in a cynical grin.

"A follow-up?" he murmured as he steadied her on the pavement. "What rich, aging legend will get the pleasure of your companionship next?"

She knew that neither John nor Erica had heard, so she smiled sweetly and said, "I think I'll do a young legend next, Mr. Lane. Of course, he'll have to be very rich and very famous."

"Ah, not like a charity case, I take it?"

"What are you doing here this evening, Mr. Lane?"

"Protecting the innocent."

"Oh?"

"My secretary. She's quite taken with your agent. You interrupted a planned night."

"I did? Damn that John! I told him—"

"Hey!" The little devil spoke himself. "It's cold out here. Let's go in!"

It was a lovely restaurant. The women were given roses and soft pillows for their feet. Their meal was to be cooked on the table skillet before them, but it was a private section of the restaurant; no other couples would join them. David and John were on opposite ends of the curved table; Susan and Erica sat next to each other.

David was to Susan's left, and yet neither of the men were really out of the conversation because of the curve. John must have thought the evening a wonderful boon indeed, Susan realized as their drinks were served, because he was politely pitching a Western author to David Lane. David listened pleasantly and promised to have one of the editors look at the manuscript right away.

"When are you going back?" David asked Susan suddenly.

"Tomorrow morning."

"So soon?"

"Mmm."

"Don't forget to check with Jerry on the security."

"I won't." Susan picked up the little paper umbrella floating in her drink and gave her attention to it. "And when, Mr. Lane, are you planning your next trip to Maine?"

He took a sip of his drink, staring straight ahead. "I'm not," he said, then he turned and spoke to her softly. "I told you, I've no arguments with you anymore, Miss Anderson. I—"

He broke off as their waitress returned, smiling pleasantly, to take their orders. While John and Erica ordered David bend his head toward Susan.

"How would you feel about the shrimp appetizer and the lobster-and-steak combination? It has to be ordered for two, you see." He tapped her menu. She wondered why she didn't say that she'd rather eat dry wood than share anything with him.

"Fine," Susan murmured, and David ordered for them.

Erica spoke to her then, telling Susan how she loved her book. She seemed much more relaxed at last, and pleasantly enthusiastic.

Their chef reached the table, greeting them, bowing, and proceeded to prepare the meal with such élan that they were all clapping and applauding his prowess with the knife and spatula. Shrimp flew with perfect aim onto their plates, then the lobster, steak, and vegetables. The chef bowed one last time, grinning with his own pleasure, then disappeared.

Susan picked up her chopsticks, which the others were all using. She could use them competently, but on her first effort she lost her shrimp. It fell on the table between her and David.

He stared at the shrimp, then into her eyes, and he smiled slowly, retrieving the shrimp himself with his chopsticks. He lifted it to her mouth, his eyes riveted to her lips, and then to her eyes once again.

"Could you, Miss Anderson," he whispered huskily, "consider this an olive branch of peace?"

Susan was barely aware of his words. It was his eyes that captured her. They were intense, seemed to probe her soul and sizzle with blue flame. The sound faded in the room, and she felt a moment's panic. It had been like this that night at the beach house when they had sat before the fire. He had had the same look in his eyes, then he touched her and she had gone into his arms as if she had belonged there, wrapped in the magic of fire and rain, spinning with the ache of desire and longing. . . .

Thank God they were in a public place, she thought as the people and laughter around them intruded on her mental wanderings.

She moistened her lips with the tip of her tongue; they had suddenly gone so dry. She smiled weakly and leaned forward to take the offering of shrimp, her teeth tugging lightly on the sticks. It seemed that his breath drew in sharply, and above those sounds of laughter and conversation it was as if she could hear the mutual echo of their hearts.

"Hello!" A soft, sultry, and friendly female voice shattered the moment.

David frowned, turning. Susan did the same. Both David and John rose quickly.

"Hello, Miss Jameson!" Erica said first.

"Vickie." David moved past the back of Susan's chair,

taking the woman's hands and kissing her cheek. John said something with his usual charm, but Susan didn't really hear him, because she was watching the new arrival with a dreadful fascination.

Miss Jameson to Erica, Vickie to David, was without a doubt one of the most striking women Susan had ever seen. Susan loved clothing, jewelry, and accessories, so she was particularly able to appreciate the other woman. From her small tilted hat to her heeled boots, Vickie Jameson was chic. She was tall and slender—but curved. Her hair was a lovely, natural blond, her eyes hauntingly dark. Her dress was silken simplicity, belted casually at the hips; her earrings and scarf were a bright blue that offset the red silk dress. She smelled subtly of a wonderful perfume, and though her smile seemed slightly reproachful and curious, it was warm and genuine.

David, Susan realized, was smoothly performing introductions. Vickie Jameson was stretching a lovely and delicate hand to her, measuring her with her eyes—just as Susan had done to her, she realized ruefully.

"How do you do?" she somehow murmured at the right moment.

"It's a pleasure, Miss Anderson," Vickie Jameson replied.

"Sit for a moment, Vickie," David said, moving for her to take his chair. She did so, still studying Susan. David leaned over her shoulder, smiling at Susan.

"Vickie, Susan is the author of the book I was telling you about. The one based on my father's life."

"Oh, how lovely! I really can't wait to read it!"

The enthusiasm was real; the woman was pleasantly real. Susan felt a little ill.

"Thank you," she said, returning the smile. "I just hope it lives up to—to everyone's expectations."

Vickie glanced up at David, chuckling slightly. "This is delightful business, isn't it?"

"Oh, it is business!" Erica proclaimed, then hushed

quickly as she received a sharp glance from David—one that was quick, but clearly denoted his displeasure. David, she realized, would never have anyone else making excuses or giving explanations for him.

Susan grasped a little desperately for her drink as she realized that Vickie Jameson and David Lane were probably intimately involved. Everything about them, the glances they exchanged, the casual way he stood behind her, the fact that a date had obviously been broken this evening, suddenly seemed to pound into her head, complicating what had already been a miserable tempest in her soul.

Oh, God! It was all so much worse than she had allowed herself to believe. Speak of casual affairs! But then, David had thought she was his father's mistress—for hire. Curiosity and whim had made him reach out in a firelit room, and she had capitulated without thought or protest. And all the while he really had had this spectacular woman back in New York, waiting, obviously with real warmth and affection, while Susan had meant absolutely nothing. . . .

She found herself talking, complimenting Vickie's clothing, listening as Vickie told her that she was a high-fashion model.

And then Susan could stand it no longer. She was on her feet, mumblng something about a trip to the ladies' room, then flying blindly to reach that sanctuary.

Susan leaned against a stall in absolute physical misery. Her hands were shaking, her palms were clammy, and she felt as if she were burning from head to toe. She hurt inside with a horrid, scratching pain that left her totally bewildered until she realized an awful truth. Against all logic, she had been falling for him; not just for the feel of his arms, of being held and loved and cherished, but for him . . . Fantasizing that she could fall in love with him; his crystal-blue eyes, his scent, the feel of his muscles, the sound of his laugh. Falling for his quicksilver changes of temper and his capability for

189

tenderness. Even his scowl and the silver flash of his eyes when his temper began to rise . . .

She had to get out of there. She couldn't change what had happened between them; she had helped him to complete his image of her. There would be no chance for truth and understanding between them now, and even if there was, that lovely woman was sitting at the table and had obviously known him a long time and known him well.

Susan bent over the sink, tossing cool water on her face. She had to get away now, but she had to do so smoothly. She stood, stared into the mirror at her too wide green eyes, and decided that she could run out into the hall, call a cab, then excuse herself by pleading a terrible headache. And it would be the truth, surely. Her head was pounding like a kettle-drum.

Susan hurried out to the quiet, carpeted hallway, dug in her bag for a coin, and slipped it into the slot. She dialed the cab number listed on the phone.

But just as a dispatcher answered, a male hand appeared on the silver receiver hook, cutting her off. Susan quickly spun around to find David lounging against the wall behind her.

"What are you doing?"

"I was making a phone call," she replied tartly.

He arched one of his dark brows. "In the middle of dinner?" He took the receiver from her hand and returned it to the phone. "Why were you calling a cab?"

"I've this wretched headache—"

"You're a wretched liar."

"It's really none of your damn business!"

He inclined his head toward her slightly. "Miss Anderson, I got you here, and I will see you back to your room."

"You didn't get me here. I'm out with John—"

"Who is out with my secretary."

Susan backed slightly away from him, tightening her long fingers around her hips. "Look, David. I'm interrupting something. I know it and you know it. I'm horribly uncomfortable, so if you want to play the gentleman, please, let me get out of here!"

He didn't leave the wall. He slowly crossed his arms over his chest. "What are you interrupting?"

"David, Miss Jameson—"

He frowned. "Miss Jameson left with the friends with whom she came."

"Well, why? That was stupid!"

"Oh? Why is that?"

"How can you be so callous! She's in love with you!"

"Vickie?" He smiled bemusedly. "No, she isn't. She's a friend who understands me." He reached out a hand to her casually. "Shall we return to the table?"

Susan sighed with exasperation. She didn't take his hand, but he cupped her elbow with it.

Erica and John were head to head when Susan and David reached them, but they quickly broke apart. "How about a carriage ride through the park?" John suggested cheerfully.

"It's a little cold, isn't it?" Susan murmured. "I think I'll pass, but you all go ahead—"

"Oh, come on, Miss Anderson. Where's your spirit of adventure?" David said smoothly, and she couldn't protest further because he and John started arguing over the bill, John saying that he was entertaining a client, David arguing that the client was his author. David won; Susan had the feeling that he would always win—charmingly.

Before they could enter the limo outside, David managed to pull Susan back against him and whisper. "Where's your empathy for young love? If you refuse the carriage ride, they certainly won't go!"

And so, fifteen minutes later, John and Erica were pulling off in one carriage, and she and David were following in another.

He was businesslike at first, asking her if she was satisfied that the book would be handled to her taste. She told him

191

quite honestly that his employees were all pleasant, enthusiastic, and very capable of inspiring trust.

"So, you see," he said softly, "it won't be such a nightmare, after all."

It was a nightmare, she wanted to scream, because she was feeling the way she had on that night they had spent together. He was against her, he was warm, his arm was draped casually around her, and his scent was a subtle taunt. She found herself staring at him and smiling ruefully, thanking him in person for the flowers. He laughed and told her that his secretary didn't always attend to his personal affairs. And for a moment, in the moonlight, his eyes looked like the frosty eyes of a mischievous Satan, and then they appeared smoky, a sensual blue. His features were dark in the shadows, and he was moving toward her, kissing her.

It was a gentle kiss, an exploration. It filled her with warmth and longing, and it made her quiver and wonder. His hand caressed her cheek while his lips moved warmly over hers, and then he moved, pulling away to watch her with eyes that were now cobalt and enigmatic.

"Susan . . ." His whisper touched the breeze, resonated with the steady *clip-clop* of the horse's hooves. It might have been a shout, and it was so light that she might have imagined it.

"I could have—"

The driver called out a command; the horse stopped. David was rising, pulling the blanket off their legs, then helping her from the carriage.

And minutes later they were all back in the limo.

They drove to her hotel first. David walked her in, and in front of her door he smiled whimsically, brushing a stray hair from her cheek. She didn't say anything. He hesitated, then took a breath and spoke softly. "I meant it, Susan. The olive-branch-of-peace business. The house is yours, and you can feel comfortable in it. I—I won't be making any sudden appearances. I don't understand any of your past, but I'm

192

not your enemy. Just do me a favor, please, and be careful. Make sure that the security is in and that it works. And if you ever need anything, call me. You know where to reach me."

He grinned, pulled her close to him for a minute, kissed her forehead, then turned and walked down the hall. He didn't wait for the elevator; he took the stairs.

Susan flew back to Maine via a commercial airline and, to her total annoyance, spent her first week home waiting for the phone to ring. It rang, but it was never David on the other end. The longer she was away from him, the worse it seemed to hurt and the more irritated she became with herself.

It couldn't be over because it had never begun.

But life had become mechanical for her. Jerry had commissioned a security company to wire the house; if anyone ever tried to break in, the police would know immediately. But she wasn't frightened; Harry Bloggs had been a fluke.

She spent time walking along the cliffs; she spent time working. She bought half a dozen new nail polishes and changed them every day.

Another week passed, and she found herself sitting at Peter's desk, playing with his pipes, thinking of him, missing him.

"Oh, Peter! Of all people, I know what it is to love and lose. I can't even think of this thing in such a light! And when you do love and lose, Peter, the therapy is to pick up the pieces and get on with your life."

There were just so many shattered pieces to her life. She didn't know where to start picking them up.

When friends called, she didn't seem to have the energy to go out. And despite the thoughts of David Lane that she could not quell, she discovered that she was spending ridiculous amounts of time sleeping.

By the end of her third week home, she determined that

193

she had picked up some kind of flu—she wasn't lovesick, she was simply sick, and if she could beat the illness, she could get going.

Susan didn't really have a doctor, so she called Harley Richmond at the hospital.

"Sue, I'm a cancer specialist—"

"Harley, couldn't you just take some blood or something and make sure I'm not anemic? I'm not deathly ill, I just think I need some vitamins or something."

"Sure, kid. Come on in, then."

Relieved, and sure that a shot of vitamin B would rid her not only of exhaustion but of David Lane as well, she cheerfully dressed for a visit to the doctor.

CHAPTER ELEVEN

Susan was dazed when she walked back into the beach house. She didn't remember the drive back; she couldn't remember thinking. All that touched her mind was the awful shock.

She wasn't sick, she was pregnant.

She should be grateful; she'd not allowed herself to really think about it, but she knew that though certain diseases weren't necessarily hereditary, they were prone to occur in certain families. And after Carl's illness she should be very, very grateful for such a totally clean bill of health. But pregnant? It was just so . . . stunning.

And then she began to think of it all as such a ridiculous trick of fate that she started to laugh in the foyer, laugh so hard that she doubled over, catching herself only when she realized she was going to start to cry.

It's not real, it's not real. It can't be real, she told herself. She could wait for nightfall, go to sleep, and then wake up and prove to herself in the morning that it was all a dream.

She didn't really feel anything. She was refusing to face this thing, she warned herself. But maybe that was good. Maybe that was a survival instinct coming to the surface. She needed some time to get over the shock before dealing with the facts.

She noticed that there was dust on the coffee table. With a whirl of energy she raced into the kitchen, dug out the chamois and polish from beneath the counter, and hurried out to the parlor to set to industriously cleaning the table. Her eyes fell on the fire—cold now. But it had been here, right here, that she had fallen. She winced, bringing the knuckle of her thumb to her mouth and biting down hard. This was it, the scene of the crime. One haphazard, stupid indiscretion in her adult life, and she was certainly being brought to task for it. Here . . . right here.

But maybe it hadn't been here. Maybe it had been upstairs. In his room. Of all the nights in the world to have gone as mad as a March hare. . . .

Susan brought her hands to her face and sank down to the sofa, feeling extremely sorry for herself and hateful toward fate. One night! If David Lane had just shown up a week later, she might have hated herself, but she wouldn't be in this predicament. If the storm hadn't come, if she hadn't walked out to the sand, if a branch hadn't broken her window . . .

If she'd had the common sense to stay away from him at all costs!

None of it mattered now. The ifs hadn't occurred.

The phone started to ring. Not really giving a damn who it was, Susan ignored it. Eventually the shrilling stopped. She continued to sit on the sofa, her thoughts a jumble, then blank again.

About fifteen minutes later the phone started up again. Mechanically she rose. Mechanics! If she could just get the mechanics down for the next few days at least! Eat, sleep, work. See people, laugh, talk. Surely then she would get her mind back and be able to deal with things.

She answered the phone with assurance, quite positive that it wasn't David Lane. Since New York, apparently he had called a truce that he intended to keep. He had decided to leave her alone.

It wasn't David. It was Joan, her sci-fi editor.

"How are you?" Joan asked cheerfully.

Just wonderful. Pregnant by a man who thought she was an exorbitant call girl who preyed on rich old men.

"Real good, Joan, thanks. How are you? Did you get away to California with your husband?"

"Yes, and we had a great time." Joan went on to tell her a bit about the vacation, then asked what she had been doing. Susan mentioned a few nights out with her friends and sounded amazingly cheerful. Joan teased her for a few minutes about working on a real-life romance, then switched the conversation to business.

"I was just calling about your last proposal and outline."

"Oh, good. I should get going on it, I guess. Is there a problem?"

"Oh, no. I love the concept! Murder on a space shuttle station. I just have a few minor suggestions. Got a pencil and paper?"

"Ah . . . yes," Susan murmured, quickly rummaging through the top desk drawer for a pad and pencil. "Can you hang on for a second? I'll find my copy."

She set the receiver down and dug into the bottom drawer, glancing quickly over the manila envelopes there. She found the correct one and straightened up. See? she thought, taunting herself. Nothing had changed. She didn't become green or sprout ten extra fingers. Keep at it, it's very calming. . . .

"I'm all set, Joan," she said.

"Great, great. Okay, chapter two, spice up the argument a bit. A little more heated. Okay?"

"Okay."

"In chapter four, I don't think your heroine would walk out like that, not without saying something. See what you can come up with, okay?"

Susan scribbled on the paper. "Okay."

"Now, chapter eight—this is my only real problem with the outline. I don't think the heroine should seem so defenseless against the enemy when she's taken and accused of the murder. She needs to be stronger, stand up to them, and fight back—even if she is scared out of her mind. Susan, are you there?"

Oh, yes, she was here, she thought hysterically. The strong, defensive, fighting back—pregnant woman.

"No problem," she heard herself say calmly. Her pencil skidded across the paper, digging into it. The point broke.

"That's it, then," Joan was saying, "I can't wait to read the complete manuscript!" She went on to say that she hoped the weather didn't get too cool too quickly, chatted a few more minutes, then hung up.

Susan laid her head on the blotter on the desk and started to laugh again. This time her laughter turned to tears.

"There's nothing to be alarmed about," Harley had said, trying to soothe her. "There are choices today. The point is that they must be made very, very carefully."

"What are you saying?"

"That you don't have to have the child."

She had even laughed then—dryly and in control. "Are you condoning abortion, Harley?"

"I'm not condoning or condemning anything. I'm a doctor, not a lawmaker, and this isn't my line of expertise. And it's certainly not my business to pry into your personal life, but you look as if you think you mated with the devil."

"You're the one who told me I needed a social life!"

"Susan—"

"Oh, Harley! It's just impossible. . . ."

"Susan, I do not believe in immaculate conceptions. Not since the Christian calendar began, at any rate."

"But—"

"Susan! You could spend every night of the month with a man. Twenty-nine of those days wouldn't matter. The thirtieth would. And even if that thirtieth was the only one, it's the one that counts. That's the way it works, kid. Look, I really don't mean to pry, but I know you so well. I mean, you must have felt . . . something. Is there still a relationship? It could all be really wonderful. Maybe he would just love to have children. Maybe marriage—"

"Marriage is out, Harley."

"Susan—"

"Hey! You promised not to pry, right?"

"Yeah, I did," he muttered.

He hadn't let her leave right away; she had been too shaken. He had given her a cold beer with a rueful smile. "I know that they're convinced alcohol is really bad these days, but this is mild and should bring some color to your face." She had sat there numbly, drinking the beer. And when she finally had risen to leave, he had cleared his throat and spoken with her one last time.

"I'm giving you two business cards. One is a friend of mine, the best OB guy I know. The other is a psychologist in family counseling—"

"I'm a psychologist, Harley."

"Every healer needs a healer now and then, Susan. See him. Talk to him. I—I well—"

"What, Harley?"

"Sue, you're young. Life stretches ahead of you, all the best now. You deserve it; you should go for all the riches and promise out there. But I don't see you—never mind. Like I said, I have no right to comment or pry."

And she smiled then, feeling so vulnerable that words had come slowly from her.

"I don't know what I'll do, Harley. I still can't believe it. I don't feel anything, and I really can't believe it's true. But I can't imagine myself doing something about it, either. Oh,

Harley! I've been around the aged so much, around death . . . This is life and I . . . I don't know." She shook her head. "I'm going home. I'm all right. I've got some time to think, right?"

"Yes, Susan. And if I can help, call me."

"You've already helped, Harley. You told me that I didn't have a stomach virus." She had tried to laugh. He hadn't. And she waved, still smiling a bit like a lurching drunkard, then hurried to her car.

And so here she was, her head on the desk, severely recognizing the fact that when she made a mistake, she certainly did it all the way.

She opened her eyes. They fell on Peter's pipe rack, and she felt a little hysterical all over again.

Oh, Peter! He wanted grandchildren so badly! Isn't this just priceless? Of all the irony . . .

She pushed herself up from the desk, that thought running through her in icy rivulets. She hadn't been able to think past the idea that she was in a serious situation. She had been able to think that she was pregnant; not that pregnant meant she was going to have a baby. An infant, flesh and blood. A human being made up of all kinds of genetic material.

She hadn't thought of David at all—beyond the fact that her mistake had been far more severe than she had ever imagined it would be.

She hadn't begun to make up her mind about what to do.

And now this thought that she didn't really want to entertain was with her, haunting her. She was going to have Peter's grandchild. How could she even entertain the thought of—

She closed her eyes again in silent anguish. This was her life—she couldn't think that way! The whole thing could be so easy! All over in an afternoon.

But it would leave scars for life. She couldn't judge for other people. Like Harley, she didn't make the laws and she didn't judge others. She was just suddenly and very miserably aware that there were going to be no easy outs for her. She had better start thinking that being pregnant and having a baby were the same thing.

She picked up the pipe. So ironic. Peter's grandchild . . .

David's child. Yes, David Lane's child. "Oh, please, please, don't be born with those eyes!" she whispered a little frantically. And then, "Oh, God! What am I going to do?"

She'd never tell him, she thought. She could just imagine herself doing so, seeing the disdain on his face. Hearing his sigh—and the assumption that she was after more money.

No. No! She felt like crying again. Through everything she'd had her dreams. It was a liberal world, and she knew it. But in St. Mary's, Pennsylvania, she'd grown up with old-fashioned ideals. A marriage with all the trimmings. Children, wanted and shared. And, oh, her grandparents might have been old when they raised her and Carl, but they'd surely had all the right stuff! So much love, so much caring.

She'd done everything so right herself—at first. She'd gone to college and she hadn't fallen in love until her last year. Then she'd met Ben Turner, and they'd gotten engaged, and like the star-struck kids they'd been, they'd planned their future with all the glowing details. And then they'd made love. Bright kids, knowing they wanted to establish themselves before starting a family, they'd behaved just like mature, responsible, sophisticated adults.

Maybe she shouldn't have then. Maybe, if she'd found out she was going to have a child then, she would have married Ben. They'd have a home near Philadelphia in a pleasant neighborhood, and she wouldn't be alone, realizing that she really had no life.

But she hadn't married Ben. First it had been Gramps to get ill, and then her grandmother. And then the horror that no one could accept: her twenty-seven-year-old brother. And Ben had been a nice guy, really in love with her, she was certain. It had just reached a point where she couldn't leave —and he couldn't stay any longer.

She didn't really remember his face anymore. Too many years had gone by since then. And though she hadn't blamed Ben, she had been bitter, determined not to become involved until sometime in the far, far future. She had been mature and responsible and everything else that she should have been. She hadn't gotten involved with anyone!

Until David Lane. Of all the people in the world!

She did burst into tears, and she indulged herself in a long, sloppy crying jag. Slowly shadows crept into the room. It was turning dark outside.

But when at last the sobs and then the hollow gasps died, she felt better. She went into the kitchen and washed her face and then put tea on. And then reminded herself that she had to eat.

When she had eaten, Susan discovered that she was incredibly tired. She laid out on the sofa in the parlor and fell asleep immediately.

In the morning she pulled on a warm sweater and went for a walk along the water, picking up twigs to toss out to the surf, loving the feel of the cool autumn breeze against her face.

Ethically she supposed that David had a right to know. Damn ethics, she decided. He wouldn't want her to have the child; he would be certain that she was out to bleed him for eighteen years and beyond. He would never understand her reasons for going through with it, the elusive thing that was her soul, which told her she could not take away life.

She felt calm. Very calm. Maybe planning had a great deal to do with it. It would be best if she moved out of the beach house, but she wouldn't go until January. That way she could save everything and not pay rent or a mortgage.

By the end of January, though, she would leave. Out west seemed best. San Francisco had always enchanted her as a lovely place to live. For a while, at least, she would have to cut herself off from all her old friends.

And what then? she thought, taunting herself. What happens when this child grows up and starts asking questions?

She'd deal with it then! she thought firmly. For now she was going to get by day by day. Thank God she was a writer! She wouldn't have to worry about survival. She could keep her job and no one would know about her personal life.

Susan tossed the last of her sticks into the sea and went back to the house to start to work.

Susan had one more bad night. A really bad night.

With the lights out and the house locked, her body weary, she discovered that she couldn't sleep. She stared up at the ceiling for hours and hours and finally dozed fitfully.

Then she dreamed, not of the man she knew so well, the one who could taunt her incredibly, but the man she had glimpsed in rare moments. The man who had told her she was beautiful, the wonder who had touched her face with awe, as if he could not bear not to stroke her cheek. . . .

The man who had concerned himself with her welfare, who had been gentle, who had carried her away from glass and bandaged her toe so gently . . .

The man who had made love to her. Passionate and exciting love, an oasis in a desert of need. He was so tall and powerful, a beautiful man, bringing her alive. Holding her and cherishing her, touching her and inflaming her, and convincing her in those moments that it was a unique magic that had brought them together.

David . . . holding her with strength, rugged and fine, all masculine. Her pride vanished in her dreams. She could long for him again, ache for him. Toss and turn with electric memory, groan softly with the inner knowledge that he had been special, that if he had smiled, if he had cared, she would have loved to have known him better, have allowed the attraction to soar. . . . Loved to have fallen in love and let the exploration last a lifetime.

She awoke, cursed herself soundly, but could not fall back to sleep. She went downstairs and made herself coffee, then tossed the pot out and made tea, distantly wondering if she should be avoiding coffee and even more distantly making a mental note that she was going to have to see a doctor because she didn't want to do anything that could harm the child.

In another week she was surprisingly resigned to the situation—and even a little excited. The child was going to be someone to love, someone to give her a sense of meaning again.

And she thought that she was behaving rather well. Her life had taken on a normal routine. She spent the mornings typing, the afternoons cleaning up and taking care of herself. She had her hair done with Mindy on Thursdays—just washed and blow-dried, but it felt good, anyway—and every few nights she went out with the others. On Monday and Saturday nights she helped out at the hospital. She was busy and almost serene.

She hadn't heard a word from David. He had promised softly that he wanted peace; he did intend it.

She had decided to go three cities inland for a doctor; her town was too small, and gossip traveled quickly. Harley would never betray her, but someone else might. She had a bottle of vitamins and a sheet of instructions. She didn't feel ill anymore; in fact, she didn't feel anything at all. The baby wasn't due until August, so the doctor—a nice total stranger —had assured her that she was quite normal.

Susan would never forget the date: It was November fifteenth, a blustery and windswept day, when the little world of make-believe she had created fell apart with a crash.

She had been typing with great concentration when the phone rang. It was John Ketchem, and as soon as she heard his voice, she experienced a sense of foreboding.

"Hi, Susan, how are you doing?"

"Fine, John, thanks."

"All caught up on everything?"

"I'm actually ahead of schedule," she said cheerfully.

"Good. 'Cause guess what? You're going on tour."

"I'm what?"

"You're going on tour."

"John, I can't possibly go on tour!"

He sighed. "Susan! What's the matter with you? Tours sell books! They're great publicity—"

"John, you don't have to go on tour to sell a book."

"But, Susan—for God's sake, why not?"

Because I'm pregnant! She wanted to scream.

He didn't wait for her answer; he went on, telling her how it meant that the company was really behind the book. He told her the cities planned: New York, Washington, Atlanta, Houston, Chicago, and Detroit. He told her how wonderful it would be and what an insane fool she was not to be thrilled by the opportunity. He reminded her that this particular book was her best shot at some good, good royalties and that its success could shape the rest of her career.

"When?" she heard herself whisper.

"January, of course. When the book is released."

It would still be early enough in her pregnancy that no one would suspect.

"Susan, are you listening to me?"

"Uh—yes."

"You crazy kid! It will be great. The company picks up the tab. They do the flights, they get the cars—the whole nine yards. All you have to do is sit back and be charming, which is something you're adept at already! Someone from the company will escort you—"

"Someone from the company?" She was certain she had stopped breathing.

"Yes. Someone from sales or publicity . . ."

She gasped with relief, then exhaled. John was still talking about how important it could all be.

"All right, John!" She said at last.

"You'll go?" It seemed as if he breathed a long sigh of relief too. Poor John! she thought. What headaches she must give him! He spent hours selling her work, and then he got to argue with her about trying to do it!

"Great, great!"

"What do I do now?"

"Nothing. You'll speak with someone from the publicity department. They'll send schedules and tickets and all that. Just sit back and get excited, kid, 'cause the world is about to be your oyster!"

"Oh, I'm excited," she murmured dryly.

And after she hung up she decided that she was. She was financially independent, old enough to know her own mind, and she had always known she wanted children. Okay, so the circumstances weren't great, but they weren't that awful, either. Many women were single parents and they did very well. She loved the baby, even if she still couldn't believe it really existed. That would be enough.

And the tour . . . well, she could buy some new clothes, have a good time traveling, and maybe discover a place where she would like to live. And maybe one day—far in the future—out of fairness to the child and David she would let him know; when enough time had passed for her to deal with things on a more mature and rational level.

Susan walked into the kitchen and took her vitamin.

She spent Thanksgiving with Harley and his family, having picked up Jud to bring him to his son's house. It was a very nice day, a family day, and she was grateful to have been invited.

The children were mischievous, underfoot in the kitchen, but so cute as they solemnly said grace that Susan felt a very welcome and wonderful warmth seep through her. This was

206

what it was going to be like! Times when discipline would be needed, times when she could look into a pair of beautiful and innocent eyes and get shivers all over with the delight that they belonged to her child. She watched Jud—a grin on his face that seemed just about to split it—make his grandson and granddaughter shriek with laughter as he gave them rides on his knees.

And when they left, she was happy again. Really happy. Face it—she had been halfway in love with David Lane. The child was his, and it was hers, and he or she was going to be very, very beautiful.

"You're going to have the baby, huh?" Jud said suddenly, and she realized that he had been studying her from the passenger's seat of her little Nissan.

"Harley told you!" she said angrily, staring at him, then remembering that she was driving and riveting her eyes back to the road. "Damn him! Of all the unprofessional—"

"Now don't go getting on the boy!" Jud advised her gravely. "He didn't tell me a thing.",

Her heart seemed to sink a little. "Then how—"

"Oh, don't go getting panicky, neither. You look thinner than you ever did. I'm just an old man with an old man's intuition."

His "old man's intuition" made her extremely nervous. The tour was coming up.

He was staring at her pointedly, waiting for an answer, she assumed. "Jud, if you whisper a word of this to anyone, I swear I'll . . . I'll see that your prune supply is cut off!"

Jud chuckled but then grew serious. "I don't tell others what they can't see for themselves. I just wanted to know, 'cause it's Pete's grandchild, and I think I'd tie you to a chair if I thought you were gonna 'take care of it,' like some people do these days."

Susan hesitated, then sighed. Jud was a lot like his old friend Peter. If he said he wasn't going to tell anyone, he wasn't.

"I'm having the baby, Jud. But how—"

"I'm old," he said cantankerously, "not dead and not stupid. Now, *you're* stupid. Stupid and stubborn and—"

"Jud, believe me, I have sound reasons for doing things my way, okay?"

"No. But it's your life."

"Yes, it is."

She'd reached his house and for a moment regretted her very sharp answer. Impulsively she gave him a hug before he got out of the car.

"You call me if you need anything, young lady," he told her.

She smiled. "I will. But I'm really a very self-sufficient person."

"No one alive is so self-sufficient that she or he doesn't need someone else sometime!" He paused, then hurried on as Sam came rushing out to the car, eager for his doggie bag. "You'll get yours in a minute, you greedy hound!" he said, affectionately scolding the dog. "And you—you should have a talk with David Lane."

"Jud, trust me. You don't know the half of it! Really, we don't get along. In truth, I barely know the man—"

One of Jud's shaggy white brows raised high, and a grin curled his lips. Susan flushed.

"Seems to me you must have known him," Jud quipped.

"I'm going home. And you promised to keep your mouth shut."

"I guess I did. But remember, I'm here."

"I'll remember," Susan said softly. And she drove home smiling because she was blessed with some very special friends.

December became hectic for her. There were presents to buy; everyone seemed to be having an open house. She prepared a dinner herself, and she had work to do at the same time. A young man from the publicity department at Puma called to give her the dates and cities on her tour on the same day that she received a large box full of presents from her cousin, Madeline, in Canada.

She was pleased to realize that she was going to Detroit, and the publicist assured her that she was more than welcome to use her free time to hop over the border and see her cousin.

Things really did seem to be moving well. She could really talk to Madeline, and it would be so nice to be open with someone! To express her fears, her worries—even her growing excitement.

Lawrence hosted a party on Christmas Day. Susan went, and it was enjoyable to be with friends on such an occasion. But it was a painful day too. There was no way out of it— Christmas was a family day, and Carl was gone . . . she had no one who was really family anymore. She would, though, she thought, encouraging herself. Next year she would have the baby.

She smiled and handed out her presents, and she received lovely little things in return. But when she returned home alone, it was to a miserable night. She dreamed that she and David were sitting before a fire with all the beautiful Christmas lights shining. He was telling her how very sorry he was for believing what he had about her. Then they were laughing and he was holding her as tenderly as if she were composed of stardust, and together they were looking at all the packages they had gotten each other, all ripped open now on the floor beneath the tree. They had bought each other things for a baby. Tiny outfits, a car seat, even a box of disposable diapers . . .

She woke up in the middle of the night, clenching her teeth together and fiercely reminding herself that David Lane was involved with a lovely and very pleasant model, that he had never been anything but suspicious and rude to her, and that she could not create a life out of one foolish night of passion.

She forced herself to think of the present and reality. She

had to do some clothes shopping. Her first tour date was in New York itself, and she was due there on the fifteenth for a newspaper interview and a book signing. Clothing . . .

It was no good. She couldn't fall back to sleep. David was as real in her mind as he had once been in this very house.

Vickie Jameson had a wonderful Christmas party. She'd invited friends from the fashion industry, and for David's sake, he was certain, she'd included a number of his employees and others from the publishing field. The food was wonderful, the eggnog perfect, and Vickie herself looked gorgeous.

David spent the evening talking with friends, standing around the piano as they sang Christmas carols, dancing with Vickie . . . and feeling restless and miserable.

There was so much warmth around him, but he felt cold and empty and irritated with himself. He couldn't always have what he wanted! He'd told himself over and over again, but that fact didn't mean that a man could change what he wanted. He wanted to see Susan again, start over and pretend that they'd never met the way they had. He could stand there and laugh, chat, answer questions, make dates, move along as he had for so long, except that it was all empty now.

After the last guest left he and Vickie sat on the sofa on the elegantly carpeted raised platform in the living room of her apartment. He leaned back, sipping his Scotch, listening to her tell him about a new play that had just opened off off Broadway.

Vickie fingered the beautiful emerald necklace that he had just given her and smiled a little sadly, a bit ruefully. She was a beautiful woman and she knew it, and everything in the world was in her favor. It was just David. He wasn't really listening to a word she was saying, and she knew that too.

"The actors are all purple ants," she told him.

"Nice," he murmured.

210

"The entire audience is asked to watch in the nude. Customary."

"Mmm."

"A large green elephant has the lead role. He dances just like a dream, but his tenor isn't up to the polka-dotted giraffe's."

"Probably not."

"David!"

"What?" He jumped at the sound of her wail, and he had obviously been so lost that she laughed—and forced herself to accept the truth with a wistful pain but also with determination. She wasn't getting any younger. And if she wasn't for David, well, there was a man out there somewhere to love her uniquely.

"David, you haven't listened to a single word I've said!" She lifted her elegant fingers when he would have politely protested. "It's the writer, isn't it?" she asked suddenly. "The woman in the Japanese restaurant."

"What?" The question had startled him; it had also hit home. She could tell by the blue glaze that fell over his eyes.

"You're in love with her," Vickie said very softly.

He shook his head. "No." She didn't believe him, and at last he continued. "It's, ah, very complicated."

"Why aren't you with her?"

"I—can't be."

"Can'ts are in the mind!" Vickie sniffed, wondering if she was crazy or not. She was practically throwing a man she adored to another woman!

He took her fingers gently, curling his own around them. "Vickie . . ." He hesitated, wincing. "Vick, you're gorgeous. You're sweet and you're patient and you're—"

She laughed more easily than she thought she might. "Yes, I am, you fool! But you're not in love with me and you never will be. Now, let's get on with this. Why can't you be with her?"

"She doesn't want me."

211

"I don't believe it. I saw her face when she was with you."

David stared up at the ceiling.

"I swore I wouldn't . . . make an appearance in her life."

"Why?"

"That I can't explain."

"Oh," Vickie murmured, then she chuckled softly again. "Didn't Erica mention something about her going out on tour?"

"Yeah. So?"

"Go with her."

"Don't be ridiculous. Salespeople go on tours."

"Don't you be ridiculous! You're the publisher and the president. You can do whatever the hell you want, David Lane."

She saw his eyes spark, become the piercing crystal blue that was like the sky, and for a moment she knew another sharp pain of regret. But she forced herself to smile.

"David, I love you, but go home."

He didn't try to argue with her, for which she was glad. At her door he touched her cheek and told her again that she was wonderful.

"Give me a kiss, David, for old times' sake."

He did. He tasted her tears and his own torment. "Oh, God. Vickie . . ."

"Don't, David. I'm going to cry tonight because I deserve it. But tomorrow—watch out! Thank you for the emeralds."

"Thank you for the watch," he returned quietly.

They smiled at one another for a moment, friends. Then David turned and walked into the night.

He was plagued by the dream again that night. It was so real that he could have sworn he was a young serviceman again. Young and in love so deeply that the sun rose and set in her smile.

He was lying on the bed, waiting. She was there, smiling,

walking toward him, reaching out her arms, sleekly crawling over him, her skin like silk, her touch like flame. They were rolling together, locked, and the love and passion in him combined to make him tremble with the wonder of it all. . . .

And then the blade struck, and he was, for seconds, too stunned to believe it. But his blood was everywhere, and when he saw her eyes, all he saw was remorse; remorse because she had failed, because he had moved too quickly. . . .

And then her remorse became fear, because he knew that she hadn't loved him at all.

David awoke, shaking and furious with himself. Why the dream now? He'd been to bed with a dozen women since, and the dream had only started—since Susan Anderson.

He lay for a long time beneath the skylight on that star-studded Christmas, pondering it all. And at length he understood.

He was in love with her. With Vickie and other women he had never been tormented, because he hadn't been in love. It was an emotion that he . . . feared. Face it, he thought.

And it was frightening, really frightening. It had gotten to the point where he didn't give a damn about the past. Or maybe he did. Maybe he wanted her to lie to him, to tell him that she'd really had no relationship with his father. And maybe he wanted it to be the truth, but he knew it couldn't be. She had admitted things too many times. Maybe it was frightening because he cared so much that none of it mattered. Caring that deeply was . . . terrifying.

David sighed and rolled over. All he knew was that he had to see her again. To hell with the decency of leaving her alone! Vickie had been right; he was the publisher and the president. He could do whatever the hell he wanted, and this time he intended to.

CHAPTER TWELVE

This—this!—was a nightmare. Susan sat near the doorway, stacks of *The Promised Place* situated neatly before her, and not a soul stopped by for an autographed copy. People looked at her in such a way that she felt like she was a display herself. But they weren't coming anywhere near her, and she heartily wished she could crawl away and nurse her embarrassment.

"Things'll pick up, don't worry!" Jarod Malone cheerfully told her. He was the young sales representative from Puma who had graciously met her at the airport, established her back at the St. Regis, and brought her to the bookstore.

"Will they?" She grimaced, then tried to smile, then actually laughed. "It has to pick up somewhat! My agent is coming by to buy a book."

"Good. The newspaper and the talk show should be a little easier. Then there's always dinner—that's usually painless," Jarod told her. "Honest. I use the right silverware and I never spit things across the table."

"Good!"

There were people in the bookstore. Lots and lots of them. Oh, God! She felt like a large green pickle! Never again would she subject herself to such misery.

"Good God! This is it, isn't it? The book I've been hearing all about! It's really about Peter Lane, the publishing mogul, isn't it? Tell me, Miss Anderson, did you know him? How well did you know him? Were there any skeletons in the family closet?"

Her eyes widened, her throat went as dry as tinder, and her palms were suddenly damp.

It was David. He stood before her, impeccable as always in his business suit, and stared at her with clear blue eyes that betrayed no recognition.

Fool! She berated herself for her reaction to seeing him. She knew he lived here. And this was one of his company's books. Besides, it was his father's story.

"Ah, come on! Please tell me. It is based on *the* Peter Lane, isn't it?"

"Ah . . ."

Suddenly all those people who had been wandering around, making her feel like a pickle on display, were grouping around her.

"Peter Lane?"

"Oh, how fascinating! They say he sold apples in the street when he first came to America."

"And that he had a horrendous time in the old country."

It was as if a small miracle had occurred. David disappeared, and she was suddenly swamped, signing away, and desperately trying to fend off questions about her personal relationship with Peter.

Only Jarod, chuckling softly behind her, gave credence to the fact that David had ever been there.

Two hours moved by quickly; John came by and was jubilant to see how well it appeared to be going. Like David, he made his appearance and then disappeared.

Her next stop was the newspaper, then she had an interview on a syndicated show. Driving from the bookstore to the newspaper, Jarod warned her that the questions would be probing.

"There's only one stop on the tour, though, where the interviewer goes for the jugular. That's Detroit. Watch out for her. Her name is Tina Shine. We call her Tacky Tina. Other than that, you'll be fine."

Her newspaper interviewer was one of the nicest men she had ever met. In his sixties, white-haired, and potbellied, he wanted to know where she had met Peter Lane, and it was, of course, a question she had expected, one she was prepared to answer. "My brother met Peter first and introduced us."

The questions were the same at the television station; her interviewer was an attractive young woman who used five minutes to great advantage. She touched on Susan's other books, on the extraordinary success of Peter's life, and on the idea of the American Dream that could, it seemed, come true.

Jarod was completely pleased with the day. "If the rest of the tour goes this well, it will be marvelous! And this was the Big Apple—a hard place to crack!"

The Big Apple had also been Peter's stomping grounds, Susan thought. And David Lane had been there, ready to rescue a disastrous situation. She tried not to think about him, to pretend that he had never walked into the bookstore. But it was impossible. It had been a long time since she had seen him, but those minutes had seemed to wash away the time.

Especially since she was pregnant with his child.

"What's the matter?" Jarod asked her over a meal of cracked crab at a pleasantly subdued fish house on Madison Avenue.

"Nothing." She smiled brightly and ate her shrimp creole.

He was a pleasant young man. He asked her questions about her brother and her family life rather than about the

Lanes. He showed her a wallet full of pictures of his three-year-old twins and his infant daughter and pretty young wife. "We're expecting again," he told her with a flush and a grin. "One last try for a boy."

"You don't like girls, huh?" Susan teased him.

"Oh, I adore them!" he protested. "We both thought we'd give it one last shot. And if it should be another girl, well, that will be great too. She can inherit all the clothing we already have!"

By nine o'clock he had her back to her hotel room. He left, reminding her to be ready early; a car would be by to collect her for a drive to the airport at eight in the morning; her next stop would be Atlanta.

"I'll meet you at the airport," he assured her.

Susan smiled, closed her door, showered, and crawled into bed. She stared at a sitcom, a cop drama series, the news, and Johnny Carson. She didn't see a thing. She kept thinking about being in New York. There might be millions of people there, but David Lane was one of them. He'd walked into the bookstore, but he'd walked out damn quickly, not even saying hello or good-bye. Damn him. She'd vowed to make her life without him, and that was exactly what she was going to do.

She rolled over but felt as if she didn't sleep until five minutes before her alarm went off. Lord, was she tired! And horribly, horribly irritable—at David Lane. Thanks to him, she was going to go off to more interviews looking like a cadaver.

She lay in bed too long and had to rush to be downstairs by eight. Running so late, she didn't have time for breakfast.

But just as Jarod had promised, there was a limo waiting for her. Susan forced herself to smile pleasantly at the portly driver.

The traffic was awful; it took almost an hour to reach Kennedy. By that time Susan was a wreck, frightened that she was going to miss the plane. She didn't want to do that;

she could just imagine Mr. David Lane's contemptuous blue eyes when he was told that his author had missed her flight. No. She wasn't going to mess this thing up in any way, shape, or form.

The limo driver turned her luggage over to a porter. Susan found her gate number and started running in the right direction. She tripped on the slick pavement, turned her ankle, and got a run in her panty hose.

She started half skipping and half limping toward the gate.

People were already boarding the plane, and only a few remained in line. Where the hell was Jarod? she wondered. He was supposed to meet her here! Maybe he had already boarded the plane? No, surely he wouldn't board without her.

She had her ticket but not a seat assignment, and so she hurried to the young man at the desk.

"Hi, I—"

"There you are! Damn. I hate shaving things this closely!"

Susan froze while her ticket was snatched out of her hands and passed to the young man at the desk. Chills raced along her spine; they became hot like a dancing fever, then ran like icy rivulets again.

It was David Lane.

"This is Miss Anderson, the ticket we discussed earlier," David said. Stunned and furious, Susan turned slowly. As usual, he was impeccable. He didn't appear at all rushed or harassed, just thoroughly annoyed.

The airline employee prepared her ticket and handed it and a boarding pass back to David. "All set, Mr. Lane. Upgraded just as you wished. Uh . . ." He paused, clearing his throat politely. "If you could hurry a bit to board, please . . ."

"Let's go," David said.

His fingers were wound tightly around her elbow, and he was practically dragging her along, forcing her to put weight on her turned ankle. Pain fed on the frantic tempest she felt at seeing him, hence flaming her temper.

"What the hell are you doing here?" she demanded harshly. "Where's Jarod? What is—"

"Would you shut up and hurry, please?" he snapped back. At the end of the carpeted hallway leading to the plane, a young blond stewardess was watching them. She was trying to maintain an expression of polite patience; she wasn't doing very well. It was apparent that she was very anxious to close the door.

Susan glanced up at David's profile. "Hurry!"

The small muscles in his jaw were contracting; his mouth was tight and harshly grim.

"Wait. I'm not going—"

"Miss Anderson, may we please argue once we're on the plane?"

Susan did shut up—not because David had suggested it, but because they were reaching the pretty stewardess and public arguments were definitely not her style.

David smiled, said good morning, apologized for keeping the plane waiting, and handed their boarding passes to the woman. She graciously indicated their seats—close to the door, since the upgrading had meant first class. Susan had been scheduled in economy.

David took her carryall from her hands without asking and stowed it in the overhead compartment along with his briefcase and overcoat. "Sit down!" he said impatiently when she remained standing in the aisle.

The 727's engines were revving. The stewardess touched her shoulders. "Excuse me, you must take your seats and buckle your belts."

David slipped an arm around her waist, propelling her none too gently into the window seat.

"Damn you, David."

Susan realized that the stewardess was still staring at them, and she felt a bit like an errant child.

She buckled her seat belt and stared out the window, seething. She was dying to verbally lash into David, but the quiet first-class section of the plane just didn't seem like the place to do it.

The plane began to taxi; the stewardess moved to the front of the cabin, giving safety instructions. Susan continued to stare out the window, very painfully aware that David was beside her.

She closed her eyes, wincing. Yesterday . . . yesterday she had been expecting him to make another appearance. She had even hoped that he would make an appearance.

But now he was here. And apparently he was now the one who was supposed to be with her for the next week. How on earth would she ever manage it?

This was going to be impossible. He hadn't called; he hadn't written. She hadn't seen him in three months—and suddenly he was next to her. If she'd really harbored any dreams for a future, they had been nothing like this. They had needed something gradual. A phone call here or there, maybe even another of his surprise appearances at the beach house. Not this.

How could she possibly act normal? Listen to him discuss a schedule in his smooth business voice, stare at him over quickly grabbed coffee and doughnuts before an interview? And all the while she would be thinking that they really hadn't known each other to begin with, they were certainly as distant as two people could be right now, and she was pregnant with his child.

Think, think, think—it didn't matter what she was thinking, she assured herself. She would just have to be careful. Very careful, because she couldn't tell him. Dear God! What a dinner conversation that would be.

"Well, Miss Anderson, how have you been?"

"Oh, fairly well, Mr. Lane. Just a little uncomfortable now and then. Do you remember that night late last fall? You don't? Well, I do. Very well. I can't forget because—it's just

the damnedest thing—but that one stupid, reckless night has caused quite a change in the course of my life. What? Oh, I'm pregnant, you see. With your child . . ."

"A drink, Miss Anderson?"

"What?" Startled, Susan turned to him. That same pretty, smiling stewardess was hovering over them, her cordial and patient expression definitely wearing thin.

"Ah . . ."

David sighed deeply. "Susan, think quickly, please. This is difficult, I know, but would you or would you not like a drink?"

Lord, yes! She needed a drink. She wanted a double, very, very dry martini. She remembered the OB's warning and ordered a light beer. The stewardess gave David a pitying glance, and Susan suddenly wanted to tear out a handful of the woman's sleekly knotted hair.

Instead she took it out on David, lowering her voice to a hushed but vehement whisper. "What are you doing here? You're the publisher, remember? Publishers have little or nothing to do with authors like me, remember? What the hell—"

"Miss Anderson," he said, cutting in coolly, "Jarod's wife gave birth early this morning. It didn't seem fair to send the man out of town at such a time."

For several seconds Susan just stared at him with shocked dismay. What had she been expecting him to say? That he just had to see her so he had changed the plans for the tour?

She turned back to the window. "Surely, Mr. Lane, you had someone else you might have sent?"

"Not really," he said remotely. "We're a small house. Besides, this book is important to me, as you well know."

"Oh, yes. That's right."

Their drinks came. Susan sipped hers in silence. She realized that David was drinking coffee, and then she remembered that it was only about ten o'clock in the morning. Oh, the hell with it all! Let him think she was a lush!

David was ignoring her, reading a paper. A little belatedly, she thought of Jarod.

"Excuse me, Mr. Lane. What did Jarod's wife have?"

His eyes flashed briefly to hers. "A boy."

She started to smile with pleasure for the man who had wanted a son so badly but turned quickly away again. She was so tired, she could feel the pinpricks of tears behind her lids. Oh, this was never, never going to work!

"Sally wasn't due for another three weeks," David continued, ignoring her back. "But the baby is fine, and so is she."

"I'm glad to hear it," Susan murmured.

A man walked by them, glanced down, and exclaimed, "David! How are you?"

David glanced up, smiled, and began speaking to the other man. He was apparently someone in the upper echelon of another publishing company. David introduced the two of them, then excused himself to look at a new book the other man had in his briefcase a few seats forward.

The stewardess came by then with breakfast. Susan stared ruefully at the beer in her hand.

"Oh, think nothing of it!" The blond said, flashing her a smile that suddenly seemed very real. "Lots of people are afraid to fly. They drink at six A.M. too!"

Susan started to protest that she wasn't afraid of flying. She decided not to and smiled a little weakly instead.

The stewardess went away; David returned to his seat. Susan started wondering how long it took to reach Atlanta. She felt as if she'd already been on the plane for a week.

"What did you do?" he demanded a little sharply, and she realized that he was looking down at her leg and the long tear in her stocking.

"I tripped!" she snapped back. "And you needn't look so appalled. I have other stockings. I'll change them before we land."

"Good."

So this was first class, she thought wryly. She tried to bite

222

into her eggs; they tasted like sawdust. She didn't think the food was the problem; she was quite sure that it was her.

She still felt stunned. Nasty. Like picking a fight. It was so nerve-racking to have him there. . . .

She leaned back, smiling acidly. "Do you know, Mr. Lane, my ticket was supposed to be economy. I assume Jarod would have flown economy. Things changed for you, I suppose."

He pushed his eggs away too. "Yes, Miss Anderson, but it's a matter of preference. Lane foots the bill for the economy ticket. Anyone who wants to is welcome to upgrade on personal expenses."

"I didn't wish to upgrade," she said waspishly.

He turned back to his paper and sipped his coffee without bothering to reply. Susan knew she was being ridiculous. She just didn't seem to have much control over herself.

Breakfast was cleared away. The flight continued. Susan was sure she could have flown to China much more quickly under normal circumstances.

"I'm surprised you didn't choose to fly around the country by yourself," Susan commented, annoyed that he could display such total interest in the news when he had no right to be there.

"Arrangements were already made," he said without glancing away from the page.

A few minutes later Susan excused herself, clenching her teeth as he smiled and helped her crawl over his legs rather than moving to allow her easy passage.

After changing her panty hose she stared at her reflection in the small mirror in the bathroom. She was white! Oh, she looked like hell, and she was supposed to be sparkling and enthusiastic. She didn't know whether to feel numb, remain furious, or hope that this could be . . . something. She didn't know what.

When she returned to her seat, it seemed that the arduous

223

journey was at last about to come to an end. The pilot was announcing their approach to the airport.

But they didn't land. There was a backup in the skies, and they kept flying around in circles, the pilot apologizing. Winter weather was causing all kinds of delays.

David was glancing at his wristwatch. It was really stunning—a new one, Susan thought, with a wide gold band and beautiful work on the face.

"We're going to run a little late for the first interview," he murmured. "But it's a newspaper, so we should be all right."

He didn't seem tense or nervous. Susan was already so nervous that she couldn't possibly become any more tense.

At last the plane glided down.

"Hurry," David urged as they left it behind and started to rush through the busy airport.

"I'm hurrying as fast as I can!" Susan grated in reply. Already her ankle was killing her again.

They reached the gliding electric shuttle, and David pushed the button. Susan stopped to adjust her shoe. "Surely these people will understand that airplanes can be delayed!"

"Come on!"

David, unaware that she was adjusting the ankle strap on her shoe, stepped into the shuttle.

"Susan!"

She looked up just as the shuttle door was closing, just in time to see total impatience and anger explode across his features. The window and the shuttle disappeared.

Susan winced, wondering what to do. There was a moving sidewalk in front of her. She rushed to it, grimacing each time her foot hit the ground. She assumed the sidewalk would take her to the next shuttle stop, but it didn't. She'd never been in the Atlanta airport before; it was immense.

"Oh, hell!" She muttered aloud, drawing a dour look from a pristine little old lady who happened to be walking by.

"Sorry!" Susan smiled weakly, then grew irritated with herself. Anyone with a grain of sense would get off an airplane and head for the baggage claim. If she went there, she decided, she would certainly find David.

It sounded perfect. It sounded fine, logical, and intelligent. Except that David wasn't there. She found her bags and tugged them toward the exit. She glanced at the clock on the wall and realized that she had been there over half an hour.

It was then that David appeared; his features more severe and dark than any storm she'd ever seen hit the Maine coastline.

"Where the hell have you been! Why didn't you get on the shuttle? I hope you realize that we haven't a prayer in hell of reaching that newspaper on time! And you're due at a bookstore on Peachtree in less than an hour! Why didn't you stay put?"

"Stay put? Any idiot would go for their luggage."

"Dammit, I've been over the entire length of this airport!"

"I did say *any* idiot, didn't I?"

His coat was over his arm, his briefcase in his left hand. He used his right to spin her around, wave to a porter, and usher them both out into a dreary day. Susan cried out as his forcefulness made her ankle buckle again.

"I just told you how late we are! Is this all being done on purpose? What is—" He paused, eyes narrowing as he took in the pain in her eyes. "What's wrong?" he asked quietly.

"My ankle!" she gasped out.

"Just now?"

"No, you imbecile!" Susan clenched her teeth together, fighting tears. "I hurt it in New York, and the way you've been dragging me around like a sack isn't helping it at all!"

He hesitated. "Can you stand?"

"Yes! I can even walk—as long as you stop trying for the four-minute mile!"

He paused, closed his eyes, and took a deep breath. The grip of his fingers on her arm eased. "I'll have to reschedule the newspaper. We'll go to the hotel and you can soak it."

"No. I'll be all right."

225

"Susan, it's not worth——"

"I will be all right!"

"Okay, we'll try it. Our car should be here somewhere."

He left her and returned a few moments later. A man with a rental agency cap on his head took her luggage while David took his own and helped her into a new Olds Supreme.

Susan had a feeling that this service was also especially for David Lane. Other people were entering shuttle buses to be driven to the rental agencies. Their car was awaiting them just like a pumpkin that had magically become a coach.

From that point on the day went exceptionally well. Susan was certain that it was because she had no more than five minutes to be near David alone. The book reporter on the newspaper was a lovely silver-haired woman who was an optimist; curious rather than interested in tearing anyone down. The employees in the bookstore were wonderfully gracious. There was an hour and a half gap between her session at the store and her five minutes on the evening news, but even that went smoothly because she sat in a café with a tea while David spent at least an hour on the phone to New York.

They had dinner with the southeastern sales manager and his wife, another very smooth event. Susan stayed in the kitchen, insisting on helping with the preparation and cleanup. After dinner she sipped amaretto, and by the time they were driving to the hotel, she was exhausted. Much too tired to argue.

Her room turned out to be a suite. Another change in honor of the publisher being on the tour, she was certain. There was a sitting room with a wet bar and two bedrooms. She was ready to go into her room and fall into bed, but when the bellboy left, David propelled her to the sofa despite her very verbal outrage.

"I ordered some epsom salts for your ankle," he replied impatiently. "Let it soak or you'll be sorry in the morning."

Giving up, Susan leaned back on the sofa, watching him with narrowed eyes. He pulled off his jacket and played with the television, paying her little attention. A few seconds later room service appeared with a bucket. David tipped the boy and he left.

David knelt down by her, pulling off her shoe. "I can get it myself," Susan protested.

"Would you quit behaving like such an idiot?" His fingers were over her nyloned flesh, and she shivered miserably.

"May I please get my stockings myself?" she asked primly. His eyes fell on her, a smoky blue, suddenly soft with amusement.

"Why, most certainly," he told her graciously.

"Well, you can turn around, or I can hobble into the bedroom."

Chuckling softly, he swiveled on his knee to stare at the television. Susan was in such a hurry to shed her panty hose that she tripped over the half on, half off nylon and fell into his shoulders. He straightened her, a half smile curving his mouth, and pulled the nylons the rest of the way off, gently setting her foot and ankle into the tub of water.

"Any better?" he asked a little huskily.

His shirt was open at the throat and his hair was slightly tousled over his forehead, but his cheeks still appeared freshly shaven. There was a subtle, pleasant aroma of after-shave lingering about him. His lips remained just slightly curved, mocking or amused, and the pulse at his throat seemed to touch an answering beat somewhere inside her.

She looked away from him quickly. "Yes."

"Good."

He slipped off his shoes, picked up his briefcase, sat at the end of the sofa, and, quite comfortable, stretched his legs out over the coffee table.

He started going over the next day's schedule.

"We'll have coffee up here first thing; it's another early

227

flight. Nine-fifteen to Detroit. Noon is lunch with the regional sales manager, two-thirty is Croft's Books, and—"

"The evening is free!" Susan said, interrupting him a little defiantly. He glanced at her questioningly, that smile still in place, and she found herself flushing. "I asked your publicity department," she said a little defiantly. "I have a cousin in Windsor, and I'm meeting her for dinner."

"Ah, yes, the Canadian cousin," he murmured, and Susan remembered that she had mentioned Madeline once. She was somewhat surprised that he remembered.

"It is all right?"

"Sure," he said smoothly, "but you didn't let me finish. Four-thirty is Tacky Tina. She's going to hit at you for everything—subtly. She'll knock your science fiction as being pure trash for illiterates, and she'll sweetly try to hang you. Think you can handle her?"

Susan couldn't help but laugh. After all, she'd been through the best of the "hangers," David himself.

"I'll be just fine," she assured him. His eyes were still on her, and suddenly he seemed very close. Relaxed and comfortable, as if he could easily reach out and slide her down to his lap . . .

If he wished to.

"I'm sorry, Susan," he said softly.

"For?"

"Snapping at you today. You were right—luggage was the most logical place to go." He grimaced ruefully, and she was suddenly very desperate to get away from him. An answer she couldn't give was at the tip of her tongue.

She wanted to tell him that she was sorry, too, for many, many things. For the way they met, for the way she led him to believe circumstantial evidence. She was sorry that they couldn't seem to start over, sorry that she was deceiving him right now. They were going to be parents, and she couldn't tell him because it would be so wrong for him to feel guilty or responsible. A relationship couldn't be forced for such a

228

reason; there either was one or there wasn't. She would love him to fall in love with her, could so easily love him, even if he did have a rotten temper and really didn't trust women for some elusive reason. . . .

"The water has gotten stone cold," she said a little desperately, noting that his eyes were still very tender as he looked at her. She felt a bit like panicking. She wasn't ready if he meant to touch her. She wasn't sure about anything.

"Could I please go to bed now?"

"Of course." He was up, bringing her a towel for her foot. She barely dried it before leaping up, desperate to rush into her own room and slam the door against him.

"Good night, Susan," he called softly.

"Good night."

Her heart leapt and sped when she had closed the door. She wondered if he would knock, if he would try to enter.

He didn't. She stripped off her clothes and fell to the bed, so exhausted that she quickly drifted off. And right before sleep claimed her, she realized that she was smiling.

Maybe there was hope.

CHAPTER THIRTEEN

She didn't look quite so bad, Susan decided, staring at her reflection in the mirror. The hollows beneath her eyes had faded along with the shadows. It was amazing what a night of sleep could do.

Not to mention a change in attitude.

She gripped the sink for a minute, closing her eyes. She couldn't believe that there had been no one else from Lane Publishing to send on a tour. Yes, the book was important to him, and maybe he had been a bit frightened that she might say or do something in an interview that would reflect badly on the last year of his father's life, but if that had been his fear, he wouldn't have arranged for the tour at all.

Which meant that he was with her because he wanted to be?

"Susan?"

She opened her eyes quickly, left the bathroom, and heard him tapping at the bedroom door.

"Coffee's here. Ready?"

"Yes. All set and packed."

She hesitated just a second, smoothing down her skirt and twirling before the dresser mirror one last time. She would do. It was her most sophisticated outfit; a red skirt suit with a white tailored blouse, slim necktie, red belt, and daringly angled hat. It should have all clashed with her hair, but it didn't at all; it brought out the dark highlights.

And she felt good! Daring and reckless and feminine. Ready to fly into the battle zone and do deadly combat with Tacky Tina.

She picked up a pair of soft kid gloves as she entered the living room. David, with his customary élan, was leaned against the window, hands in his pockets, a slightly brooding expression on his face. He looked like something out of *GQ*, and Susan smiled. If nothing else, they looked like a perfect couple.

He turned to her, raised his brows, grinned, and slowly assessed her from head to toe. She spun around for him, returning a slightly haughty gaze, then laughing delightedly because she liked the glint in his eyes and wondered if her own mirrored it.

"Shall I handle Tacky Tina, do you think?" she asked pertly.

"Beyond a doubt, Miss Anderson. Beyond a doubt."

He left the window to bring her a cup of coffee, already poured and steaming hot. He lingered near her, hands in his pockets.

"And you smell good too. It's a shame they can't get a whiff of that over the television tube."

"Why, Mr. Lane, thank you. And may I return the compliment? You smell . . . divine."

They were flirting, she realized. Like strangers who had just met, were attracted, and getting their toes wet.

He moved away from her, stacking things into his briefcase and closing it. "It's too bad we can't have breakfast up here," he muttered regretfully. "But the porter's already on

231

the way up, and"—he hesitated, shooting her a warning glance—"I really do hate them slamming the door behind me on a plane before I'm on it."

"It wasn't my fault!" Susan protested. "I wasn't driving, remember? You had a car pick me up, and the traffic was deadly. I wrecked my body to make it on time!"

A soft curl played at the corner of his lip. He paused, surveying her very slowly again. "Your body looks okay to me."

"I'm talking about my ankle!"

He started to respond, but there was a rap at the door. The porter was there; they had to get to the airport, leave the car and keys, and get on the plane.

It was the first-class section again. David admitted a preference because of the length of his legs. "I feel like an accordion when I sit in the back," he told her. "You really don't mind, do you?"

She looked at him, sipping tea that morning, and shook her head. "I'm willing to suffer for professionalism, Mr. Lane."

They really didn't speak that much on the plane. David read the paper again; Susan did a crossword puzzle. But it was nice to have a comfortable silence between them. Toward the end of the flight David folded up his paper and pointed out the river separating Detroit from Windsor. He asked her casual questions about the beach house and wanted to know how Jud was doing out in his hunter's lodge. With a little catch in her throat Susan cheerfully talked about Christmas, how pretty the pines had looked, coated in snow that had frozen over to glitter like panes of glass. She asked him about his Christmas; he evaded the question and told her that John and Erica seemed to be getting quite serious.

Despite some miserable drizzly weather, things began quite well in Detroit. Again the newspaper people were charming. The young man doing the interview had done a

232

short piece for the previous day's issue on Peter Lane—with speculation about the book—so her stint at the bookstore was marvelous. Lunch was a quickly grabbed sandwich between appointments. David spent time on the phone again, and Susan bought a horror novel to entertain herself during the in between moments and plane rides. She called Madeline, promising that she would be at the Cock's Crow in Windsor by eight for dinner.

And then it was time for Tacky Tina's show.

The "tacky," Susan quickly realized, definitely had to do with the woman's barbarous tongue, because appearance wise she was quite stunning. Her hair was so dark, it was almost black, and it was cut in a very contemporary pageboy. She was tall and lanky, dressed in the height of fashion in a beige silk dress that clung to her with a savvy negligence. She had a lovely smile, a low, cultured voice, and dark, dark eyes that carried a pure streak of either mischief or malice.

The studio was like any other: large, cavernous, filled with cameras, cameramen, and production assistants. Susan was quickly miked and told to get comfortable on a white sofa that faced her hostess's chair on a dais. Tina assured her the questions would be chatty and easy, and then they were given a ten-second warning.

And ten seconds later Susan learned that Tacky Tina did indeed plan to skewer her. In her introduction to her audience Tina allowed her voice to drip with insinuation. "Neither Miss Anderson nor Lane Publishing try to hide the fact that the book is based on *the* Peter Lane. And when we come back, we're going to get to the . . . nitty-gritty, shall we say?" A delicate little laugh, a lowering of her voice, a movement that brought her conspiratorially closer to the camera. "We're going to delve here today and find out just how well—and how intimately—Susan Anderson actually knew Peter Lane."

There was to be a sixty-second commercial. Tina smiled at

233

Susan, and Susan smiled right back, certain that she could handle the woman. She felt as if she had been challenged to a fight, and there was nothing like that feeling of being armed for combat—righteously!

But something happened in that sixty seconds. She didn't see exactly how, nor could she understand why or quite what happened in that short span. Before the camera rolled again, however, David Lane was miked and sitting next to her—to her surprise and apparently to Tina's surprise, as well, for there was definitely a glint of annoyance in her eyes as she saw David sit.

"What—"

"I'm David Lane, Tina," he said smoothly, and he managed to look as if he hadn't acted on the spur of the moment, as if he hadn't moved like the speed of lightning to be where he was. He smiled, and that smile was a better warning and challenge, Susan was quite certain, than any that Tacky Tina ever had been given in her life.

Tina tossed her head and smiled plasticly to the camera. "A surprise guest! The late publisher's son himself, Mr. David Lane. Now, Mr. Lane, do come clean! What are we hiding here?"

"Hiding?" David managed to sound completely surprised and innocent. His smile deepened. "I don't think there's a thing to hide. My father's life is an open book, which you can discover by opening the pages." He went on and on—smoothly, silkily. Tina was as lulled by the sound of his voice as Susan was amazed. He was managing to keep her included in the interview, and somehow keep Tina out of it. He also managed to imply that anyone looking for skeletons in closets surely hid a few of their own—that, or they were dreadfully bored with life.

The interview ended with Tina furious yet not sure exactly what he had done.

And Susan wasn't sure what she felt herself. A certain anger because, dammit, she could have handled it herself.

234

And because, she thought, wincing as he led her out of the studio, he had stepped in simply because he had believed exactly the opposite of what he had said. In his eyes Susan Anderson did have a whole packet of sins to hide—sins that might degrade his father's memory.

"What's the matter with you?" he asked sharply as he opened the passenger's seat to the Camaro they were driving in Detroit.

"Nothing."

She sat in the seat, anxious to get back to the hotel—and then anxious to get away from him. In just a few hours she could find a harbor in this strange storm, the company of her open and honest cousin.

He folded himself into the driver's seat and turned on the ignition, his teeth grating like the motor. "Don't tell me nothing. What's the matter?"

"All right!" She spun in the seat. "I'm supposed to thank you, right? For saving me from her clutches? Well, I'm sorry! I resent what you did! You implied that I was a bumbling fool! And you didn't come up there for me, anyway! You came up to save the very precious Lane name because you're so damned convinced that there's something to save it from!"

"There is, isn't there?"

"Go to hell."

He shot her a glance, his eyes crystal blue with anger. Susan noted a taxi jamming on its brakes ahead of them. "David! Watch the road!"

"I know how to drive!"

"You almost hit him!"

"Then shut up!"

She did, compressing her mouth tightly. He watched the road, and she stared straight ahead until they reached the towering hotel. She was out of the car before he could help, striding toward the lobby to call a cab.

"Susan—"

"I'm off, Mr. Lane. I have a dinner engagement."

"I'll drive you."

"No thank you."

The doorman was signaling a cab. David narrowed his eyes on her very sharply and spoke softly, "Suit yourself, Miss Anderson. But remember, please, that we leave Detroit at ten A.M. The weather is bad—leave yourself enough time to get back here at a decent hour tonight."

A cabbie sprang out and opened the door to his battered taxi for her.

"Thank you very much, Mr. Lane. I do live alone, and I'm quite capable of looking after myself. Good night!"

Susan gave the cabdriver the address to the restaurant in Windsor. He sighed and told her that he would have to charge her an arm and a leg to drive her over the Canadian border. Susan was sure she could have found someone who wouldn't rip her off so outrageously, but she wasn't about to get out of the cab with David still watching her from the doors of the Westin Hotel.

At the border she was questioned. Susan mused that if she were carrying a pack of explosives, she certainly wouldn't admit it. But maybe the bored guard was more experienced than she could imagine; maybe he knew from her face that she wasn't the type to be an international weapons smuggler.

She arrived at the restaurant thirty minutes early, yet was glad that she had. The night was a dark and ominous one; snow fell from the sky and turned to slush on the ground. A little guiltily, she made a mental note to start back to the hotel early, no matter how she and Madeline got to talking.

Sitting by herself and sipping a seltzer while she waited for her cousin, Susan felt her temper cool. The restaurant was a nice one, filled with warm, varnished wood tables, the walls lined with pewter trenchers and tankards, like an old English establishment.

She leaned back, closing her eyes and taking a deep breath. David hadn't said anything at all to her this time

236

around that could be construed as mocking or demeaning. Oh, they'd argued over his appearance, her tardiness, and all, but he'd apologized too. It was as if he wanted to forget the past, almost as if he cared, even though he still believed that her "sordid past" did exist.

There had been moments so special and so nice between them! If only she could tell him the truth. But to what avail? Why should he believe her now? To convince him she'd have to tell him where she had really met Peter; she would have to tell him that his father had known he was dying almost a full year before the heart attack had struck. And no matter how angry she had been, she had never wanted to hurt him in such a fashion.

"Praying? Or meditating?"

She opened her eyes at the sound of her cousin's warm, amused voice.

"Madeline!" With a little cry Susan was on her feet, hugging her tiny cousin. Madeline was in her mid-thirties but looked as if she were twenty-two. Her eyes were the same sparkling green as Susan's, and she, too, had inherited the dark, flaming hair from some distant ancestor.

"Oh, kid, it's so good to see you!"

For a few moments they stood there, laughing and hugging each other. Then Madeline sat down opposite her, and Susan plunged into a spate of questions about Madeline's husband, Bill, and their children, five-year-old Timmy and two-year-old Amy. Madeline told her that Bill just hadn't been able to get out of work, that the kids were fine, and they couldn't wait until she could make a real vacation visit.

"Oh, you're a liar! Amy's too young to remember that I exist!" Susan accused her.

Madeline denied it with a grin, then ordered a glass of burgundy from the waiter. She frowned slightly as Susan hesitated and then ordered a light beer. They decided to split a giant prime rib, the house specialty, then continued to chat over idle things for a time. After the food had been served, however, Madeline sat back, studying Susan.

"You look awful."

"Thanks a lot. I thought this was one of my better outfits."

Madeline shook her head. "You look too thin and pale."

"It's winter. The Caribbean isn't on my tour schedule."

"Mmm," Madeline murmured, sipping her wine. "And you've been on tour so long already, you're even avoiding me! Hey, we only have a few hours here, so spill the beans, sweetie!" She tensed and asked slowly, "God, Sue, you're not . . . sick, are you?"

Susan shook her head vehemently. "No, I'm fine, really. I'm . . . pregnant."

"Thank God!" Madeline murmured, not batting an eye. She took a bite of her prime rib.

"That's it?" Susan asked incredulously. "I make an announcement like that and that's all you have to say?"

Madeline continued to chew serenely, then swallowed and took another sip of her wine. "Well, you're either going to tell me about it or not, aren't you?"

Susan laughed then, feeling as if she had come home in a way. "Yes, I'm going to tell you all about it. I'm desperate to tell someone all about it!"

And she did, leaving out nothing except for David's name and his connection with Peter. Madeline informed her without mincing words that she was a fool. "Where have you been? That child is his responsibility! And"—she paused—"it sounds to me like you're in love with the guy."

"I don't know. Maybe. But, Madeline, don't you see? I refuse to be a responsibility." She told her cousin about the pretty model she was certain held some kind of sway with him, and that she was equally certain he would never believe a word she had to say, anyway, that he was capable of being judgmental, arrogant, and opinionated, a condition which she had certainly contributed to by being so flippant instead of indignant.

Madeline didn't say anything else—nothing pressuring, at any rate. She was very glad that Susan had decided to have the baby and convinced her to come to Windsor instead of going somewhere else where she would have no family or friends.

"I'll protect you," Madeline promised, half joking, half serious. "Really! It will be fun and wonderful. We can make it so. Except I still think that you should look at the other alternative."

"Like?"

"Like telling the father the truth."

Susan hesitated. "I can't, Madeline. Not unless he can fall in love with me for myself—and believe me because he believes *in* me."

Madeline shrugged, then glanced at her watch. "Sue! It's past midnight. I promised Bill I'd meet him at the tunnel at twelve. He didn't want either of us getting into a taxi alone, you see."

"Oh! We'd better get going."

Sue insisted on paying the check, then she and Madeline slid into their coats and rushed out to the street. The slushy snow was still falling, yet the street was filled with traffic. Madeline managed to hail a cab, but they were in it for fifteen minutes and had barely moved a block.

"What the heck is going on?" Madeline asked the driver.

"Don't know," he mumbled. "I'll turn around and take the bridge."

"No, you can't! My husband is meeting me at the tunnel," Madeline told him.

"Lady, the meter's running, but it's your money."

They sat a while longer, thankful for the heat in the cab. Still, the traffic didn't move. The radio gave out static; horns beeped so loudly that the night seemed a cacophony.

At last the driver turned to them, having understood some

239

of the static on his radio. "Seems the bridge is blocked by an accident—a lumber truck. That means all the traffic is headed for the tunnel, and we've got heavy traffic 'cause there was a big political banquet today—a huge thing, hundreds of Americans coming over."

"Great!" Susan murmured.

They sat a while longer, then the driver finally suggested that they could reach the tunnel faster by walking.

They walked awhile, then Madeline's heel broke off her shoe, so they ducked into what seemed to be the only lounge still open and ordered a drink. Madeline miraculously managed to find a waitress who carried glue and repaired her shoe—for the time being, at least. But then the waitress disappeared into the disgruntled crowd. Susan took her American Express card from her purse to hunt down her waitress. She paid the bill, but when she came back, her purse was gone from the booth. Madeline hadn't seen anyone, so they crawled around on the floor and at last gave up, Madeline admitting that she had been so involved in pressing her heel into her sole that she might not have noticed if someone in the bar had reached over to snatch the purse.

They reported the theft to the restaurant; they called the police. The police couldn't get there, it seemed, and so they had to leave with nothing more than a promise that as soon as possible something would be done.

"What am I going to do?" Susan wailed once they were on the street.

"It will turn up."

"I have to fly out in the morning!"

"I've got money."

"Thanks. I'm going to need it to get back into the States!"

But the night was intended to get worse. When they reached the tunnel, Bill wasn't there. Susan talked to a woman at the customs cubicle and was told that there should have been a bus back to the States but that it hadn't shown up yet.

240

"Oh, God! I think I'm going to have to walk back."

"Wait!" Madeline told her. "I see a guy over there. Maybe he's a cabdriver!"

"Madeline!"

But Madeline was already rushing over to the bus terminal, so Susan followed.

"You can't walk through the tunnel," the apologetic customs agent told her. "You'd asphyxiate from the fumes."

"I've got to get back!"

"I'm sorry, I really am. This night is just an awful mess. The only way you're going to get back over to Detroit is to hitchhike."

Susan turned to her cousin.

"Well, we've got to get you into something, huh?" Madeline said, smiling in a manner that meant she was trying really hard to find the bright side of things.

"What about you?"

"Bill will show up eventually."

Susan was finding it hard to believe that she was standing in the middle of all the honking traffic, all dressed up, and that no one—*no one*—would pick her up. "Oh, God!" she said with a moan. But a truck went by then, with a pair of farmers in it. She smiled at them. They looked at her suspiciously. She would have gladly gone in the truck, but they said that there was no room.

"Maybe I do look like a weapons carrier!" she muttered.

"Show some leg," Madeline suggested.

"I think I'd strip naked if it would help," Susan said, moaning. "You go out there and try some leg! I don't believe this!"

Just when Susan was about to absolutely give up, a horn blared at her. She turned around, shielding her eyes from the sudden flare of lights. Her heart lifted and soared. It was the rented Camaro, and David was driving.

"A car!" Madeline cried out. "Oooh, and he's cute! Oh, no —he's too good-looking. Maybe he's a mass murderer or—"

"He's not a mass murderer," Susan muttered. "Not that I know of, anyway. It's David Lane."

"Oh! And I'll bet that—that's *him!*" Madeline muttered.

David rolled down his window. "Get in!" he yelled at Susan. She ran around to obey, much too frustrated to resent his tone or worry about Madeline's words.

"Hi. I'm her cousin Madeline," she said, introducing herself, stretching out a hand graciously despite the cacophony all around them.

"Need a ride?" David asked.

"No, I'm safe by the customs agents. My husband will get here eventually."

"Good night, then!" David rolled up the window and inched ahead with the traffic.

"Were you following me?" Susan snapped suddenly.

"No. Other people have friends and relations in Canada, too, my dear."

Susan leaned back against the seat, exhausted and at the edge of her temper. She tried to stare ahead through the tunnel. David was doing the same thing.

"Damn!" he muttered. "Of all nights for someone to try to play Dirty Harry at the border!"

She didn't understand his meaning until they came closer to the end of the tunnel. Then she realized that the border guard was taking his duty very seriously. He seemed to be searching every car.

"You do have your ID?" he asked.

"I—uh—" Oh, God! It was all in her purse. "I have my American Express card!"

"What? Oh, my Lord! You've been watching Karl Malden too often. Susan, an American Express card is not an ID!"

"My purse was stolen!" she shouted back.

He took a deep, deep breath. It was finally their turn at the border. He snapped out his identification and got out of the car. Apparently he had a way with men as well as

242

women; the guard began nodding, then actually smiled at Susan. "You are an American citizen, right?"

"Right! Right!"

"Where were you born?"

"Philadelphia. No. St. Mary's. Pennsylvania. St. Mary's is very, very small, that's why I said Philadelphia. Honest to God, I swear it! You see, my purse was stolen—"

The guard was shaking his head, looking at David as if he were insane to be with such a scatterbrain. "Drive through."

David did just that, casting her a glance that assured her he thought he was insane himself to be with such a scatterbrain.

"You don't know where you were born?" he asked softly.

"Oh, shut up! It's been an absolutely miserable, rancid night, with everything in the world going wrong, and if you say one more word, I swear I'll—"

"What?"

"Explode! Right here and now. But I'll tear every hair out of your head first!"

And for a second she thought that it would happen—that she would tear into him with all her pent-up frustration, anger, hurt, and fear. Or that he would forget all about the wheel and throttle her.

But it didn't happen. He stared at her, and then at the road, and then he glanced at her again and burst into laughter, and to her amazement she did too.

And he reached out, putting an arm around her shoulder, pulling her close to him. "Your purse was stolen, huh?"

"With everything but my credit card," she said with a moan.

"Well, everything can be replaced," he said, trying to soothe her. Her smile remained. She allowed herself to close her eyes and nestle close to him.

They reached the hotel and had to bang on the glass doors; apparently Detroit closed up at night. The guard told them that the main door was always open. David smiled and

243

thanked him even though it didn't matter since they were leaving in the morning.

His arm was still around her as they wandered up to their rooms, another suite.

"Want me to order a nightcap?" he asked a little huskily.

She shook her head—she'd already had the two beers, and she was too nervous about the baby to drink more. But then she smiled again.

"I'd love a strawberry shake," she told him.

"A strawberry shake?"

"Yep."

"Well, at Lane we do try to please."

He picked up the phone to see if room service was possible. Susan tossed off her coat and shoes. "I'm going to take a bath," she told him.

He nodded in her direction. She walked into her room, closed the door, went to the bathroom, and ran water into the tub. She shed her clothing rather sloppily, wrapped her hair into a knot, and stepped in, feeling a rush of physical pleasure as the nearly hot water soothed her. She rested her head against the rim of the tub and mused that she really was crazy about David Lane.

Idly, languorously, she began to lather her legs. And then she froze, not languorous at all, when she heard his voice. Very low and husky, and so sensual that her breath caught just as her eyes flew open.

"I'm going to drop this thing before I get it to you if you keep that up."

How long had she been in the tub? He was freshly showered with a towel around his waist, standing in the doorway with a pair of paper cups.

There were a million things she could have said, starting with, "Get the hell out."

She didn't say it. She watched him move across the room to her. Kneeling by the tub, he ran his fingers over her soapy leg, then smiled as he handed her one of the cups.

244

She even took it. Watching him, she sipped the frothy shake while he ignored his own and stared at her, grinning ruefully while he spoke.

"I didn't follow you tonight. I did come over, though, when I heard about the accident, hoping I'd find you if you were in trouble."

"Oh . . ."

He reached for her shake. "Do you really want this?"

Susan didn't think she replied.

"Come on out of there," he told her, and his fingers, long and bronzed, closed around hers, pulling her up. Then she was standing, stepping from the tub, and murmuring ridiculously, "I need a towel."

"Take mine," he offered, and it was suddenly ripped from around his waist and set around her shoulders. David held on to the ends, using them to urge her closer to his naked body until her flesh was crushed to his, alive with a warmth, beautifully aware of his body and . . . desire.

"Tell me, my dear Miss Anderson," he whispered, his eyes smoky and fiery, passionate and tender, "could you feel tonight, perhaps, just a wee bit of charity for a man who's desperately in need of your touch?"

She shivered as she stood there, trembling deep inside. But she couldn't resist the whisper of his voice, the power of his eyes. Because, against all logic, she believed him. She also believed that what there was between them went far beyond the petty spats that rose between them, even went beyond the mistrust and the anger and . . . anything that either might have known in the past.

She lifted her hands slowly, feathering her fingernails lightly over his torso to place her palms against his cheeks.

"Yes," she said simply, and then she might have melted, for his arms went around her tightly and his lips were on hers. It was not gentle, yet it was caring. His kiss ravaged with the need and desire of his soft-spoken whisper, de-

245

manding entrance to hers, searing her to the core with the thrusting movement of his tongue.

Her hair slipped from the knot, cascading over his fingers like tresses of silk. A jolt of yearning rippled through him, a jolt of wonder. It was as if a mist surrounded them, shimmering like gossamer, creating enchantment. It was the same as it had been that first night he had touched her, looked into her eyes, stroked her flesh. And he wondered if it would be like this always, erotically sweet and gripping just to hold her, a sensation of purity even while it seemed that jungle drums began to pulse within him.

He barely remembered moving; he had her in his arms. They fell to the bed together, and he was entangled in the length of her legs, agile limbs that drew his touch, the stroke of his fingers, the brush of his kiss. He rose above her, saw that mist in her eyes as they searched his. Arms braced by her head on the bed, he lowered himself to kiss her again. She welcomed him, slipping her arms around his neck, pulling him down, embracing him with her touch, with the undulation of her body, moving, touching him, thrilling him . . .

He was in love with her. And she touched him with the will to give, to love in return. For one bitter moment he held her stiffly; he knew that he had been the one unwilling to give, unwilling to trust. He had been afraid, but he could be that way no more; not if he wanted to hold on, not if he wanted a chance to keep the magic.

He pulled away from her once again and saw the magic of love in her eyes. He had to tell her.

"Susan . . . I love you."

Her eyes widened, an emerald fire against the night, sparkling and radiant. And he thought that there might be tears in them, but he would never be sure, for her lashes lowered quickly. The sweet pressure of her lips fell against his throat, and then she showered his shoulders with little kisses and the graze of her tongue, and her nails stroked like a sensual

246

spell against his back, raising the shuddering pulse inside of him to a thunderous pitch. He rolled, catching her to him, burying his head against her to lave her breasts with adoration, catching the nipples, stroking them, teasing them, loving them with tenderness and passion until the beat of his heart joined the thunder of her own, and her whispers were of both love and desire. Ah, and she was more than memory had told him, more slender, more rounded, her breasts fuller, her hips more wanton.

Yes . . . he was in love.

But it was she who cried out the words as he thrust into her, she who kept whispering incoherently, she who matched the wild splendor of his ecstasy and longing. He took the lead, and then she, moving over him, proud and straight in the night, her breasts a fascination that drew his hands, the arch of her throat making her ever more beautiful, her touch, her cry . . .

And his hands moved from her breasts to her shoulders, sweeping her beneath him again as all was lost but the driving desire of the body. The feeling, the sensation that grew like a winter storm, raging and passionate and . . .

Susan cried out his name. Her beautiful body went suddenly rigid beneath his, then shuddered again and again. He let himself go, soared like the winter wind to his own climax, and he knew that his body shuddered like hers, trembled and trembled again in the aftermath.

He lay beside her, lacing his fingers with hers. Light from the bathroom spilled out upon them, reflecting on their locked fingers, on the length of her body, the swells of her breasts, the curves of her hips. When he met her gaze, her eyes were filled with a secret confusion.

He touched her cheek, smiled, and only lightly qualified his words. "I am in love with you, you know. A response would be nice."

She looked at him and smiled a little sadly. "I think I've been in love with you for a long time." Susan closed her eyes

247

and shook a little—relieved as well as incredibly ecstatic. She'd been so terrified that he would know. The doctor had assured her cheerfully that first-time mothers didn't necessarily show until they were a full five months. Some women gained weight immediately, but she seemed to be the type who did not. But there were differences; differences she could feel. There was a slight swell to her belly, and her breasts were definitely rounder, darker.

But then the room was dark, and he wouldn't be looking for such changes. And when he had touched her, nothing had mattered but the will to serve the promise of his words, the tenderness and passion in his eyes. And then, somewhere in it all, she knew she had received even more than the startling power of his lovemaking. She had received something from his soul.

"David?"

"Hmm?"

She bit her lip lightly, then ran her fingers over the lower side of his back where she found the scar. "What happened?"

He was silent for a long time. For so long that she was convinced he had no intention of answering her.

Then he turned to face the ceiling, running his fingers slowly and lightly over the length of her arm.

"When I was young, just before my stint in the service was over, I had one of those wild and wonderful affairs." He hesitated. "I'm going to say this, Susan, but then I want your promise not to talk about the past. Your past or mine. Promise?"

"But—"

"Susan?"

She nodded, innately aware of what he wanted: a new beginning, time to find each other.

He ran his hand through his hair and spoke dryly. "This girl was a lovely Eurasian, and like I said, I was young and disastrously in love. I wanted to marry her. She was living in

248

Hong Kong, and I saw her every time I could get there. I don't think she ever realized quite what I was worth—financially, that is. She did know all about payday, and she knew how to whisper I love you in two dozen languages. Anyway, I was about to leave for home, and I'd asked her to come with me one last time. She wanted to make love and promise that she would marry me—without words. I'll never forget the way she looked that night." He rolled back to her and smiled. "She'd intended to kill me that night for the money I carried. She had a full-time lover who didn't mind sharing her for the money they could get from servicemen. They didn't kill everyone; I was a special case because she warned her friend that I'd come after them if—if I lived to do so."

"Oh, David!"

"Don't! Please, don't!" He laughed. "I think it only haunted me because I did love her. I haven't loved anyone since. Not—not until you."

"Oh, David!" she whispered, gratitude and love shining in her eyes.

"You can 'oh, David!' me that way anytime you want," he told her huskily. She reached out and stroked his cheek.

He kissed the line of her throat. "So let me love you, okay?"

She could only nod. And then whisper and whimper . . .

And cry out his name, again and again, with wonder at the beauty of it all. And just before falling asleep, she sighed with happiness and gave a silent little prayer of thanksgiving.

It was a new beginning, Susan thought deliciously as she awoke four days later. They'd been through most of the cities on the tour, and now there was only Seattle to go. Busy days . . . wonderful nights.

She stretched, reaching out a hand across the bed. They'd talked about so many things in little spurts. Lane Publishing, her classes in college, her writing, his work, her agent, his

249

secretary, Maine, Jud—even the troublesome Sam. She'd talked a bit about Carl, told him all about Madeline and Bill, and he'd described his penthouse apartment in New York.

They hadn't talked about Peter; they had never veered too far into the past. Susan had seen to it that they made love in the darkness because she hadn't mentioned the most pertinent fact in their lives—that they were quite shortly to become parents.

She winced; she just couldn't do it. Not yet . . . not until she knew for certain that this was what she wanted it to be, the type of relationship that demanded marriage, and even more, the total commitment of the heart.

With a soft sigh she closed her eyes and envisioned the past few days with wonder, then winced again. She was holding out. There were so many important things that she might have said to him. And yet she didn't. This thing between them, this new relationship . . . this love . . . was so fragile. Susan trusted him; she wanted to trust in his feelings for her, and yet she was afraid. Always afraid that the truth would not be believed, that it might appear so convenient that it couldn't possibly be believed. David had said he hadn't wanted to talk about the past—and it had been easy to agree.

And then there was that dread inside her that she might hurt him. She couldn't talk about her hospice work; she didn't dare. She wouldn't tell David that Peter had known about the cancer claiming his life and had chosen not to involve the son who loved him so deeply. . . .

Magic. She closed her eyes tightly, aware deep inside of her that they just had to make the magic last. They had to grow together, gain strength together, if the truths were ever to be known. Especially that most pertinent truth: the child she carried. His child.

Her fingers kept floundering across empty sheets, and she realized with a smile that David was already up. His watch was on the hotel nightstand, though, and she smiled again, thinking that it meant he hadn't dressed yet. He had a habit of putting his watch on before his clothing.

She picked it up, just like any lover who touched her beloved's belongings as an extension of touching him. It was such a beautiful piece. . . .

Her heart pounded slowly, and she stopped winding the band around her fingers. Inadvertently she caught her lower lip between her teeth and drew a trickle of blood as she read the inscription: "To David, on Christmas. My love forever, Vickie."

A tempest of emotions raced through her, pain foremost. He might not have loved a woman in over a decade until he had met her, but he'd sure as hell had something hot and heavy going with Vickie Jameson! Christmas? When she'd been so lonely—and pregnant with his child.

Rage pushed aside pain, and then the pain came back, and then an awareness that bordered on both panic and serenity.

She'd never pretended that he hadn't been having an affair with Vickie Jameson. She'd known it the moment she first saw the model. It had been an affair that had long preceded her own.

And if he loved her, he would come to her. He would stay with her, eventually ask her to marry him. Love had to endure the test of time, and she only prayed that they had the time.

She put his watch back where it had been, rose quickly, and ran into the bathroom with her clothing. She didn't want to be scrutinized too closely by the morning's light.

David still wasn't in the bedroom when she had finished showering and dressing. Frowning, she hurried out to the suite's small parlor. He was wrapped in a towel, stalking around while he talked on the phone. He saw her, smiled a greeting, and kept talking. Susan assumed it had to be his office, but then she heard him say Jerry's name and she frowned, wondering if it was Jerry from Maine with whom he was talking.

251

He hung up quickly, threw his arms around her, and gave her a kiss, but when he released her, he appeared brooding and upset.

"Was that Jerry from Maine?" she asked.

"Yeah. There was a message from him at the office. I called him. He just wanted to warn us both that Harry Bloggs's trial is coming up in early February. They want us both to testify."

"Oh," Susan murmured. David handed her a cup of coffee. She shook her head with confusion. "So why are you upset?"

He sighed. "I have to get back to New York right away. There's been an attempt by another house to hustle some stock, and I'll be damned if I'll wind up under someone else's control."

"Of course you've got to go!" Susan said with forced cheer. No! she cried out inwardly. No . . . not yet. She wasn't ready for the time to be over.

"Susan, Jarod is on his way out—"

"Oh, David! I'm an adult, I know how to get on an airplane! Why did you make him come when he has a brand-new baby?"

"It's only another couple of days." David grinned ruefully. "It's okay. He was with Tracy in the hospital and during those first few days. His mother-in-law is down now, so he's eager to get out a bit."

"Truth?"

"Truth."

He pulled her against him. Susan wished that he was dressed in something more than a towel. He started to kiss her, very deeply, his fingers moving against her throat and cheeks in a way she found horribly evocative.

"David!" She broke away from him breathlessly. "If you've got to get out of here, don't do that!"

"I guess not," he murmured regretfully. Still he hesitated. "Yeah." He glanced at his wrist and realized that he wasn't wearing his watch. "You've got a radio appointment in an hour and a half and I have to rush."

But he pulled her back to him one more time. "See you soon?"

She tilted her head back and tried to give him a sultry smile without breaking into tears. "You know where I live."

David sat at his desk exactly two weeks later, flourishing his signature across the last of the documents that secured Lane Publishing from outside intervention. With the last of it, he shoved the document from him, leaned back with a smile, and planted his feet on his desk, definitely pleased. It had been a hectic time; he'd moved more money around than he knew he had. But it was over. He could fly out this afternoon and be with Susan that night.

Maine. The beach house.

"You know where I live."

Her whisper had stayed with him night and day, even haunting his dreams. Jarod had told him that the tour had finished as smoothly as it had begun. Sales figures were trickling in, and they'd hit a number of the best-seller lists already.

He hadn't called her. He'd been so busy, he'd barely gone home at night. And besides . . . a phone call wouldn't have been right. Not now. He had to reach her. . . .

His buzzer was sounding. He punched the intercom button and picked up the receiver. "Erica, I am done!"

"Oh, great," she replied. "I'll get a messenger up right away. You've got a call on fifty-four."

"Who is it?"

"I don't know."

"Erica!"

"David! I think you should answer it. I think it's a woman. It's kind of a muffled voice. But she says it's urgent and personal."

"Erica—never mind. I'll take it."

He punched the extension button. "Yes?"

"David Lane?"

"Yes?" He was growing impatient; he wanted to get out of the office.

"Excuse me, Mr. Lane, but you are a blind idiot! Solve your silly problems and go marry that woman before the baby is born without a father!"

The phone went dead in his hands. He dropped the receiver as if it were on fire and clutched his temples between his hands. Idiot! Yes . . . How could he have failed to see it? She had changed, her breasts were fuller, and—oh, hell, he'd been so damned blind!

Pregnant . . . a baby. Life. His child. He groaned softly, with pleasure, with pain, with incredulity. Remembering the night, the very first night, so long ago now that it seemed like another world, a fantasy played out of wind and storm and mist. He could remember so clearly how she had looked, so exquisitely beautiful, so beguiling that neither promises of heaven nor threats of hell could have veered him from his need to touch her. To love her.

And from that night, that first night of both tempest and passion, there would be . . . life. Dear God in heaven! Why hadn't she told him?

The answer struck him slowly, slowly and painfully. Pregnant. For quite some time. Obviously for quite some time. Which meant . . . that it might be his—and might not. And he loved her so much that it didn't even matter except—

He didn't even think about his father. She might have lived with Peter, she might have really loved him. David knew inside that she had never hurt Peter; he knew what Peter had known, the beauty that Peter had seen. Whatever her real feelings had been, she had never used Peter.

It didn't matter. None of it mattered except that he had to know—and that she hadn't even come to him with the news! And, oh, God, it was just like another knife digging into him, only this one carved around his heart and into his soul, and he knew damned well that he just wasn't going to be able to handle it well at all. . . .

Winter was having a heyday in northern Maine. Susan didn't care. She needed to be outside. Outside where the wind rushed by her, where she could walk along the sand, see the pines, the water.

She went outside every day and walked. It was good for her. And she prayed every day that he would come.

He had to come to her. He had to. . . .

CHAPTER FOURTEEN

Susan saw a red Porsche parked in the driveway and her heart began to fly. David had come back to her.

Her fingers were trembling; she clasped them together. She felt like laughing and crying, felt lighter than air. He was back! Their days together had not been a simple game, and his whispers of caring had been real. They had been apart a full two weeks, but he was back.

Susan walked to the door and entered the beach house, trying to control her elation and hope. He was sitting in the parlor, staring into the blaze in the hearth. The fire danced warmly, snapped and crackled and hypnotized.

David knew she was inside. He had heard the door but hadn't turned.

The urge to run to him died within Susan's heart, and suddenly the fire didn't seem warm at all; its crackle had become tension. She felt as if she had been struck, yet she had no idea why or from where the blow had come. She stood still, watching his dark head.

He stood up, hands in his pockets, and sauntered slowly to the mantel. He kept staring into the flames, resting an elbow against the ledge, then turned at last to her.

His eyes . . . she had always known they could look like that. Dark blue and hard and glittering in the fire's glow . . . icy fire. His features were so tense. He appeared as firm as a rock and weary to death at the same time.

Her heart seemed to soar, then to cease beating; she wanted to reach out to him, to cry out and demand to know what was wrong. How could they have parted so closely and come to this in a matter of days? She wanted to speak; she couldn't. She just stared at him, stunned, lost, waiting.

A slow, rueful smile curved his lips, a jeer against himself. And at last he spoke, so softly that the crackling fire almost eclipsed his words.

"So that was it, Susan. I wondered why you became so gentle. Why you were suddenly so eager for my touch, for me. Eager to talk, eager to listen. But I fell in love, you see, so I didn't want to question your motives."

He hesitated, his eyes falling to the flames again, then rising once more to hers as a pained, dry laughter came from him.

"Well, Susan, am I expecting a son—or a brother?"

It felt as if a hammer had slammed against her, robbing her of breath and power. She wanted to slap him, to tear into him with her nails like a savage, wounded hawk. But still she couldn't move; she stared at him, feeling ill, unable to comprehend that he could believe what he was saying. After all this time, after all they had shared, he still didn't understand.

"It doesn't really matter, of course," he said flatly, drained of emotion. "You didn't even have to undergo your charitable charade. I'll marry you—I would have married you without it. I wouldn't want my son or brother labeled a bastard for life with a blank space under 'father's name' on a

257

birth certificate. After all, one way or another, the child is a Lane."

She could move; at long last she could move. Her rage was a very cold thing, astoundingly under control, like the pain that ripped her apart but left her standing.

"No."

"No what?"

"Your proposal was unique, but no. You don't have to worry about a Lane being a bastard. I don't know where you got your information, but it isn't anything that should concern you. The last man I'd have raising an Anderson is an arrogant, judgmental bastard like you."

She turned around and slammed out of the beach house. Susan heard him shout her name furiously, but that was all she heard. The roar of the surf clogged her ears; the wind picked up, and her heart thundered as she ran. Her breath tore from her, and that, too, was loud. It was interspersed with laughter and sobs, and she had never felt closer to hysteria in her life, never felt more torn, more desperate to get away, to lick the wounds of a hurt beyond death.

"Susan!"

She heard him again but distantly, because she had already reached the high ground, the pines and boulders, and had never welcomed that sandy forest more. Twilight was coming, and it was a place that she knew, a place where she could hide in the darkness.

Bits of snow clung to the trees and the ground. Susan paused, gasping for breath. He would follow her; him and his self-righteous determination to do the right thing. She leaned back against the trunk of a tree and sank slowly to the ground. She started to cry softly, but the air was so cold that it felt as if her teardrops turned to ice the moment they fell from her eyes. She looked up through the sheltering pines; darkness was coming, but so was a storm. He wouldn't find her, not when the shadows protected her. Eventually she would have to go back. Or forward. She could probably reach Jud Richmond's cottage before the storm broke if she hurried. She stood up and started walking.

He called her name by instinct. David didn't move right away; he felt numb and more confused and tormented than ever.

What had he expected from her? It wasn't what he had expected, it was what he wanted, longed for: Susan, hearing him, disputing him, running to him to tell him that she knew the child was his, that she loved him with all her heart, that . . .

At last he moved, shaking himself severely. He knew her so well. She didn't beg, she didn't plead, and she had a pride that never quit. And with his own wounded pride and terrible fear he had attacked her with guns blazing. Why the hell hadn't he managed things decently for once? Talked to her, held her, admitted that none of it mattered at all, that he loved her.

Because, he answered himself, he loved her but hadn't been able to trust her yet. Because it was still there, after all the years, the horrible feeling that love made a man vulnerable, that it bared his back to a thousand knives in a thousand different ways.

He reached the door and called her name again, frantically. The phone began ringing, but David ignored it.

"Susan!" He looked up at the sky and bit into his lip, unaware that he gouged it. Storm clouds were gathering, roiling and dark like the coming of the night.

He had to find her. He loved her; if he wanted a chance for them at all, he had to find her. And he couldn't fail her—or himself—this time. He had to find her, hold her with all the love and the strength that he could, and admit that he was afraid but that nothing else in the world mattered if she could only love him in return. . . .

The phone was still ringing. David stepped back into the

foyer to grab his coat out of the closet. The phone was such a damned annoyance, he barely gave it a thought. She'd headed for the pines, and he had to find her before the storm broke.

But right before he walked out the door, some sense of foreboding stopped him in his tracks. No sane person let a phone ring for that long unless they were desperate.

David hurried into the library and answered the summons.

It was Jerry, and he sounded surprised to hear David's voice, but then he went on—with relief. "David! Thank God you're there! He's out."

David shook his head in confusion. It sounded as if he were supposed to know what Jerry was talking about.

"Who's out? What are you talking about?"

"Bloggs! Harry Bloggs! That psycho you caught at the beach house! Hell, how can you forget such a thing?"

"I didn't forget. I thought he was in jail—"

"He was! But there were only two guards on duty; Bloggs slipped the key from one of them and locked him in the cell. He knocked out the sheriff. David—he was issuing all kinds of threats against you and Susan. Is she with you?"

David looked down at his palm. It was soaking wet with sweat, but a chill of fear was making him shiver at the same time.

"I'd better find her—fast!"

"David! Wait!" Jerry yelled.

"What?"

"I think he's already up there! Jud Richmond called in a short time ago. He was out in the woods and came back in to find his old dog, Sam, dead on the porch. His place was a mess, but only one thing had been stolen, his old sawed-off shotgun. David, listen to me, listen good, please!" Jerry begged. "The deputy's trying to get some men through, but the storm has already started here. The road's impassable.

You've got to watch it like a hawk until they can get through! Be careful!"

Jerry was screeching, almost as if he were in tears. David was shaking, shaking so badly that he wasn't sure he could walk, much less use extreme caution. He had never been so frightened in his life.

Got to find her, got to find her, got to find her . . .

The words took hold. He raced up to his bedroom, found his revolver, and then he was racing into the pines.

Jud's house was dark. But he never locked his doors, so he'd just come home and find an unexpected guest. Susan frowned, berating herself furiously. The storm was about to break any second; she just hadn't really given a damn because she'd been so upset. She paused in the clearing before the old log cabin, looked up at the sky, and suddenly realized that she cared very much. Rash, reckless emotion had made her leave the beach house knowing a storm was brewing, and she hadn't given a moment's thought to the baby.

Once he had just been a thought, a catastrophe that struck her life and had to be dealt with, accepted . . .

But now, standing in the clearing, she accepted that she was pregnant, realized how very much she wanted the child . . . David's child. Peter's grandson, Carl's nephew. Life! And no matter what David had to say, no matter what he felt, she was going to have the baby, love him with all her heart, and give him all the wonderful things and people that were a part of him.

A snowflake touched her cheek, and she hurried up to the porch. But as she reached it, narrowing her eyes against the fall of darkness, she frowned. There was something large by the door.

Susan hurried closer and bent down, her fingers reaching out. It was only Sam. But Sam didn't bark, and he didn't wag his tail. He didn't move at all.

Susan pulled her fingers away, fear razing through her like

261

a bolt of lightning. Her fingers were all sticky; they were covered with blood.

"No!" she cried out, and then she gazed around in panic, straining to see through the shadows. Someone had killed Sam! Someone who was lurking in the shadows, someone who might be in the old hunter's lodge, someone who might be . . . anywhere.

She closed her eyes for a moment while terror gripped her. She opened them again. In the darkness the pines had taken on grotesque shapes; they stood etched against a dead gray sky, swaying, reaching, transforming before her eyes into a thousand demons.

She blinked; they were pines, just pines. But she didn't know what to do—slip into the lodge or go back through the pines? In the lodge she might find Jud, just as she had found the dog.

No. *No!*

The pines, she had to get back to the pines. Susan stood slowly. The snow had begun in earnest.

She stepped off the porch, and then she ran. But just as she began to breathe more easily as shelter seemed to reach out to her, the forest was shattered with a harsh, alien sound. She looked at the tree in front of her; the bark was burned and blistered. She realized numbly that the shattering noise had been the sound of the bullet.

She turned slowly, very slowly. He was there, just behind her, laughing. A big man, full-bearded now, and even in the darkness she could see that his eyes were red-rimmed and bloodshot, as if he'd been helping himself to Jud's liquor cabinet.

"Where's Jud?" she heard herself ask.

"Don't know, missy. The old codger is out somewhere."

He spoke so casually, she was certain that he hadn't lied. He would have told her that he'd blown off Jud's head just as casually.

She didn't back away from him; it wouldn't have done any

good. The blast from the sawed-off shotgun had hit the tree in front of her; she couldn't possibly run fast enough to escape it.

"I'm worth a lot of money," she told him. "Enough to buy you freedom. If I'm not hurt—" She broke off because he was laughing again. It seemed so absurd, both of them standing there, the snow falling all around.

"I don't really want to hurt you, but if I have to, I will. I like you. I like the way you smell. I like the way you look. I like the sound of your voice."

He took a step toward her, and she didn't give a damn about the range of the shotgun. She turned to run.

His fist closed around her shoulder, jerking her back. She knew that she screamed, but the sound was cut off quickly as he dragged her to the ground. And then she fell silent because the muzzle of the gun was against her throat, scratching her flesh, pressing into her windpipe. His face was right up to hers.

Bloggs smelled more like a tomb than a jail. Like something old and decrepit and horrible. "You're so white," he crooned to her. "As white as the snow. But don't pass out on me. Not yet. We have to find the tough guy first. And when I finish with him, you'll be ready to jump before I can even whisper."

He stood up, dragging her along with him, the barrel of the gun at her spine. "Don't pass out!" he hissed.

She wasn't going to pass out. She thought that she might be sick. She was terrified for David—unsuspecting David, enwrapped in his own torment. She thought she might well die, and she was afraid that she would burst into tears that would strip her of all awareness, all chance. The baby . . . She'd been so close to death so many times. . . . Oh, Carl, Peter! she thought, wincing against the prod of the shotgun. Was it like this? Was it like this? But, no, it hadn't been terror for them, it had been a certain peace. God, I can bear to die! she prayed silently, but not the baby. Please, not the baby. . . .

Which meant, of course, that if her prayer were answered, she'd have to live herself.

"Come on! Start walking, real quiet." Bloggs's voice was like the hiss of a snake.

She swallowed and moved. And kept praying.

There was movement: a crackle of dead branches. David straightened against a pine, leveled his revolver, and whirled around. The shadow was still distant. He didn't pull the trigger.

Why the hell couldn't it be light? Why was a blinding snow falling? He narrowed his eyes, felt a headache begin as he tried to see. And then he relaxed. The shadow was tall but very thin.

"Jud!" he whispered hoarsely.

"David?" A whisper came back to him. David moved away from the tree so that Jud could see him and come to him. The old man looked like death itself, gaunt and strained.

"Where's Susan?" David demanded anxiously.

"She ain't with you?"

"No!"

"Boy, there's a killer out in these woods! The son of a bitch killed my dog!"

"Oh, God, Jud, I know," David whispered in anguish.

Jud's eyes leveled on him. "Why aren't you with her?"

"I'm not! It's that simple."

"You argued?"

"She's out in these trees somewhere."

"Hell!" Jud spat. "She's on her way to my place. You argued about your kid, huh?"

"We've got to find her."

"Let's head for the lodge."

"Jud, you're too old—"

264

"I can move just as smooth as you, boy."

They started off together, hugging the pines. "You gonna marry her?" Jud formed the words more than voiced them.

"Yes, yes," David said distractedly. *If she lives!* "Yes, whether it's mine or not. . . ."

He didn't know that he'd spoken the words aloud. Jud suddenly stopped in his tracks, staring at David. They should have kept going, silently, but Jud was too incensed.

"What are you saying? She isn't the type of woman to sleep around!"

"Shut up, Jud! I wasn't talking about her sleeping around. I was talking about my own father, if you must know!"

"Your father?" Jud was so stunned, he stopped again, still whispering vehemently. "Why, you young ass! Where'd you get an idea like that?"

David sighed, worried and determined to go on. What the hell difference did any of this make unless he could find her before Bloggs did? "Jud, he was paying her a salary for her services! She—"

Jud spat on the snow. "Author services! He knew he was dying; he wanted his words down fast! He met her at Harley's clinic the day her brother died."

For a moment the world swept away, the pines, the forest, even the fear. All David could feel was the cold. "Dad . . . knew he was dying?"

"You weren't ever supposed to know; them were his wishes. But seems to me Pete would want to think of the living, not the dead."

David doubled over suddenly, shot through with pain, aware again of the pines, of the darkness, of the snow, falling even harder now. God in heaven! She'd led him on! Because Jud was right: He'd been such an ass! And no matter what the provocation, she'd never hurt him with the truth that his father had been dying, and David's own obstinacy had kept him away when . . .

Bloggs was out there. Susan was out there.

265

He gripped a pine and Jud at the same time. He heard footsteps, footsteps against the snow. He practically jerked Jud off his feet to get him off the trail and into the shadows of the trees.

And then he saw it all clearly. Susan was walking past him. Bloggs had his elbow crooked around her throat, and Jud's shotgun was pressed against her spine.

Susan. Everything he loved. Everything that gave him a chance in life. He needed her forgiveness for so much; he needed her, and he was so damned scared. . . .

He let them move on by, horribly aware of Jud's breathing behind him. No sound, no sound . . .

He waited until they had moved past, then motioned to Jud. Melding with the trees, they followed behind. Bloggs and Susan were getting closer to the beach. The snow was turning to a drizzling rain. The boulders on the sand rose like sentinels as they neared.

David motioned to Jud, who moved next to him. Jud listened to his words, then nodded. David skirted around through the trees, and Jud moved spryly, rushing up to hide against one of the granite boulders. He waited and listened.

And then he called out, "Bloggs! Harry Bloggs!"

Susan was jerked around and slammed in front of the man just like a human shield. Jud realized with real pleasure that Bloggs wasn't at all sure in the darkness and rain where the call had come from.

"Is that you, tough guy?" Bloggs called out.

"No, it ain't!" Jud replied. What the hell did he do now? David had just said to keep the man talking.

"It's me—Jud Richmond. You killed my dog, you no-good bastard. That dog didn't do nothing to you!"

"Tried to bite me, you old geezer!"

Good for Sam! Jud thought with a pang. The dog knew garbage when he saw it and fought to the end! He remembered he was supposed to be talking without becoming a target himself. "Why don't you let go of that young lady? You hurt her and the law—"

"The law!" Bloggs sneered. "*I'll* worry about the law. You want the girl released, you get me her boy!"

Jud didn't see anything but a blur—a dark blur that ran from the shadows. The blur cut off Bloggs's speech. Susan screamed. When Jud heard her fall forward, he flew out from his boulder, racing down to the sand. She was soaked; snowflakes were on her shoulders, melting in the rain. It was so damn dark! And the wind was howling.

But he saw her eyes. Green as emeralds in the night.

"David?" she whispered, and they turned around together. Susan ran toward something in the sand and picked it up. It was the sawed-off shotgun. But David hadn't shot Bloggs; he hadn't dared because he might have hit Susan.

"Oh, God!" Susan gasped, swirling around with Jud. They could see the two men, rolling in the sand, but they were nothing more than blurs again, movement, shadows in the night.

The wind picked up. It screamed with the roar of the surf.

"Give me it!" Jud told Susan. "I can hit a squirrel in the eye!"

Susan gave him the gun. They raced together to the shore, but even Jud was forced to stop, aim, and stop, and try to aim again.

David and Bloggs were involved in a deadly wrestling match, trading punches, falling, rolling again. They moved out into the water where crashing waves combined with the wind and rain to blur vision and make the men appear as one again and again.

"Do something!" Susan screamed to Jud. He shook his head.

"Can't shoot! I can't shoot!"

They were going farther and farther into the water. Oh, dear Lord, Susan thought in rising desperation and panic. If

267

David survived Bloggs, he would freeze to death in the winter waters!

She raced toward the surf and let out a long horrible scream.

Both men had disappeared beneath the waves.

Cold. It was so cold. Harry Bloggs had gone down with the last blow, gone down deep, and now seemed to be gone. But David might have been gone himself; all he could see or sense or feel was the cold water. It seemed to beckon and whisper to him: Sleep, David, close your eyes and sleep. There's no need to fight. Just close your eyes. . . .

He saw his father. Peter's secretive grin, his brilliant blue eyes, his cap of white hair.

Hi, Dad! Dad, it's so damn good to see you now! I missed so much. I was so wrong, so out of line! Can you forgive me? Ah, Dad, why didn't you set me straight? Why didn't you give me a punch in the jaw? I would have deserved it. . . .

Swim, David. Move your arms! Kick, son—you can swim. Come on, son, reach out, reach out your hand. . . .

David stretched out his hand and reached, again and again. Peter was in front of him, ready to help.

He touched the hand. It wasn't Peter's at all; it was slim and delicate but filled with a surprising strength. He opened his eyes, shot through the water, and was stung with salt and wind.

He saw her eyes, green, sparkling emeralds, filled with moisture, with tears. "David! David, come on . . ."

He shook himself. The cold was still with him; it was frigid, piercing, terrible. But it had ceased its whispering, and reality was all around him. She was helping him to stand in the shallows, bracing him as he stumbled to his feet against the sand and surf. He looked at her and smiled.

A second later Jud was there, supporting him. Together they lowered their heads against the wind and stumbled back to the house.

CHAPTER FIFTEEN

He'd been in the tub long enough to feel as if he'd thawed out when he heard the door open. With his eyes closed and his head rested against the edge, he smiled. It was a rueful smile, touched by pain and regret yet hinting of hope.

He didn't open his eyes. She cleared her throat a little nervously. "Jud's sitting on the sofa in the parlor with his shotgun across his lap. I got him to put on some of Peter's socks, a pair of slippers, and a cashmere robe, but I can't get him into a hot tub. He says that if you came out of the water, Bloggs just might too. He says he'll watch for the first half of the night, then wake you." She hesitated. David didn't speak. He kept his eyes closed, listening to the tone of her voice, feeling it flow around him.

She cleared her throat again; he heard her take a step toward the tub. "David, Jud said he told you about your father. I—"

David lifted a hand to her. After a moment she took it, kneeling down beside the tub.

He stared at their hands, laced together. His fingers so brown, hers so pale and slender locked within them.

Then he looked into her eyes. "Can you ever forgive me?"

Susan lowered her head, quivering so inside that she was afraid to speak.

"Susan?" He touched her chin, raising it gently. His eyes were light and clear, as naked as a cloudless sky, filled with tender emotion.

She took his hand between both of hers, squeezed it tightly, then brought his palm to her lips and kissed it.

"I love you, David."

He stroked her damp hair, gazing at her with that tender, rueful smile. "Can you really?" he asked softly. "After everything . . . can you really?"

She was still shaking. So badly that she was afraid to keep staring into his eyes, afraid to realize the love that was really there, deep and tangible and humble and strong.

"David, I—I didn't help matters much. When I first met you, I was infuriated. If I'd been a better person, I would have stayed no matter what you said. I would have told you the truth—"

"You came to tell me that my father was dying—despite his wishes—didn't you?"

She nodded. "I didn't know if it would be right or wrong."

"Oh, God!" David said with a groan.

"David, he loved you so very much. He was so proud of you and your relationship with each other. Can you understand? He didn't want you to know because you never failed to treat him like an adult. He didn't want you to start treating him like an old man, like a child. Oh, David . . ."

He stood, stepping dripping wet from the tub, then kneeled down beside her and took her cheeks gently between his hands, bringing her eyes to his once again. "I understand, Susan. It hurts, but I understand." He smiled at her, seeing tears brimming in her eyes, determined not to let them fall. "What I don't understand is why he never set me straight about you. Or why you let me believe you had been my father's mistress."

She managed to smile back through the haze of tears. "Pure nastiness—and you deserved every bit of it!"

"I definitely did," David replied ruefully. "But why didn't you tell me about the baby?"

"I couldn't, David. First, I think I was in too much shock. And then . . . well, I did live in this house with your father. No one could really prove to you that I hadn't been what you thought I was. Then, after I'd encouraged your beliefs at every point, how could I go back and try to convince you that I had been lying when it would look so expedient?"

He started to laugh, pulling her against his wet, naked body. "Oh, Susan! I was dying for you to come to me and tell me that! You little fool! I was in love with you. I would have believed you!"

She smiled wistfully, savoring the words, allowing her fingers to trail through the dark hair on his chest. Then she straightened, pushing him away. "You're damned lucky you didn't die of exposure! Get back into that tub—"

"Not alone!"

"David! Jud is in the house!"

"Oh, Jud would condone every movement! Besides, you're soaked too."

She couldn't really protest; he was pulling her sweater over her head; his fingers felt like lightning trailing over her back, tugging at her bra strap.

She laughed a little breathlessly, wondering how a day that had brought such terror could produce such a magical night.

She was suddenly set on her feet, but he was not. He still knelt before her, his fingers moving in a tender, sensual caress over her breasts, then lowering to snap open the button on her jeans and pull the zipper. He tugged the jeans over

271

her hips along with her panties; she stepped out of them and he tossed them aside, but still he remained there, stroking her flesh so lightly and reverently that she began to tremble. His fingers moved with that same tender and exotic appeal over her abdomen, and at last she dug her fingers into his hair, demanding that he look up at her.

He was smiling, bemused, tender. "We're going to be parents."

"I know."

His grin widened devilishly, and he whispered huskily, "You are the most beautiful woman I've ever seen."

"You've used that line before!" she said breathlessly, teasing him.

"Yes, and it worked."

"Too well! By the way, who gave me away?"

"I'll never tell."

"It had to have been Harley or Jud."

"It was an anonymous phone call."

"I don't believe you!"

"It's true! And I don't think it was Harley or Jud."

"My cousin!" Susan gasped. "Why, the little rat!"

"She wanted things to work out. She knew we were made for each other—even if we were being too stubborn to get around to that realization."

His smile faded, but the love remained in his eyes. Then they closed, his arms wrapped around her, and he pressed his face to her naked belly, planting a gentle kiss there.

He looked up at her again, taking both her hands, bringing her back down to him, on her knees before him. "I honestly can't understand why you're willing to forgive me. I'm just so very grateful that you are. Susan, I love you. Will you marry me?"

She threw herself into his arms, burying her face against his shoulder. "Of course I'll marry you. As long as you love me!"

His arms tightened around her. He drew back and kissed

her, long and hard and passionately, and Susan felt the heat
in her body soar, and the longing to be a part of him burned
within her like a fierce blaze. Laughing slightly, she pulled
away from him, unaware that her breasts were gleaming
with the moisture from his body, deliriously oblivious to the
effect her body had on his.

"David! You've got to get back into the tub or dry off and
get dressed. One or the other."

He arched a brow, then rose quickly, carrying her along
with him to sink back into the steaming tub so that she was
leaning with her back against him, his legs embracing hers.
He could lock his arms around her and tenderly play with
the weight of her breasts, rake the nipples with a negligence
that just might belie his fever and ignite her to his level of
desire. . . .

The touch of his hands was casual; the proof of his desire
was not—not the way she was sitting! Susan trembled, leaning back against him with total elation, smug, content, and
feeling deliciously cherished and loved—and thrilled beyond
reason at feeling his male passion pulsing against her flesh.

"Are you all right?" he asked, a hoarse whisper that
teased her earlobe.

"Of course," she murmured innocently. "You were the
one in the ocean."

His voice became tense and strained. "You were the one
that Bloggs was holding. Susan, if—"

"I'm fine!" she interrupted, twisting slightly to assure him
with her eyes and her smile.

He grinned back. "Want some soap?"

"Soap?"

He gave her that rakish, sensual devil's grin that wouldn't
quit. And then she discovered why. A bar of soap he had
been holding bobbed to the surface where he quickly retrieved it again and began very slowly to move it over her
breasts, causing her breath to catch beneath and her heart to
pound like thunder against his touch.

273

"After all," he murmured, "we are in the bathtub."

"After all . . ."

He moved the soap over her belly, slowly, lullingly. And then his hands moved again, bringing the slick bar along her thighs and between them until she gasped, trying to spin, encountering his heavy-lidded, smoldering eyes once again.

"David!"

When he laughed she snatched the soap from him, wriggling from her position to lather his chest. He pulled her close to him.

"You're sure you're all right?"

"Absolutely."

His arms wound tighter, and he stood, causing Susan to cry out in laughter and panic. "The soap! You're going to slip! You're—"

But he was already standing by the tub, bending to cut off her words with a kiss. She wove her fingers through his hair, never so enflamed by the passion and need. His kiss left her lips to fall against her throat, and he was walking, heedless that they were still wet. In his room he laid her on the bed, falling beside her to cover her with his body, with warmth, with new tremors of longing.

"Oh, David, I'm so very happy."

His lips covered hers, then broke away, and he surveyed her eyes, tangling his fingers in her hair.

"It's just like fire. The first time I touched it, it was fire and silk, and I think I knew even then that I was lost."

She locked her fingers around his neck, pulling his mouth back to hers, taunting his lips with the tip of her tongue until he invaded her mouth with new hunger. His hands started caressing her breasts, feathering over her belly, stroking along her thighs and between them.

Her body writhed against his, her kisses fell to his shoulders, she nipped his neck, and then raked her fingers lightly, lovingly over his back. And then her nails dug suddenly because he was over her, thrusting into her, and she clung

274

hard against him, whispering his name, gasping, loving that first shattering moment of having him a part of her.

"Love you . . ."

"So much. So, so much . . ."

And then she was gasping again, swamped with the erotic pleasure that rose and rose as his whispers became more graphic, telling her how he loved each of her movements, the feel of her, her breasts against his chest, her thighs wrapped so tightly around him, her hips, fluid . . . fantasy.

She'd never made love like this. One glittering pinnacle was not enough; she fell against him, exhausted, only to feel a desperate new fever begin to burn at his slow touch, his finger moving sensually along her spine, his whisper against her ear, his kisses falling suddenly upon her breasts, her hip, her lips. . . .

They were both sleeping when Jud rapped on the door, grumbling that he was too old to stay awake all night. They both sprang up a bit guiltily and took Jud's place before the fire while Jud fell asleep in Peter's room.

It didn't seem at all difficult to stay awake, though. There were still so many things to talk about. The fire blazed before them; Susan curled against his chest, and they sipped tea, occasionally silent, bursting into speech again when something would occur to one of them.

"Tell me everything about my father," David urged her at one point. She hesitated but then said, "I met him through Harley Richmond. Carl was receiving treatment at the hospital, and I was always with him. Because of—or in spite of —my psychology background, I wound up working hospice, helping others there deal with their diseases, with death. I think I was able to help a number of people, but when it came to Carl . . . well, I fell apart at the end. Peter found me on the day Carl died, and the patient was suddenly the doctor. He was so gentle, David. It was quite a while before I discovered that he was one of Harley's patients. Then he found out that I was a writer. He had read a number of S. C.

de Chance's sci-fis, and he broached the subject of making a fictional work out of his life. He was so delighted with the thought of it all! I wasn't at all sure, but Peter convinced me that I needed to be away from the hospital, on the beach, working on my craft, as he put it. And he needed me, David. His love for you was very great; he certainly never meant to hurt you in any way. . . ."

David stroked her hair over her forehead, his eyes not on hers but on the flames.

"How did he die?"

"We were south of here, out on a little fishing launch, as you know. His line was in the water, he was talking, and then suddenly he wasn't. It was . . . very quick and peaceful, David. And a gift, really, because he never had to suffer through the final, painful stages."

"Then I'm grateful," he said very softly. He shook his head. "How on earth could I have thought—" He broke off, wincing, and Susan laughed, then very shyly told him about her one and only, very youthful affair.

David smiled tenderly down at her, stroking her cheek, then he chuckled. "Well, thank God, then, that you were deprived! I wouldn't have managed to seduce you so easily if you'd been more experienced!"

"I thought I seduced you!"

"Maybe. Maybe you'd been dealing so long in fantasy on paper that you were able to create real magic," he whispered.

Susan frowned suddenly. "David . . . what about Vickie Jameson?"

His gentle, reflexive smile caused her a moment's pang of jealousy, but his words eased it away.

"Vickie is a lovely lady. She's the one who sent me back to you—in a way."

"Really? How?"

He laughed, playing with a lock of her hair. "She said that I was in love with you and asked me to leave so she could get her own life back on track." He hesitated, then smiled. "She suggested that I tour with you."

Susan laughed. "You lied! You said that no one else could go!"

"Vickie reminded me that I was the publisher, president, and majority stockholder. If I thought I was the best one to go, then I should!"

Susan made a mental note to send Vickie Jameson flowers and the nicest thank-you note she could manage to compose. Then she smiled, amazed with it all again, and threw her arms around David, kissing him heatedly. His hands slipped through the folds of her robe, caressing her bare flesh, stroking her breasts. But when the wonderful, silky heat of her form threatened to overwhelm his senses, he pulled away, reproachfully locking his arms around her, and returned her sedately to his lap.

"We're supposed to be on guard duty!"

Susan grimaced. "He's not coming back. It's a miracle that you're alive and well."

"Mmm. But Jud did his stint—it's our turn now."

Susan smiled. It didn't matter.

And in seconds she was asleep on his lap, which didn't matter at all to David. He was pleased just to hold her, to listen to the roar of the weather outside and bask in the warmth of the parlor, in the warmth that held his heart.

Susan awoke because she heard people talking. She was alone on the sofa, and the fire had died down to embers.

Frowning, she straightened her robe, tossed back her hair, and hurried into the kitchen, flushing slightly as she saw that the small room was full. Jerry was there, Mindy, Carrie, Lawrence, and even Harley Richmond and his wife, as well as Sheriff Grodin and Jud, who apparently had decided that it was safe enough to shower and looked exceptionally dignified in one of Peter's satin smoking jackets.

"Ah! The heroine has arisen!" Mindy cried with laughter, but she hugged Susan fiercely, and Susan, startled by the gesture, staggered back, only to be caught from behind by David, who stared down at her bemused look with amusement and affection.

"What . . ." Susan began, and then everyone was explaining that, of course, in a village the size of theirs everyone had been frantic, and as soon as the roads were cleared, they had all hurried out. Susan had slept through their arrival, but in the kitchen Jud had dramatically told them all about the night's events.

Susan smiled, accepting a cup of tea from David, glad to nestle back against him again where he leaned against the counter. Susan lifted her cup to them all, thinking again that she was a very lucky woman. Not only was David standing behind her, but through Peter Lane and Harley she had acquired a host of caring friends.

"Actually," Susan murmured, smiling ruefully, "I wasn't a heroine at all. Jud and David are the heroes."

"Oh! Heroines aren't supposed to solve the thing!" Mindy teased. "They're supposed to be saved—"

Susan laughed. "Trust me! I write the stuff! She should be strong! She should—"

"Actually," David said, mocking her tone and breaking in as he tenderly nuzzled her ear, "heroes and heroines are supposed to survive together—trust me, I'm in the business."

Everyone chuckled, but then the mood grew somber again as Sheriff Grodin informed her that Harry Bloggs's body had been found about two miles south. Susan shivered; she wondered if she shouldn't have felt something, some remorse for a life lost. She didn't. She couldn't help it, she just felt relieved.

Maybe she could feel something for the younger man he had surely once been. Things happened to people in a lifetime, things that touched their behavior—she knew that. She had studied behavioral sciences, and there were influences . . . as with David. Loving and being betrayed when he had

278

been so very young. It had taken him so many years to learn to love and trust again.

She trembled a little, realizing that their pasts made the present so much more precious. They hadn't said it aloud, but Susan knew that they were both aware that what they had was special. In the days and in all the years to come, they would value what they had.

Susan started as Mindy suddenly raced across the room to kiss her enthusiastically again. "Oh, how wonderful! Well, let's get out of here, then, and let them get dressed and into town!"

She had been musing, and she hadn't heard a word spoken. As everyone filed out of the beach house, kissing her, shaking hands, saying good-bye, she was still at a loss.

David stood back in the foyer, arms crossed over his chest, laughing as he watched her close the door.

"All right. All right!" she wailed. "So I wasn't listening! I haven't the faintest idea what's going on!"

He smiled, enveloping her in his arms.

"I just invited them to the wedding. Three days from now in the chapel in the village. You don't mind, do you?"

"Mind? Why, not at all, Mr. Lane."

EPILOGUE

"Don't you understand?" Race shouted to the captain. "They were all shot by lasers! Captain, that means one of our own. A traitor on this very ship . . ."

Susan paused, her fingers over the typewriter keyboard as she heard the front door open. She smiled slowly. He had called to tell her he was running late, but he must have hurried, because he wasn't very late at all.

He'd been disappointed, of course. It was a big night for them, the one-month anniversary of their marriage. They'd planned on dinner and show and dancing, but Susan had understood, and she hadn't been terribly disappointed. Between the wedding and their two-week honeymoon in Hawaii—where the beach water was warm!—David hadn't been giving Lane Publishing all that he should be giving.

And she didn't mind at all that they weren't going out. The February weather was bleak. Snow was falling, soft, delicate flakes that hit the skylights like magic. On the streets, the flakes would melt to slush. Here they remained magical, creating a night of stardust above the huge bed.

"Susan?" David called from the entry of the penthouse apartment.

"In here!" she called back.

She lowered her head over the keyboard, smiling secretively. She was glad that they originally had been planning on a night out. She'd spent the afternoon in a perfumed bath, washed her hair, polished her fingernails, and literally dusted herself from head to toe in a new powder guaranteed to seduce. She felt very lazy and sensual . . . and sweetly aroused just by the sound of his voice.

He pushed open the bedroom door. His dark head was slightly damp from the snow; he'd shed his coat and appeared impeccable in a dark three-piece suit. He started to speak but paused, smiling as he leaned against the door for a moment, then slowly moved toward her. Was it in her eyes? she wondered. The invitation that had given him a demon's pleased grin and sent him to her with such an assured sway?

She smiled, then gazed blankly back to her paper, her heart racing while he planted his arms around her, hands on the desk, and nuzzled her ear while he spoke.

"Working?"

"Mmm-hmm."

"Traitor on Alpha Five?"

"Mmm." She twisted around to look at him. "You really don't mind, do you, David? I love these things."

He laughed. "You mean because it isn't Lane? No, I don't mind. I'm glad you like what you do. You shouldn't do it otherwise. I still think you should try a murder-suspense. Bloggs was perfect material."

Susan shivered. "I'm not up to Bloggs yet. Maybe in another few months."

He tilted her chin to him, stroking her cheek. "It's definitely all over with him, Susan."

"I know." She bit her lower lip, studying his face, finding

281

that she was absurdly pleased with herself because of David. Because she loved everything about him so very much and he loved her. If only Peter could have known that this would be!

"What is it?" he murmured softly.

"Oh, I was just thinking about your dad." She sighed. "He would have been so happy, David. He so wanted grandchildren. If only he had known."

He tweaked her nose lightly. "Maybe he does know, Susan. I always thought of him as a really great fellow. If there is a heaven, that's where he is. And maybe—just maybe—he does know."

Susan caught his hand where it lay on her shoulder and kissed his palm. He stroked her throat softly with his thumb.

"Are you finished there?" he asked huskily.

"Just about."

He was close behind her, lifting her hair to plant a kiss against the nape of her neck. She tried to fill in the last sentence but couldn't. Laughter and a swift fire stilled her fingers as his hands cupped over her breasts, erotically teasing her nipples.

"David!"

"Just thought you might be on a sex scene. I wanted to give you a hand. I don't mean to disturb you. It's just that, after all—"

"You can't write on memory forever, right?"

"Something like that."

"I'm just about—"

"Uh-uh. You are done," he told her. Her chair rasped back over the carpet, and she was laughing as he plucked her into his arms to deposit her on the bed beneath the skylights.

"David!" She meant to protest, but she was laughing too hard.

"Susan!" he said, accusing her back and recklessly shedding his jacket, kicking off his shoes, tugging at his tie, and tossing off his socks. "My dear Miss Anderson!" His vest

282

landed on the floor, and he plunged to the bed beside her, working on the buttons of his shirt. "No wife awaits her husband so clad, or unclad as the case may be"—he fingered the gossamer material of her teal gown—"unless she wants to be disturbed!"

He was being atrociously slow with his buttons. Susan shifted to help him. Impatiently he ignored her efforts, cradling her cheek, kissing her lips, her forehead, her throat. His mouth moved lower, over the flimsy material, hot and moist through it. He caught her nipple lightly between his teeth, and the snow's enchantment, high above them in the velvety night, seemed to touch her whole body.

She brought her fingertips to his hair, then clutched his shoulders.

"You're definitely disturbing me," she murmured.

He rested his head against her swelling abdomen for a minute. And for that moment his touch was infinitely tender. But then his eyes met hers, and they were dark with passion.

"Helping you," he told her. He rolled to sit beside her, shedding his shirt quickly. He stood to rid himself of trousers and briefs. Susan smiled slowly, sensuously, lazily, alive in every sense as she awaited him.

"Helping me?" she murmured as he came back beside her.

"Research," he assured her, nipping her earlobe.

"Oh!" She turned into his naked chest. "Well, I admit . . ."

"What?"

"Feet."

"Feet?"

"I've always wanted to write something erotic about feet."

"Oh."

He kissed her instep, proving beyond a doubt that an instep could be a highly erogenous zone.

"How about ankles?" he asked.

"Ohhh . . . surely."

283

"Kneecaps?"

"Hmmm."

"Thighs . . . hips . . . intimate, intimate places . . ."

He asked her no more questions, and she could have given him no more answers. Snowflakes continued to fall against the skylight; warmth burned below it.

At long last they were aware of the sky again, aware of the snow that fell beyond.

"It's another anniversary, you know," he told her.

"Is it?" she murmured, languorous and sated.

"It was exactly a year ago today that you walked into my office and threw water all over me."

"It's exactly a year since you first accused me of being your father's mistress!" Susan retorted.

He smiled ruefully. "It wouldn't have mattered if you had been. I was head over heels in love." He rolled over, pinning her beneath him, smiling mischievously. "But I am rather glad that you did become my mistress instead."

"Mistress?"

"Mistress, friend, lover, wife. Mother of Carl Peter or Peter Carl Lane—whichever we decide. Is that better?"

"Much! But there is one problem."

"What's that?"

"Carl Peter or Peter Carl just might be a girl!"

"True," David mused. "Ah hah!"

"What?"

"Carla!"

"But what about Peter?"

"Well, that won't really matter. Because one way or another, my love . . ."

"Yes?"

"He or she will be a Lane."

"Yes," Susan agreed.

"Well, since that's settled . . ."

"Mmm?"

"Think you could handle a little more research?"

"David, one should never, never tire of research."

┌───┐

Now you can reserve July's
Candlelights
<u>before</u> they're published!

♥ You'll have copies set aside for *you*
    the instant they come off press.
♥ You'll save yourself precious shopping
    time by arranging for *home delivery.*
♥ You'll feel proud and efficient about
    organizing a system that *guarantees* delivery.
♥ You'll avoid the disappointment of not
    finding *every* title you want and need.

ECSTASY SUPREMES $2.75 each

☐ 129 **SHADOWS OF THE HEART**, Linda Vail 17794-4-13
☐ 130 **CONTINENTAL LOVER**, Cathie Linz 11440-3-48
☐ 131 **A MAN FOR AMY**, Blair Cameron 15314-X-18
☐ 132 **A FORBIDDEN REFUGE**, Eleanor Woods 12733-5-26

ECSTASY ROMANCES $2.25 each

☐ 442 **FEVER PITCH**, Pamela Toth 12505-7-30
☐ 443 **ONE LOVE FOREVER**, Christine King 16608-X-11
☐ 444 **WHEN LIGHTNING STRIKES**, Lori Copeland 19420-2-29
☐ 445 **WITH A LITTLE LOVE**, Natalie Stone 19546-2-10
☐ 446 **MORNING GLORY**, Donna Kimel Vitek 15567-8-12
☐ 447 **TAKE CHARGE LADY**, Alison Tyler 18478-9-22
☐ 448 **ISLAND OF ILLUSIONS**, Jackie Black 14147-8-14
☐ 449 **THE PASSIONATE SOLUTION**, Jean Hager 16777-9-32

 At your local bookstore or use this handy coupon for ordering:

DELL READERS SERVICE—DEPT. B1111A
P.O. BOX 1000. PINE BROOK, N.J. 07058

Please send me the above title(s) I am enclosing $ _____ [please add 75¢ per copy to cover
postage and handling] Send check or money order no cash or CODs. Please allow 3-4 weeks for shipment.
<u>CANADIAN ORDERS</u> please submit in U.S. dollars

Ms Mrs Mr _____

Address_____

City State_____ Zip _____

└───┘

Fans of

Heather Graham

*will delight
in her boldest
romance to date!*

Golden Surrender

Against her will, Ireland's Princess Erin is married off by her father to her sworn enemy, Prince Olaf of Norway. A Viking warrior, Olaf and his forces are needed by the High King to defeat the invading Danes.

Nevertheless, the proud princess vows that her heart and soul will never belong to her husband, although her body might. Until one day that body, together with the life of her young baby, is almost destroyed by the evil Danes. When her husband *proves* his deep and abiding love for Erin by braving a desperate rescue attempt, she is forced to admit that her heart also holds a fierce love for her brave husband.
$3.50   12973-7-33

Don't forget Candlelight Ecstasies and Supremes for Heather Graham's other romances!